DEATH ON THE HIGH SEAS

Anna Legat

Headspace Books

CONTENTS

Maggie Kaye and Samuel Dee

in

The Shires Mysteries

Book 4

DEATH ON THE HIGH SEAS

Anna Legat

CHAPTER 1

Cruising across the North and Baltic seas in the middle of winter wasn't exactly what Sam had in mind when he suggested a holiday. His idea of a holiday location was somewhere exotic: sandy beaches, palm trees and the lapis lazuli oceans of the Tropics. He also rather favoured getting there by plane. Cruises were for the elderly. Sam didn't yet subscribe to that age bracket. He needed action and adrenalin. Being cocooned for two weeks in a small cabin while the ship bulldozered through iron-grey waters of the monotonous northern seas didn't appeal.

Maggie however found the prospect singularly alluring.

As soon as she had forced upon him her outlandish idea of a cruise, she had gone ahead and chosen the most obscure – and the chilliest – of all routes: *The Cities of the Hanseatic League*. The ship would take them on a merry-go-around misadventure to Amsterdam, Gdansk, Riga and Helsinki. Crowning it all would be a foray into the confines of Siberian winter: St Petersburg. In December.

Sam had mooted the possibility that Maggie was experiencing a minor breakdown which had transformed into a fully-blown death wish. Who in their right mind—

'Use your imagination, Samuel!' She had waved a glossy brochure at him, where, on its penultimate page, she had circled a small segment about the Hanseatic cruise. How on earth she had found herself attracted to it in the first place was anyone's guess. The segment was buried among spellbinding full-page ads featuring the historical cities of the Mediterranean and the tropical islands of the Caribbean. Maggie had snubbed the attractions that any reasonable traveller would find irresistible. Instead, she had dug out of obscurity some ancient league of some God-forsaken towns on the frontier of the Arctic Circle. Why, oh why!

'Just picture having a white Christmas, the world blanketed with snow, and the two of us in the golden city of St Petersburg – drinking champagne, eating caviar and dancing. Waltz, foxtrot – whatever tickles your fancy!' Maggie's eyes shone with the glitter of her unbridled imagination while Sam sat, unstirred, uninspired and – unimaginative.

'I'll have you know that I can't dance.'

'We'll do millions of other things, then.'

'Like?'

'Like whatever we feel like.'

'Could we not do those things somewhere else? Somewhere nicer and warmer.'

'No, not really.' Her face had crumpled, ready to fold in altogether. 'I've never been to St Petersburg...'

'You've never been to Barbados either.' Sam resisted her folly valiantly, hoping that common sense could yet prevail.

'But that's not the same!'

'Precisely! Barbados isn't just different – it's better.'

'It has to be St Petersburg. I've set my mind on St Petersburg. Anyway, it'll be a blast, Samuel. Trust me. Something you'll never forget.'

'That's where you're probably right.' He had given in. He knew when he was beaten. He wouldn't have won the argument. Anyway, the last thing he wanted was for their escape from murder, ghosts, gossip and the general mayhem of Bishops Well to start – and end – with a row. But most significantly: he had his designs on Maggie.

This seafaring expedition would be the romantic backdrop to their courtship. He had long resolved to win Maggie's heart. He adored the little minx, and would follow her to hell, never mind St Petersburg. He would do it even though he hated winters and the voyage was scheduled for December. He would brace himself for the stormy, northern seas. He would brave the unrelenting waves knowing full well that he would suffer from sea-sickness. Yes, it would be trying and bloody awful, but Maggie was worth the trouble.

Unaware of Sam's ulterior motives, Maggie was triumphant. She had convinced herself that Sam's unconditional surrender was solely down to her persuasive powers. Again, she had assured him that he would not regret it and could trust her superior judgment. Having won that battle, she had embarked on extensive sea-voyage preparations. She had travelled by rail to London, where she had spent a week shopping for *necessities.* She had returned to Bishops saddled with bags and bags of random stuff, plus a trunk. It had taken Sam and two other passengers to help unload the trunk onto the platform (based on his previous experiences, Sam wouldn't tackle voluminous luggage on trains on his own).

On the day of their departure, Sam, Michael and Dan Nolan, as supervised by Maggie, had hoisted the trunk into the boot of Sam's Jag. Despite their ingenious efforts to reposition the monstrosity inside the boot in a way that would allow shutting it, they failed. The boot would have to gape open all the way from the Shires to Southampton.

'What do you keep in there, Maggie,' Dan

inquired, irate, after the cursed thing had nearly crushed his hand, 'a dead body?'

'Just a few items of suitable clothing, Dan, nothing more.'

'So why is this thing so heavy?'

'It's a seaworthy trunk, if you must know. It's waterproof, mahogany with a wrought iron frame and hinges. It came highly recommended.'

'By who? A funeral director?'

Maggie snorted and let the remark pass unanswered. She hugged in turn her friends who had come to see her off. That meant a sizeable proportion of the village population. It had taken twenty minutes and a few tears to say goodbye and *bon voyage*, but at last they hit the road. Sam had Maggie all to himself.

Once they had gone through the check-in and passport control formalities, Maggie's trunk was wheeled onboard the cruise liner by a forklift operator who had been commissioned for this task by the porter. Maggie and Sam (who was carrying his own suitcase of modest dimensions) followed the porter down a long, carpeted corridor to their respective cabins. The porter pushed the trunk off the trolley and bid them good-day. He limped away massaging his lower back. It looked like his career might have been cut short by the seaworthy casket holding just a few items of suitable clothing.

Their cabins were identical: each with a

twin bed despite their single occupancy, and standard hotel-type furniture. They had blind windows featuring fantastical scenes with pink orchids and waterfalls. Oversized dragonflies and busybody humming birds wrestled for supremacy in the foreground. Due to his anticipated sea-sickness Sam had insisted on rooms within the core of the cruiser, for stability. That had been his only condition. Maggie's longing to awake every morning to squawking seagulls and shoals of migrating herring would not hold sway over him on this occasion. Maggie had conceded to his terms and now they stood arm in arm in front of their cabins.

'So, we are still next-door neighbours,' Sam reflected affectionately.

'Aren't we just!' Maggie beamed.

She followed her trunk into her room and shut the door. She intended to change into something more appropriate and would see Sam on deck in fifteen minutes. She wished to wave goodbye to good old Blighty when the cruise liner left the harbour.

Fifteen minutes later, she emerged on deck, dressed in a pearl-white, puffy jumpsuit. Ensconced inside it and with her thrilled, wide-eyed expression, she looked like someone who had just landed on the Moon and was taking their first steps on its surface. Sam concealed his amusement in an improvised cough.

A small crowd of those staying behind on

dry land was gathered on the quay. Relieved, smiling faces mouthed *bon voyage* to the crowd of intrepid travellers waving to them from the ship. The crowd on the quay appeared immeasurably more sensible to Sam than the crowd on deck. And in that crowd Maggie stood out as the least level-headed. Her cheeks were burning red (probably due to the heat generated inside her thermal jumpsuit) and she was thrusting her arms excitedly. Then to add to her air of incongruity, she leaned over Sam's shoulder and shouted in his ear, 'I wonder how many of the people I'm seeing here and down there are only spirits. There seem to be awfully big crowds – they can't all be alive.'

'It's an awfully big boat, Maggie.'

'You can say that again! You know what it reminds me of, don't you?'

'I wouldn't presume for one minute to know what you're thinking.'

'The Titanic, of course!' Maggie laughed. 'You can see it, can't you? A big, unsinkable ship on her maiden voyage, hundreds of passengers looking forward to a new life in the New World. Only she sunk, didn't she, poor thing? And took everyone down with her.'

'Let's hope we can avoid that fate.' Sam didn't even try to figure out what had brought this unfortunate analogy to Maggie's mind. The cruise ship had by now been manoeuvred away from the quay and set off on its straight and narrow course into the English Channel.

'Come on, let's go to the bow.' Maggie pushed her way through her fellow passengers. Their numbers were already thinning on deck, people returning to their cabins – or more likely, to the bar. The spectacle of farewells was finally over and the voyage across the seas began in earnest.

Sam would have liked to stop at the bar for a quick drink, but Maggie was unrelenting. She led him to the top deck and leaned against the guardrail, her arms and her chest thrust out. She expelled a shrill of delight. That pose instantly brought before his mind's eye the iconic scene with Jack and Rose at the bow of the Titanic. Just in case Maggie got any ideas about flying and tipped over the rail, Sam held out his arms ready to catch her. He was suddenly overcome by an irrational anxiety. He fought off the images of the sinking Titanic and prayed to God Almighty that Maggie's words would not prove prophetic. One could never be too sure of the actual extent of Maggie Kaye's supernatural powers. Even she was unsure on this score.

CHAPTER 2

All the waking hours on the cruise liner were punctuated with regular and frequent meals. The moment the ship left the harbour, afternoon tea was served.

Maggie packed her plate full of cake – so full that one would be forgiven for thinking that she was hiding a starved stowaway in her cabin. Alas, it was all for her personal sampling. Unable to make a choice between the cakes on offer, she grabbed one of each kind. Her plate was like a cakey Noah's Ark. Sam carried a measly scone with butter on his plate. That gave him a spare hand for the cups and saucers.

The restaurant was abuzz with hungry customers. Maggie spotted a table for four occupied by a lone elderly man. He was stooped intently over his tea, stirring in sugar with an unsteady hand. His hair was the colour of dust – neither brown nor grey, but it was thick for a man in his mid-seventies. He wore a navy-blue jumper over a white collar, and a pair of tawny corduroys.

'Are these taken?' Maggie asked immediately after planting her posterior in a chair next to the man. She twirled her fingers at Sam, 'Here, Samuel, I saved you a seat!'

The elderly man smiled benignly and invited them to join him, not that Maggie required any invitation to invade his personal space. She pushed her plate to offer the man one of her cakes, considering that he had none. He declined politely. Maggie retrieved her plate and went for her first treat: a mini lemon tart. Introductions followed. The man's name was Sidney Worsley. He was from Stroud. A retired veterinarian and a collector of rare stamps. A widower. Maggie unearthed all of the man's personal data between sitting down at his table and the waiter re-filling their cups with tea, which was a matter of ten minutes.

'I'm sorry to hear that,' she quipped. 'Samuel is also a widower.'

Sam wasn't sure if that was intended to make the man feel better, but he nodded and smiled reassuringly.

'Has it been long since your wife's passing?' Sidney inquired.

'A while - over four years now.'

'Eleanor passed away six months ago – at the beginning of June.' Sidney sipped his tea, his hand still quite shaky, his tea rippling in the cup.

'Was it sudden – your wife's death?'

'Oh no. Not at all. She died after a long illness. I had time to prepare. In fact, we planned this cruise together.'

'You did? For the two of you?' Maggie enthused. She loved a tear-jerker love story with a tragic ending.

'At first, yes. We'd been thinking of something like this for years. Eleanor had always wanted to visit St Petersburg. Her great grandmother, three times removed, was a Russian countess, or so Eleanor was told as a child. Family tales, you never know how much truth there is to them, do you? Still, there were heirlooms and old photos from St Petersburg. Eleanor dreamed of seeing the place for herself, but life conspired against our best laid plans. She got ill and we knew she would only get worse. So she made me promise that I'd take this trip on her behalf as soon as I was free to do so. It took me a few months to make the arrangements, and here I am.'

'Fulfilling your wife's dream?'

'Exactly. It was her dying wish.'

Maggie put down the uneaten half of her chocolate eclair and wiped the cream from her lips. She looked up and skimmed over the faces of people around them. 'It's odd then,' she observed, 'that she isn't here with you.'

'What do you mean?' Sidney was taken aback by her pronouncement. Hadn't she been listening to a word he'd said? 'Eleanor is dead. She can't be here - it logically follows.'

'Not really—' Maggie was just gathering speed to roll poor Sidney over with her outlandish logic.

Sam could not let her do that. He grasped her hand and squeezed it. 'What Sidney means is that she can't be here in body. She may well be here in spirit, of course.'

'But that's what I mean: she isn't here in spirit!' Maggie started flogging the dead horse again. All that sugar must have gone to her head and wiped out the rest of her sense and sensibility.

Sam fixed her with a stern glare, 'If that's what you mean then we all agree.'

'Oh that? Yes, of course,' Maggie was catching on painfully slowly. 'Would you have a photo of Eleanor? Sorry, just curious to see what she looked like. Maybe I've missed her – so many strangers around here...'

Sidney scowled with suspicion, but he pulled a photograph from his wallet and handed it to Maggie. 'This is Eleanor on our wedding day. I've been carrying it for fifty-two years.'

Maggie took it and scrutinised the picture, then scanned the lounge. Sam realised what she was up to – she was looking for Eleanor's spirit. She didn't find it. Her disappointed face said as much. She returned the photograph to Sidney. 'I love that full-skirt dress. If I were to get married,

I'd wear a similar one.'

Sam's heart skipped a beat.

The waiter returned with the tea and the three of them had a top up. Maggie had left most of her cakes untouched. By her own account she felt full just by looking at them.

The chatter drifted towards the joys of winter at sea, dressing sensibly, not overeating (Maggie concurred vehemently), drinking in moderation (Maggie looked away, distracted by something) and of course the promise of entertainment and extravagance that the cruise held for everyone.

Sam's thoughts travelled on a tangent – to Alice. She would have hated it here, confined on a boat, surrounded by food, booze and seagulls. She would be bored to her back teeth and itching to set foot back on dry land. Maggie, on the other hand, relished every minute, and almost every cake. She was different from Alice in every single way. They were like chalk and cheese, but then Sam never sought Alice's faithful replica in Maggie. Alice was irreplaceable and she was now a closed chapter. Maggie was a new beginning, untainted by Sam's past. She wasn't just a new chapter – she was a new book and in a completely different genre.

They worked up an appetite for supper by circumventing the decks twice. Maggie led the charge, dressed appropriately in a fitting velvety tracksuit and a pair of hiking boots. Along the way, they explored every door open to the public and found two swimming pools, a well-equipped gym, a cinema, an auditorium with a large stage fit for the Theatre Royal, five bars, each with its own unique ambience which Maggie resolved to explore thoroughly as the cruise proceeded, and three different restaurants. There were also doors that would not open for them and those were marked STAFF ONLY, something Maggie struggled to accept.

By the end of their hike Sam was knackered and ready for dinner.

'You see, I told you that you would be,' Maggie self-congratulated. Sam could not, for the life of him, remember when exactly she had told him that.

They returned to their respective cabins to refresh and agreed to reconvene in an hour.

Precisely an hour later, Sam knocked on Maggie's door and was invited in. He was confronted with Maggie's seaworthy casket gaping open at him like the mouth of a toothless sea monster. It was spewing strings of pearls and other jewellery, skirts of crushed velvet and shawls of silk bristling with colour and glitter.

'My God, Maggie, have you robbed Madame Tussauds?'

'Don't be impertinent, Samuel. It's just my evening wear.' She emerged from the bathroom and stood before him in all her sequin-enhanced glory.

Sam had never seen Maggie dressed to kill. In Bishops Well she would ordinarily sport her pre-millennial dungarees, mildew-green wellies and a roughed-up straw hat, resembling a scarecrow. Sometimes, when on a temporary engagement with one of the village schools, she would make an effort and put on a skirt and blouse, and substitute pumps for her wellies. But never anything like this! The sparkling deep-blue, off the shoulder number undulated between her ample breasts and along her luscious curves, rippling with the excitement of being so close to her milky skin. Sam's imagination ran wild for a few passion-infused seconds.

'Is something wrong with this?' She bit her lip.

'On the contrary – you look stunning, Maggie. I love… it!'

She exhaled. 'Oh goodie.' Then she gave Sam's jumper with patches on his elbows a perfunctory glance, and added, 'Tomorrow we'll find something more appropriate for you to wear.'

CHAPTER 3

A huge Norwegian fir adorned with tinsel, baubles and flashing lights was the restaurant's centrepiece, but it bore no comparison to Maggie. Sam was spellbound. They were shown to their table by their waiter. He was a small Asian man with spiky black hair and sharply trimmed moustache. He introduced himself as Pi Lam.

Though the table was set for six people, only five were seated at it. Apart from Maggie and Sam, there were the husband and wife, Hywel and Stacey Edwards, and a sweet old lady, Barbara Hancock who was travelling alone. The sixth seat remained empty throughout the supper.

Over the entrée, Maggie promptly dispelled everyone's misconception that she and Sam were a couple. 'We're business partners,' she informed the table, 'and neighbours. In fact, we've been neighbours for longer than we've been business partners, haven't we, Samuel?'

'Yes. Our business, a B&B, hasn't officially opened yet.'

'But it's ready to go. We've spent months renovating the place – it used to be my parents' house but was well scorched a bit in an arson attack. Long story. Never mind.' Maggie flicked her wrist and took a swig from her wine glass. 'Anyway, we're now taking time off to recharge our batteries. And naturally, to see St Petersburg in winter. Isn't that right, Samuel?'

'Yes – more or less.'

'Dear Lord, an arson attack!' Barbara looked horrified, so Maggie proceeded to strike while the iron was hot and conveyed -with many embellishments and exaggerations – the story of her wayward sister and her arms-dealer boyfriend. Everyone at the table, including Pi who had just arrived to clear the plates and stayed on to hear the tale, was suitably impressed. Maggie drank to that.

'Did I mention that we – Samuel and I – were instrumental in helping the police to solve that crime. We do a bit of sleuthing on the side. It wasn't our first case actually. But it was special. By golly, it was something else! You did go further than just solving the crime, didn't you Samuel? You did cross a few lines—'

'Well, I… Let's not go there, Maggie.'

'He's so modest, this man, but he's my hero,' she exulted, refilled her glass and asked everyone to join her in a toast to Sam. Pi was requested to bring another bottle of the same vintage.

Over the main course, it was the Edwards' turn to introduce themselves – Maggie insisted. Hywel was a burly Welshman with ginger-tinted curly hair and small brown eyes with irises dotted with golden specks. He was in his early sixties while his mouse-like wife Stacey couldn't be older than forty-five. Everything about her was self-effacing. Her clothes were a pale shade of beige. Her simple cashmere jumper blended with her skinny jeans and riding boots. Her hair was pulled up into a pony tail. She wore minimal makeup and gazed at her husband adoringly whenever he spoke. If he didn't speak, and only then, she would, but it would be all about him. Their reason for embarking on this cruise was to celebrate their fifteenth wedding anniversary. They lived in Guildford. She still worked, commuting every day to London. She was a youth worker. Hywel was a retired estate agent, and an active campaigner for fathers' rights. They had met on the London tube, travelling to work on the same train every day, until he invited her for a drink. They had no children together in spite of several IVF cycles which had nearly bankrupted them. They had given up trying when Stacey turned forty.

'I've no children,' Maggie informed them. 'I don't know if that's what you would call *by choice*, but I never got around to developing maternal instincts. In fact, I never got down to getting married, so at least you're one step ahead of me.' She raised her glass and drank her wine, after which her attention drifted to her plate. She shuffled her vegetables around the beef wellington without attempting to eat any of it.

Sam had detected an undertone of regret in her voice and the same was apparent from her body language. He had never thought of Maggie as someone plagued by regrets. It would usually be him wallowing in self-pity and Maggie pulling him out of it with her wacky take on life. She consistently presented the façade of a woman with no regrets who had lived her life on the hoof and spent little time analysing wasted opportunities. And yet here she was.

'I can't have children,' Stacey said, equally desolate, if not more so.

The two women gazed at each other warmly, an understanding of some kind forming between them.

'I don't know what's worse,' Hywel interjected, 'not having children in the first place, or having them but being prevented from ever seeing them. At least if you don't have them, you can't get hurt when they're taken away from you.'

'Hywel has a son. The boy's mother refused to acknowledge Hywel's paternity. He was blocked from any contact from the moment the boy was born. In fact, he didn't know he had a son for a good few years – he missed his whole childhood.'

'I've lost every court case against her and in the end run out of money. The law is behind her. She gets to decide if I meet my son, and she decided that I won't. Biological fathers have no rights whatsoever. But this is going to change.'

'Hywel is the chairman of EFF. It's a charity – Equality for Fathers. They're bringing a petition to parliament to change the law – to give biological parents the same rights. It will happen, I'm sure it will, and we can both be parents to Hywel's boy.' Hope shone in Stacey eyes. Being a mother – even if only by proxy – seemed to matter a great deal to her.

'He's not a boy anymore,' Hywel said. Overcoming a small quiver in his voice, he added, 'Let's not get bogged down in that all over again, love. We're on holiday and we don't want to bore everyone to death.'

Whimpers of denial ensued, but weakly. Hywel ordered another bottle of wine and deflected attention towards Barbara. 'And what about you, Barbara? How did you land on this boat?'

'Thanks to my children, as it happens,' Barbara sounded apologetic, presumably for bringing the subject of her offspring into the equation at this juncture of the conversation.

'How's that?'

'They paid for this cruise for me. I couldn't

possibly afford it on my pension.'

'That's really lovely of them,' Maggie perked up, and in the same breath, knocked down another glass of wine (refilled by Pi).

'I suppose…' Barbara didn't sound half as enthusiastic as Maggie. 'It's my Christmas treat.'

'Wow, wow, wow! There's still goodwill in this world. I will drink to that!' Maggie slurred drunkenly.

'Then again,' Barbara took a lady-like sip from her glass, 'James – that's my son – wanted to take his family skiing this Christmas and my daughter travelled to New York with her new partner. Apparently New York is magical at this time of year. Anyway, they felt obliged to send me away somewhere, otherwise I would have expected them at mine on Christmas Day. This way they don't have to feel guilty.' Barbara smiled dolefully. It was obvious she would rather be at home, entertaining her family with roast turkey and mulled wine by the fireplace.

Pi materialised to cheer them up, 'Will you be having coffee?'

'You bet we will!' Maggie gushed. 'I think we could all do with some strong Irish coffee.'

As they were leaving the restaurant, Maggie spotted Sidney Worsley. He seemed uncomfortable sitting amongst a group of people in their thirties. They were laughing, and he was not. Maggie caught a snippet of their conversation – something about a new comedy show on Netflix. Sidney seemed more like a Radio 4 man who wouldn't miss a single episode of *The Archers.*

Maggie pointed Sidney out to Sam. 'Look at him, poor sausage...'

'What makes you think he needs your sympathy?'

'Wouldn't you if you were surrounded by those... those drunken booze-cruisers?'

That was rich coming from a woman who could hardly stand up straight after the amount of wine she had guzzled. Sam did not make that observation out loud.

'We need to rescue poor Sidney. Come on, Samuel.' Maggie staggered towards the table. Sam followed, unsure what to expect, but ready to act.

'Sidney, darling,' Maggie babbled. 'Long time, no see!'

Since this afternoon, Sam commented inwardly. Sidney gawked like a possum caught in the headlights, probably trying to remember their names.

'You must – you absolutely have to – join our table! We have a spare seat. I won't take no for an answer. We're over there.' She waved her arm vaguely in the general direction of their table, which now featured Pi throwing on a fresh tablecloth. 'Say yes, and I will see you there tomorrow for breakfast.'

Sidney looked gobsmacked as did his fellow

diners who had stopped laughing to critically scrutinise the drunken woman before them.

'Is that a yes?' She insisted.

Sam smiled his encouragement at the old man. Sidney nodded.

'Excellent!'

By the time they reached their cabins, Maggie was clutching Sam's arm, using him to stabilise herself. She was carrying her shoes draped over her wrist. She was thoroughly sozzled and this was only the first day. Sam's plans to start his romantic offensive tonight had to be put to bed, next to Maggie. Even if she'd said *yes*, she wouldn't remember it the next morning and he would have to repeat himself. A proposal was one of those once-in-a-lifetime utterances. Well, perhaps twice in a lifetime in some cases. Sam had to wait for the right moment to make it.

Tomorrow, when she was sober, he would have a word with her.

CHAPTER 4

Maggie's Journal

I had committed myself to writing a travelogue for the Sexton's Herald online magazine, and further to contribute my entries in daily instalments. I fell at the first hurdle – my first day was a blur. I woke up feeling queasy and only got better when I threw up.

As a rule, I am not a thrower-upper, but this – I concluded – had to be a severe case of seasickness. I wasn't going to surrender to it or to, God forbid, cut this holiday short because of it. I was going to manage it. Less cake, for example, and more liquids. Hydration was the name of this seafaring game.

Having conquered the seasickness, I was feeling optimistic. We were to spend one day on dry land in Amsterdam. No nauseating bobbing on the choppy waters of the North

Sea for twenty-four hours. I showered, brushed my teeth and dressed, appropriately. I packed my notebook and pen in my rucksack. I was determined to mend my ways and to apply myself with diligence to note-taking. I would make it up to *Sexton's Herald* for the day I had missed, and to myself for the money I had lost. They were paying me a set fee for every entry: no entry – no pay. Considering that I had bled myself dry buying the necessities for this trip, I was in financial dire straits.

Samuel knocked on my door at 9am. There was something unimaginative and infuriating about his punctuality, but I wasn't going to tell him that, was I? I had planned this holiday carefully, with Samuel in mind. I was doing it for him. He had been my knight in shining armour on a number of occasions in the past. It was my turn now. Sweeping him off his feet on this wild Viking adventure was a token of my appreciation.

After this trip, his status would return to that of an ordinary man. I couldn't continue having a hero for a business partner indefinitely. That just wouldn't work, and I intended to make a great success of Badger's Hall, that being our joint B&B enterprise back in Bishops Well.

Samuel squinted at me and made a particularly insensitive remark, 'You look green, Maggie.'

'Well, thank you, Samuel!' I chose to take that

on the chin. 'I've been feeling a little sick, but I'm much better now. Seasickness, I'm afraid.'

'Seasickness?' He stared at me, incredulous.

'Or food poisoning,' I said on reflection. 'Something didn't taste quite right – I'd say the cream in that éclair wasn't as fresh as I'd wish it to be.'

'Cream?'

'Yes, cream, Samuel.' He seemed a bit slow. 'Are you feeling okay?'

'Absolutely fine.'

'You see! That's because you didn't have the éclair.'

Samuel opened his mouth to say something, but thought better of it, and closed it. We – I – decided to skip breakfast on the account of seasickness, and proceeded to the main deck in order to disembark.

I found Amsterdam the way I had left it some fifteen years ago when I last visited. I would even venture to say that most of the bicycles in view were the exact same bicycles as fifteen years ago, still lined up in an orderly, tight formation, chained to the rail in the wall, some sporting the same baskets and very few equipped with helmets. I had quickly learned to look left and right before crossing the streets as I had nearly been mowed down by murderous cyclists who seemed to own the roads. Not only did they not apologise or ask after my welfare, but they scowled at me, and a couple of them reprimanded me in no uncertain terms for getting under their feet, or rather wheels. For a brief while, I found myself missing the sleepy dirt roads of Bishops Well.

Leaving bicycles and cyclists behind us, we sought shelter away from the deadly streets and visited every gallery worth visiting in Amsterdam. Let me tell you, there are many worthy galleries in Amsterdam. I was taking detailed notes for my travelogue.

Soon the paintings of famous battle scenes and the faces of city merchants and their chambermaids began to melt before our eyes. It had all become one bleary composite of a blobby shape and a nondescript shade of grey. We decided it was time to stop for coffee. And to sit down – our feet were killing us. At least, mine were, and they were doing it loudly and rancorously. Samuel isn't one to complain about his creature discomforts so he made no comments about his feet when I complained about mine.

We emerged into the chilly dusk of the mid-December afternoon. It was tempered by multi-coloured lanterns suspended from bridges and exuberant Christmassy décor bursting out of shop windows.

We walked for a short while along a narrow, cobbled street parallel to one of the many Amsterdam canals. In the basement of one of the tight tenements lining the street we uncovered a café. It was dark and dingy, lit only by the feeble and languid flames of gas lamps, with huge barrels for tables and medium-size barrels to sit on. There was some sort of ventilation pipe hanging overhead, making bizarre knocking sounds. As we descended the spiral stone stairwell into the café, I had the strong impression that we were entering the first circle of hell. I was thrilled.

The strange, part-smoky part-musky scent hanging over the place began to make sense to me when I read the menu. It featured cannabis and a few other varieties of weed in assorted forms: edible, drinkable and smokable. The little hairs on the back of my neck stood up on end. I had never been to a drug den!

I inhaled deeply, but that would be my only partaking in drugs. I have an addictive personality and that means I have to steer away from anything habit-forming. This way I remain in charge of my faculties, with my feet firmly on the ground and my head as clear as the morning dew. I ordered a pot of tea and a slice of poppyseed cake. Samuel made his order too.

Soon after our cakes and beverages arrived I began to wonder whether Samuel might be indulging in something hallucinogenic. He was having a mysterious herbal infusion and a pink-and-brown cake the likes of which I hadn't seen before. And then he started acting oddly. He rolled his barrel closer to mine so that our thighs were now touching. He pressed his chin into the cup of his hand and leaned on it, gravitating his upper body towards me. Our shoulders met too. At first I thought he was trying to inspect my cake, but that idea was banished when Samuel began speaking – well, mumbling incoherently – into my ear.

Quoting him word for word would not make any sense, so I can only transcribe and interpret his mutterings here.

To begin with, he seemed unspeakably (in more ways than one) grateful to me for agreeing to sell him half of Priest's Hole and becoming his neighbour. I attempted to explain that it had been a pretty straightforward commercial transaction and he had nothing to be grateful for: he had paid me a fair market price for it. He disagreed by way of a snort. He then continued in the same vein of *looooving* Bishops Well (*the best kept secret in the whole of England*), *loooving* his new life – next door to me being mentioned again as an added bonus, *loooooving* me always being there for him (I would say it was the other way around, but didn't bother to interrupt him as he was in full swing of just *looooving* a long list of items yet to be declared).

I must say I was dumbfounded by the blooming *loooove* Samuel was teeming with, and didn't know what to do with it or how to respond (if response was required, which wasn't quite clear from his monologue). I looked away, searching for help. I feared medical help might be called for as Samuel had evidently succumbed to a drug-infused trance.

My eyes were attracted to a man wearing a distinctly out of date outfit: a pinstriped suit and the sort of wide-brimmed hat men used to wear in the early sixties. And not just any men. That kind of attire belonged in London's East End in that era, sported by gangsters and gigolos. This man was in his twenties, lean and tough-looking, self-possessed and puffing on a cigar. The smoke from the cigar clouded his face.

Next to him sat another man in his twenties. This one wore common twenty-first century gear of skinny jeans and a grey top. This man was real and very much alive, I realised, while the other one was a spirit of someone long dead. The living young man appeared familiar unless I was also hallucinating due to my second-hand weed inhalation. I blinked through the fumes.

It was the unusual combination of his Mediterranean olive complexion and his ginger curls the likes of which one would expect to find on a full-blooded Scotsman. I knew him! And I knew the (living) woman who was with him. I let my eyes shift to her: an older but still beautiful woman with shiny black hair, sculpted thick eyebrows, a Roman nose and sensual lips (possibly surgically enhanced – the lips. The nose seemed like the authentic article). That was it – I had it!

'What a small world!' I interrupted Samuel's drivel. 'They are from Bishops Well.'

'Who?'

I pointed them out to him. 'Oh, what's her name? It's on the tip of my tongue.' I meandered through the smoky corridors of my fallible short-term memory. 'Oh, damn it! She lives in Forget-Me-Not – bought the house last year. I forget her name. A very rich woman – an internet banking queen, or something to that effect... Oh, come on, Maggie, try to remember!'

'Cordelia Conti Lang, of course!'

'You know her?'

'Everyone does. At least everyone has heard of her. Especially if you're a Londoner.'

'Why is that?'

Samuel proceeded to enlighten me about Cordelia Conti Lang, our fellow Bishopian. He seemed fully coherent all of a sudden. I gathered that the effects of the drugs he had ingested in his cake were wearing off. I was amazed at the extent of his knowledge of the woman, but as he went on I realised why. Cordelia Conti Lang was famous – or more to the point: infamous.

She had been married to the notorious East End mobster, Lenny Lang. That was when everything fell into place for me: the cigar-puffing spectre, his pinstriped suit and wide-brimmed hat. The apparition was that of Lenny Lang.

He had met Cordelia in a seedy Soho bar when he was in the twilight of his illustrious criminal career and she was an up-and-coming escort. It had been love at first sight despite the thirty years age gap between them.

Cordelia Conti wasn't just a pretty face and loose morals. She was a well-educated woman. She had a degree in economics from the University of Padua. She also had a sharp mind and a ruthless heart. She had the scruples of an alley cat. Under her influence Lenny had graduated from violent to white-collar crime: organised, untraceable and much more profitable.

Lenny had half of the Metropolitan Police in his pocket, and the other half were too scared or too hapless to do anything about his and Cordelia's activities. From the mid-nineties onwards, they had built an impenetrable world of fraudulent pyramid schemes and fake investment scams. The early noughties had seen them inducing unsuspecting victims to invest their life savings, pensions and bonds in the bubble of the property boom which had burst in 2008 sending most of those victims to their early graves.

Auspiciously for Cordelia, Lenny had joined his victims by suddenly passing away in that same year, at the age of seventy-three. He left Cordelia well provided for, her fortune estimated (for no one would ever know the exact figure) to oscillate in the region of half a billion pounds sterling.

Despite her riches, Cordelia had not rested on her laurels. With the instincts of a money bloodhound, she had sniffed out good money in the internet market, and thus she had become known as the Bitcoin Queen. By now, the woman had doubled her wealth.

'Blimey!' I exclaimed. 'And she lives next door to us! Maybe we could make her acquaintance and see if she would be willing to invest in our archaeological projects?' I feel I should mention at this point that Samuel and I are members of Bishops Well AA, that being an *Archaeological Association*, and we have so far uncovered a Bronze-age settlement with burial grounds in Sexton's Wood and set up a museum. There are many more priceless artefacts to dig up as Bishops appears to have been built on an ancient treasure trove, but we ran out of funds. We could do with a rich benefactor.

'I don't think that's a good idea, Maggie. She's not the charitable type. She is a criminal, plain and simple. If anything, she would strip you of any spare cash you have.'

'Good thing I haven't got any.'

I scrutinised her and her son discreetly from behind the menu. Last time I had seen them, and that had been at The Old Stables Café in Bishops, the boy looked like he was high on drugs. This time however his demeanour was calm and composed, his eyes clear and the fact that he was engaged in an animated conversation with his mother meant that he was fully compos mentis. Perhaps he had given up using drugs and taken to dealing them instead, I speculated. I wouldn't put it past him, and his mother in particular. I whispered to Samuel, 'What do you think they're doing here? In a drugs den? Do you think what I'm thinking?'

'And what is that?'

'They're dealers – wholesale drug dealers. Lenny is here too, probably showing them around, introducing them to his old contacts.'

'Lenny Lang?'

'Yes, Samuel. Keep up! Lenny's spirit, of course – the man is dead.'

'Ah that,' Sam rolled his eyes, a gesture which I didn't appreciate. He was dismissing me and my ways.

'Didn't you just say that he was a drug lord?' I reminded him.

'Yes, I did but Lenny wasn't selling drugs in Amsterdam – he had his hands full in London. Anyway, what makes you think they're doing anything untoward?'

'It's blatantly obvious that they are. Why else would they be sitting in this particular type of establishment, of all the cafes and restaurants in the whole of Amsterdam? With their money, they could afford the Ritz.'

'They may just be enjoying the ambience,

like us.'

'A little over a year ago that young man was a junkie. I saw it in his eyes. And from what you're telling me about Mrs Conti Lang, she doesn't frequent places on the off-chance of enjoying the ambience. Something fishy is going on, and we must find out what.' I was fired up for sleuthing action.

Samuel clapped his hands against his head and seemed to squeeze his temples alarmingly hard. 'No, Maggie. Please don't start again. Can we just forget about crime and criminals? Just these two weeks? Can we simply have a good time instead?'

'We will. Of course, we will,' I assured him. 'That was the whole idea of bringing you on this cruise – so you can have a good time.'

He blinked at me rapidly, as if he were having an episode. I feared it may be a side effect of him ingesting his mystery cake.

Cordelia Conti Lang and her son rose from their table and headed for the exit, with Lenny sauntering behind them, enveloped in vapours of cigar smoke.

I jumped to my feet and summoned the waiter. I paid him, leaving a tip I couldn't afford only because I had no time to wait for my change. I waved to the blinking Samuel.

'Come on, Samuel, get up, let's go. We can't lose them!'

The streets of Amsterdam never sleep. It was night-time but the dark was dispelled by many bright lights and a flurry of nocturnal activity. Our suspects led us to the legendary red-light district. They meandered aimlessly, Mrs Conti Lang's arm hooked over her son's and her head inclined towards him cosily. They seemed deep in conversation and rather too relaxed and unconcerned to be drug dealers on the prowl. Still, I concluded, appearances could be deceiving, especially when one was dealing with hardened criminals.

Whenever they stopped, we did too and if there were no deep alleys to dive into, we tried to act nonchalantly like a pair of harmless tourists. A few times we ended up staring at display windows with young ladies in different stages of undress pouting their lips, blowing us kissing (aiming primarily at Samuel) and shimmying their abundant breasts. One such lady, when I perhaps stared for too long at her knees-wide-apart unlady-like pose, mouthed some fruity abuse and waved her fist at me. We moved on.

Before long the subjects of our invigilation (closely followed by Samuel and me) left the Sodom and Gomorrah pit of the insomniac city, and carried on towards what seemed like the harbour. I was intrigued as to where we would end up, and astounded to find that it was our very own cruise liner. The notorious Bitcoin

Queen and her offspring were apparently our travelling companions. And so was the ghost of the notorious London Mafioso.

CHAPTER 5

They were late for supper and joined the table just as everyone was finishing their mains. Maggie was delighted to see Sidney, and, at the same time, remorseful for not being there at breakfast to welcome him. She was forced to skip the morning meal due to seasickness, she claimed.

'Don't you fret about that, young lady,' he dismissed her apologies with an affable smile. 'Everyone's been very accommodating. I daresay we're chums already.' He sent a furtive glance towards Barbara, whose cheeks coloured faint-pink as she demurely lowered her gaze.

Unwittingly, Stacey gave Barbara time to recover her senses by babbling about everyone's love of the game of bridge. Stacey and Hywel were apparently regional champions and indulged in playing at every opportunity. Sidney and Barbara had offered to join them for a few games. That was rather auspicious since many evenings of uneventful sailing were – so to speak – on the cards, and not everyone was fond of karaoke nights.

'Excellent! That's exactly what I was hoping for.' Maggie exulted. She then promptly embarked on some strange manoeuvres under the table. Her head momentarily disappeared.

'Maggie?'

'It's these rotten boots, Samuel.' Her voice rose from the floor. 'They're killing me. They're coming off now.'

Pi approached with care. 'Is madam all right?'

'I'm fine. And please call me Maggie. All that *madam* hogwash makes me feel like we're on the set of a Victorian costume drama.'

Pi blinked his bafflement, but obliged her with: 'As you please,' followed by a half-whispered, half-mouthed,' … madam.'

She heard it and grimaced her displeasure, 'For the last time, *Maggie* please!'

'Are you ready to order… um… Maggie?' The discomfort in Pi's voice was palpable.

'Samuel, darling, could you order something for me? I've got my laces in a blinking knot!'

'The pork belly is first class,' Hywel suggested helpfully. Sam ordered two of those, resolving to give the starters a miss.

Over her pork belly and a glass of chilled Pinot Grigio, Maggie blabbered with renewed energy. She had monopolised the conversation, acting on her customary notion that the things she had to say were incomparably more fascinating than anything anyone else wished to talk about. To Sam's shock, she falsely and without batting an eyelid accused him of indulging in hash cakes and weed tea, *going off his rocker and talking utter tosh* to use Maggie's exact phraseology.

Over the poached pear and vanilla ice-cream, she relayed to the table their cloak-and-dagger pursuit of the *internet-banking diva* and her *offspring*. She dismissed Sam when he corrected her to point out that the lady in question was known as the *Bitcoin Queen*, but acknowledged that her actual name was Cordelia Conti Lang.

'The famous widow of Lenny Lang?' Sidney was both impressed and intrigued.

'Yes, the very one. As it happens, she lives in our village, literally next door to us. Although we aren't as close with her as we were with Richard Ruta who owned the estate before her.'

'The film director?' Barbara asked.

'Indeed. And a dear friend of mine.'

Sam cocked his eyebrow in salient protest to that barefaced lie.

Maggie didn't notice his facial contortions. She was on her high horse, charging further and further into her fantasies, 'We have reason to believe that Mrs Conti Lang and Son are up to no good.'

'No, we haven't,' Sam tried his best to keep

things in perspective.

'We do, Samuel.' Maggie softly placed her hand on his arm and gave him an admonishing squeeze. 'Let's not beat about the bush – you could tell they were up to something. We followed them – a bit. Actually, we had no choice but to follow them. They happen to be our fellow passengers on this very boat.'

'You followed them here, onboard this ship?' Stacey appeared disconcerted. She looked at Maggie in disbelief, then transferred her gaze to Hywel. 'They're here?'

'Are we really sharing this vessel with two dangerous criminals? I say!' Hywel winked at Sam behind Maggie's back. Sam rolled his eyes in reply.

Stacey gawped, speechless. At least she believed Maggie and thought that her revelation was newsworthy.

'I know!' Maggie cried. 'We were rather surprised to see them embark.'

'So where are they? Should we be afraid?' Hywel made as though he was looking nervously about him.

'We lost them.'

'So you didn't actually tap them on the back and go *Oh, hello there! What a small world!*'

'No, of course we didn't approach them. Like I said, we think they are up to something.'

'That'd be the royal *We*,' Sam clarified. 'Personally, I think they're just taking the cruise to St Petersburg like the rest of us.'

Maggie scowled at him. Even when she scowled she looked delicious: like a little, plump hot-cross bun.

Sam harboured high hopes for the evening. The night was still young. There was a magic show at nine, followed by karaoke. He groomed himself in his cabin like a love-stricken teenager: showering, moisturising and spraying himself with gallons of expensive cologne. He even put on a silk shirt and tie. All to woo Maggie.

He was ready for her with twenty minutes to spare. He knocked on her door, and just like in Bishops Well, she shouted from within that the door was open and he could let himself in. *Anyone* could let themselves in, Sam despaired at her recklessness and blind trust in people. He entered and waited for Maggie to emerge from the bathroom. When she did, she took his breath away. She was wearing a black, body-hugging mini dress with a white collar and white cuffs. It brought to mind a naughty French maid. All that was missing was a feather duster. Maggie's shapely legs screamed for a compliment but all Sam could muster was to look.

'What's wrong now?' Maggie inspected her tights in search of holes and ladders.

'Um, it's just the getup – it's… it's—' Sam was bumbling.

'OK, so what's wrong with my getup?'

'Nothing. I mean, another new dress! I wonder, do you have a different dress for every day? That'd explain the size of your trunk.'

No, that wasn't what he wanted to say. Not at all. What he really wanted was to deliver a killer-compliment to show Maggie his appreciation of her efforts. And how fond he was of her. What he achieved however was questioning the size of her wardrobe – again!

'What if I do?' She snapped – quite rightly. 'Are we ready? Let's go.'

Sam hung his head and shuffled behind his shapely neighbour down the corridor and two flights of stairs to the auditorium. Sadly, Maggie was unaware of her effect on him.

The place was packed and not a free chair in sight, but their dining companions were already there and had saved two seats for them in the front row. Hywel waved and gestured towards the space between him and Sidney. Sam ushered Maggie to the front, and they sat down after thanking Hywel.

Maggie crossed her enchanting legs and gazed at the stage, taking in the layout and the gothic décor. Sam was taking in Maggie's knees, and more. He tore his eyes away from Maggie's thighs and turned to Hywel to occupy his straying mind with small talk.

Hywel's attention was elsewhere. Sam followed his gaze to the door that led behind the stage. There stood Mr Conti Lang Junior in the company of a pretty young lady dressed in the theatrical finery of net-stockings and a ruby-red bodice with a black ostrich-feather tail. The two young people seemed to have eyes only for each other.

'That's Conti Lang's son,' Sam told Hywel.

'Oh, is he? Yes!' Hywel startled. 'Sorry, I was miles away. Yes, I gathered this much – Oliver Lang, and a pretty girl on his arm.'

'It's good to see that. At least the lad has other interests than accompanying his mother everywhere she goes.'

'She's nowhere to be seen,' Hywel agreed.

'And those two are very cosy with each other.' Sam and Hywel grinned as the young man and the pretty young lady exchanged a surreptitious kiss, after which the girl disappeared back-stage.

The show was about to start. The lights were dimmed and the stage was hit with bright spotlights. The compere announced the grand entrance of Maestro de Norte – or *Morte*, Sam couldn't quite make that out.

The Maestro burst onto the stage in a puff of white smoke. He was wearing a top hat and a cape, and altogether resembled Count Dracula. He was tall and lean, with sharp but handsome features. His hair was uncannily black – probably dyed. The hair and the heavy eye makeup rendered the man creepy, in Sam's opinion. Even more so after he noticed that Maggie was utterly hypnotised by him. She stiffened in her seat, pushed her chin forward, squinted and gaped like a possessed groupie.

'Ladies and Gentlemen, welcome to a night of magic and mayhem!' De Norte spoke in a deep baritone. 'Let me introduce my glamorous assistant, Mademoiselle Coco.'

The pretty young lady with the tail of ostrich feathers glided onto the stage and took a wide and low bow. The audience applauded. The spectacle commenced in earnest.

Everyone's eyes, particularly Maggie's, were on de Norte who was performing a card trick; Sam's eyes were on Maggie's legs. They stayed there throughout the spectacle of rabbits pulled out of hats and knives flung at a rotating target board with Mademoiselle Coco spread-eagled across it. Sam's eyes didn't leave Maggie's lap even when Mademoiselle Coco was being sawn in half in a sarcophagus which she had entered dressed in feathers and re-emerged mummified in bandages. Maestro de Norte's vanishing act in a Tardis-like box and his puzzling re-appearance in a small explosion hardly registered on the periphery of Sam's vision. Only when the magician conjured a bouquet of blood-red roses and strolled off the stage to approach Maggie, plunge on one knee and present her with the flowers did Sam shift his gaze away from Maggie's legs.

He stared gobsmacked as Maggie timidly

accepted the flowers. Her cheeks blushed as red as those rose petals. De Norte rose from his knee, kissed Maggie's hand with the panache of a real count and bent over her to whisper into her ear (and within the earshot of the still gobsmacked Sam), 'You're beautiful as ever, Maggie Kaye…'

A few ohs and ahs rippled through the captive audience. The Maestro leapt back onto the stage, light-footed as a frisky springbok. He summoned Mademoiselle Coco to his side and they jointly executed the final bow – he with a swish of his cape and she with a twerk of ostrich feathers. Enthusiastic applause rewarded their efforts. De Norte blew one last kiss from the stage – directed at Maggie! – before diving behind the curtain.

Sam looked to Maggie for an explanation, but she wasn't offering one. She was still spellbound, staring at the empty stage, red roses in hand.

Sam lay in bed with his eyes wide-open. He was unable to settle into sleep. He had been lying like this for a good couple of hours.

After the magic show, Maggie had suddenly resolved to return to her cabin and give the karaoke a miss. She wouldn't be persuaded to stay. Her change of heart had alarmed Sam. Maggie loved singing, loudly and badly, and what better opportunity to indulge that hobby than a karaoke session. And yet, she had fled to her cabin, quoting the need for an early night due to a headache. Sam had offered to escort her and had done so despite her protestations.

He was now feeling guilty and inadequate. He had failed in his knight-in-shining-armour gallantry. He'd shown no flair and no imagination to his lady. His courting efforts were laughable. He was like a bull in a china shop: tongue-tied and clumsy.

And there was more to his discomfort. There was jealousy and suspicion. Who was Maestro de Norte? More to the point: who was he to Maggie? How did he know her name – her full name? Why did he single Maggie out from an audience full of single ladies falling over each other for his attention and a chance of a holiday romance? They were swooning over him, yet he went for Maggie – Sam's Maggie! Why?

Was that cold-blooded lizard trying to seduce Maggie right under Sam's nose? And why was Maggie so cagey about it? She hadn't explained, had in fact refused to talk about the man when Sam had asked. She had said she wanted to be left alone. *Left alone by Sam,* but did the same apply to Count Dracula?

Sam wasn't just suspicious of the magician - he was also angry with himself. Why couldn't he come up with something as simple and effective as a bouquet of red roses? Why couldn't he squeeze through his throat any flattery, any compliments or declarations of his undying devotion? It would all be true: Maggie was beautiful to him in every single way, she was great to be around, she had helped him deal with grief over Alice's death, and he loved her – loved the damned woman to bits! He just couldn't say it.

He tossed and turned on the one half of his wide bed, wishing Maggie was lying on the other, and acutely conscious of the fact that she wasn't and that, as things stood, never would be.

Sam fell into deep and dark despondency. He stood no chance against the charming and mysterious magician with a knack for pyrotechnics – Maggie's type.

He rolled sideways and stared at the painted window with bright pink orchids, dragonflies, humming birds and waterfalls, all of which was just an illusion. He whispered, 'Oh Alice, I can't remember how to do it. Help me here. Remind me how it's done.' But Alice didn't reply. She wasn't even there. Sam's torment continued through the night.

CHAPTER 6

Maggie's Journal

I can't tell if I was dreaming or remembering. It was something in between, something on the verge of surreal.

I had fended off Samuel with a rude but effective, *I just want to be left alone,* and shut myself in my room. I actually flicked the lock on. I listened at the door to make sure Samuel wasn't lingering. He was – for at least five minutes. Then, I heard his door click shut.

At first, I tried not to think about Benedict Rawbotham. He was a blast from the past and I was determined that he would stay there. It had been many years. I wouldn't know what to say to him. I didn't care to know what he had to say to me. The time for explanations had long passed. I resolved to avoid him. This was a big ship – it was perfectly possible for our paths to never cross again.

The starched collar of my dress was stiff and scratchy. My neck was red-raw. I unzipped the dress and wriggled out of it. I chucked it into the trunk. I sat in my underwear, feeling lost. Perhaps I would be better off sitting shoulder to shoulder with Samuel, drinking a nightcap. I decided against it. Firstly because Samuel was bound to ask questions and I really didn't wish to discuss my unglamorous past. And secondly because I re-discovered a bag of Rum & Raisin Extravaganza fudge. I was too distressed to share it with anyone.

It was peering at me from the depths of my trunk. I had purchased it from Kev and Jane Wilcox at the Thursday market two days before the cruise. Of all the bare necessities I had acquired for this trip, the fudge was the best. I had my creature comfort which I could rely on to cheer me up. I would let Samuel sleep in peace. I crawled into bed. There, curled up with the pillow under my cheek, I stuffed my face with the comforting fudge and let it take its effect. I fell asleep. At least I think I did.

When the images of Benedict began to flood in, I wasn't sure if I was fully awake or fully immersed in dreams. I was in that nebulous twilight zone that was neither reality nor fantasy.

It had been a meeting of minds and hearts – love at first sight. Somebody's birthday party – I can't remember whose. I think it was one of my girlfriends from uni. It may have been Eleanor, but what does it matter anyway?

I was in the second year of my teaching degree. We were mainly women, and a couple of nerdy boys not worth a second glance or already taken. We were starved of a true alpha-male, testosterone-rich presence in our midst. Not that it bothered me. I had given up on men, still smarting from the rejection I'd suffered at the hand of my previous boyfriend (at least, I'd thought he was my boyfriend after our one and only night of passion; he'd had a very different take on the matter. Let me tell you – it hurt like hell). So, understandably, I was absolutely convinced that I didn't need a man in order to be happy. I was even contemplating engaging in front-line feminism. I had already stopped wearing bras and shaving my armpits. Benedict changed all of that.

He glided into my life like a beautiful black swan. He was charming. He was funny. He was an adventurer. I was an adventurer, I fancied. It therefore followed that we were soulmates.

Within three months we moved in together, renting a studio flat in Shepherds Bush. Benedict was studying acting at RADA. He was a talented actor. He'd even appeared in the Motorola ad. He was also a budding entrepreneur. There were times when he could afford to light his cigarettes with five-pound notes. Indeed, money tended to burn holes in his pockets. There were also times when his pockets were empty. Never a dull moment in the life of Benedict Rawbotham.

I often felt like an ugly duckling to his glamorous swan. He was heading for film stardom and I for a village school classroom. But he knew how to dispel my insecurities. He treated me like a lady and was perfectly in character in the role of a gentleman. Now, with hindsight, I suspect it was just an act.

He hadn't changed that much. His manner. His panache. His black hair and sharp grey eyes that could pin you to the wall, ravage you and leave you wanting more, like a vampire's bite. He was still hypnotising – perfectly placed to become a magician. Then again, he could be anyone. I wondered how he had landed the role of performing magic tricks on a cruise liner, but I wasn't going to ask him.

My neck was sore. The discomfort woke me from my dreams – or my reminiscing. I felt the tender skin of my neck. I checked it in the mirror. It looked angry. There was some swelling. I applied moisturising cream to it, but it stung back. I decided to wear my old Christmassy turtle-neck dress. It was soft merino wool, gentle on the skin, and it had Rudolph the Red-Nosed

Reindeer on the front. That nose would go perfectly with my red neck.

It was eight-thirty in the morning. To my surprise I wasn't feeling hungry. I was wretched and tired, and hung over. I was bracing myself for the second day of my unabating seasickness.

At breakfast I worked tirelessly to evade Samuel's questioning glances. I didn't want to interact with anyone. I decided to let my table have a go at socialising without me. As a result, the conversation didn't sparkle with wit or humour. A few loose remarks were made about last night's show. Barbara asked me if the flowers were real. I had to think hard and long before realising she was referring to the bouquet of roses Benedict gave me.

'They were artificial – paper roses. Nothing special.' I shrugged and poked my egg benedict with my fork. It was cold. I'd barely touched it.

'Are you OK, Maggie?' Stacey asked. 'You look a bit peaky.'

'And you left quite suddenly last night. I thought you were staying for the karaoke.' Barbara too had to throw in her two pennies' worth. 'Something not agreeing with you, dear? Is it the food?'

What is it with us, women, jumping out of our skins to show concern and compassion every chance we get? As if it's our business. As if we care. Men don't give a monkey's and they don't pretend they do. The world doesn't fall apart because of their indifference. It carries on regardless – bruised and uncared for, but it just goes on. What doesn't break it, will make it stronger.

I was mulling over those disjointed and bitter notions, and growing altogether world-weary and fed up. I wished I had stayed in good old Bishops Well for Christmas instead of galivanting around the Arctic Circle, with the Ghost of Christmas Past breathing down my neck and a couple of well-meaning strangers trying to read my mind.

And then there was my itchy neck crawling with ants under my stupid Rudolph the Red-Nosed Reindeer dress. I gave in and sunk my nails into it. Full steam ahead, no holds barred.

Barbara peeked over and gasped, 'Oh dear, that looks bad! Is it a rash? Maybe Sidney should take a look at that?'

I glared at her, 'Sidney is a vet.'

'Still, he'd have an idea about what may be causing it, wouldn't you, Sid?'

Sid? Oh, so it was *Sid* now, I noted. My two elderly travel companions were getting cosy. I would have rejoiced to hear that at any other time, but right now I felt rotten and couldn't care less about bringing those two together. I just wanted to scratch my neck to death and then go home.

Sidney opened his mouth to clarify his

vocational credentials, but our attention was drawn away towards none other than Cordelia Conti Lang, the Internet-Banking Prima Donna. She stormed in like a charging buffalo, a wild look in her eyes. It was impossible not to notice her. She stopped Pi in the execution of his duties and demanded to know if he had seen her son. Pi offered her a few respectful *madams* and a profuse apology, because no, he had not seen the young gentleman this morning. She pushed him aside and continued to blunder around the tables, searching for her offspring. Her agitation was irreconcilable with the fact that we were confined on a ship, in the middle of the sea, with nowhere to go. The young man had to be somewhere on this boat. The likelihood of him jumping overboard was slim, unless of course she knew something that we didn't – something that gave her cause for concern. She darted about madly until she came to our table.

She startled and stared. It was uncanny how she had stopped in her tracks and just stared at us. Her eyes were glazed over with something visible only to her. I wondered if she had suddenly remembered where she had left her son, but her lips weren't smiling with relief. They were curled down, revealing her bottom teeth. She looked like a wolf, motionless, hungry, about to pounce on its unsuspecting prey – us.

I tried to smile, even raised my hand to signal my friendly intentions towards her, but she didn't seem to register me at all. She was looking, but she wasn't seeing.

This bizarre moment lasted for a good half a minute, if not longer. It certainly felt longer. When she finally huffed at us and stormed out, we all exhaled.

'That was odd.' Sidney cocked his eyebrow.

'Indeed.' Samuel cocked his.

The rest of us said nothing. Barbara looked shaken to the core, Stacey white as a ghost and Hywel inscrutable. It seemed as if he had been turned to stone. I was the only one relieved by Ms Conti Lang's intrusion – she had taken the heat off me.

CHAPTER 7

Maggie's Journal

We soon discovered that Conti Lang Junior was still onboard this ship, in one piece, and reunited with his mother. Samuel persuaded me to accompany him to the top deck to admire the Kiel Canal.

It was indeed glorious: its banks were dusted with fresh snow which made everything look clean and fluffy. We were passing through the town of Schleswig-Holstein. It was pretty and festive, and sprinkled with lights. I could tell Samuel was doing his best to just enjoy the view, but his urge to interrogate me was stronger.

'You know I care about you, Maggie, don't you?'

'Of course, I do. As I care about you. We are, after all, business partners.'

'We're more than that, I should think.'

'And neighbours. And, yes, you're right, we are good friends. If I'm honest with you – but don't repeat this to Vera – you've overtaken Vera as my closest confidante. I don't mean it's because you live next door, but because… because… well, I don't know how to put it.'

'Just say it!' His eyes shone – burned even – with encouragement. I had no idea what exactly he was expecting me to say.

I said, 'Because we have a history now, the two of us. We're as thick as thieves. I mean, we've been through so much, and— You know what, Samuel? You never let me down.' That revelation dawned on me before I finished the sentence. I looked at my best friend with new eyes.

He seemed slightly less expectant, nodded pensively and compressed his lips. Perhaps he had not heard what he wanted to hear. Still, it was true. I beamed at him. I was chuffed to have him in my life, right next door to me.

'I'm sorry if I was a bit offish last night. And this morning.' I apologised and felt a heavy weight lift from my chest. At that moment I experienced the precise physical sensation behind the phrase of *getting it off my chest.*

'You know you can always talk to me? About anything.'

'I do, Samuel, yes. There's nothing to talk about though.'

'What about that magician?'

'Benedict?'

'Is that his name?'

'Benedict Rawbotham. Forty-six, maybe seven. An actor by trade, upgraded – or downgraded, depending on how you look at it – to a magician. An ex-boyfriend. Ancient history. I never envisaged bumping into him, so it came as a shock. I'm fully recovered now.' It felt good. I had put Benedict into perspective and he came down to his normal size. I'd purged him. I grabbed Samuel by the shoulders and bear-hugged him.

'What was that for?'

'I don't know. I just felt like it. Anyway, have we cleared the air? Are we friends again?'

'We never stopped, Maggie. But if I am your friend and if my judgment means anything, let me tell you – something is fishy about that Benedict Rawbotham of yours. He's bad news.'

'You can say that again!' If only he knew the half of it, I pondered ruefully.

'I don't trust him. He's a showman – a confidence trickster. I know the type only too well.'

I had the distinct impression that Samuel was jealous. It sent a fuzzy, tickly current down my spine.

'I don't trust him either.'

'He's trying to seduce you. He's like a big black spider, weaving his web around you. I mean, those roses! Cheap trick. That was ludicrous. What does he want, you have to ask yourself this—'

'Didn't you hear what I said?'

Samuel's answer froze on his lips as raised voices burst on to the deck from the fire escape stairwell. It was Cordelia Conti Lang and her son, and they were having a proper go at each other.

'You had no right to send her away like that, Mother. She's not one of your chamber maids!'

'She's a harlot, Ollie!'

'Don't ever call her that!'

'Then what would you call her?' Cordelia's tone lowered to a growl. 'What self-respecting girl would entertain a stranger in her bedroom on the first night she met him? A common whore.'

'Say that again and I'll kill you!'

Samuel and I ducked. It was an impulse. Ollie sounded like he meant it. We were squatting on the floor, eavesdropping on the pretty explosive row which was taking place just round the curve of the prow.

'Look here, my darling boy,' Cordelia executed a sharp change of tack. She sounded almost soothing, 'you are infatuated by a pretty little thing in a fancy costume. You got carried away, thought it was for real. But it's an act. She's smelt your money and she wants it. There're thousands of slimy whores around – take your pick. Just don't get emotionally involved. Okay? And next time do tell your mother that you're going to be out for the night. I can take it – as long as I know.'

'I'm not your darling boy anymore, Mother. I'm twenty-three.'

'Still a baby. Always my baby.' Her voice was soft like lavender talcum, or whatever that powder is that you sprinkle on babies' bottoms for nappy-rash.

'And I'm not infatuated. I love Emilia.'

'You've only just met the little—'

'We've been together for nine months, Mother. She saved me from the drugs – from you! We are in love. We're going to be married, and there's nothing you can do to stop us.'

For the first time, Mrs Conti Lang was speechless. No response came from her for a frighteningly long time. I assumed she had fainted. But then I realised she couldn't have because Ollie was still speaking so she must've been conscious in order to listen.

'Why do you think I booked this cruise for your birthday? Why do you think I'm tagging along and putting up with you? This isn't my idea of a holiday – sightseeing with my bloody mother! I'm not that sad! You need a reality check. So here it goes: it's all because Emilia is here and I can't bear being separated from her, even for a couple of weeks.'

Ollie was beginning to grow on me. The boy had balls. Only slightly taller than his mother, he looked her straight in the eye and laid down the law, 'You'll treat Emilia with respect. You will not call her names. She is the woman I love and I want you to meet her, but you must—'

Cordelia howled. I peeped over to check that she hadn't transformed into a werewolf. She still looked human – just. Lenny Lang, her dear-departed husband, was also there, watching the scene of mother and son verbal carnage with unease. It was all too much even for him – too much for a heartless mobster, imagine!

Cordelia raged on, 'I won't have it! She's a harlot, a showgirl, a whore – she'll use you, steal from you and throw you to the wolves when she's done with you. Like all of them! She's no diff —'

'Don't paint her with the same brush as yourself,' Ollie's voice was cold and brimming with menace. 'Just because you did it, Mother, married Dad for his money, used him, stole from him, and threw him to the wolves—'

That was when she slapped him. It was more like a punch with an open hand. His head literally bounced to one side and had it not been for his neck, it would have flown overboard. I recoiled and crawled back to Samuel.

'You ungrateful little shit,' she hissed. 'Over my dead body – hear me? I'll sooner disinherit you. You won't get a penny from me, and neither will your little whore.'

Despite the blow Ollie had suffered, he was still able to parry her thrust, 'Feel free. I don't care about your money.'

'But she does. Wait till I tell her you haven't a penny to your name.'

'Leave her alone, Mother. Don't go near her. I'm warning you.'

'Don't make me laugh!' And she stomped away, turned the corner and nearly tripped over the two of us squatting on the deck. She regained her balance and glared down at us as we scrambled to our feet.

'Oh, Ms Conti? Small world!' I chimed, idiotically. 'We're from Bishops too. Bishops Well, remember? You don't recognise us, do you?'

'Pardon?'

'I'm Maggie Kaye. We haven't been formally introduced. And this is—'

'Let me pass,' She scowled and pushed by me. Before taking the stairs, she looked back over her shoulder. I feared that she was going to accuse us of spying, or worse yet, shoot us dead with a small lady revolver she would pull out of her clutch bag.

I decided to improvise. I dropped down to my knees and started feeling the floor with my gloved hands, 'Where's that damned earing, Samuel? It must be somewhere here.'

The door swivelled behind her and without further ado the witch was gone. Lenny's ghost floated loyally behind her like an eccentric pixie in a pinstriped suit.

CHAPTER 8

The cruise liner paused in Gdansk for half a day. A city steeped in history, Gdansk featured enchanting medieval architecture peppered with cranes, mills, cobbled streets and gold-encrusted gates and fountains. To see the panoramic views of the city Maggie and Sam visited the Basilica of St Mary's. Maggie complained that it was chock-a-block full of spirits, all in their best patrician attire. The ghost-packed church felt – to Maggie, at least – like Paddington Station at the start of the Christmas festive season. The spirit overcrowding was soon explained. It turned out that the church had been built on a graveyard, a fact duly verified by their tour guide.

'I'm not surprised they're so agitated,' Maggie quipped. 'How would you feel if thousands of feet were trampling over your grave every day?' Maggie shivered and rubbed her shoulders.

Sam was a reasonable man. The answer that would naturally fly off his tongue was that he wouldn't feel anything because he would be dead. However, he bit his tongue and held his peace.

After leaving Gdansk, the cruise liner had entered the rough waters of the Baltic Sea. Twenty-four hours later it got worse. A full-blown storm was raging outside. Strong winds were taking the heads and arms off those few kamikazes who ventured on deck. Lead-stained clouds compressed overhead and were spewing up gallons of freezing water. The passengers were asked to stay below deck until further notice. Life onboard the ship evacuated to the higher ground of the restaurant.

'Ladies and gentlemen, may I please have your urgent attention!' A male voice, amplified by a handheld megaphone, disrupted the noisy social interaction.

The whole restaurant fell silent. Astounded gazes travelled to an old man in uniform, with the Cruise Liner logo on his breast. He was tall and well-built, but a bit hunched and hollowed – an undeniable sign of his ripe old age. His face was ploughed with deep ruts of wrinkles. His hair was as white as a pigeon. Yet, despite his advanced years and stooped posture, he commanded authority.

'My name is Vincent Hatton. I am the Chief

Security Officer onboard this ship. An hour ago, two of our crew witnessed three red flares in the distance. That signifies a *mayday* distress call. Someone at sea is in danger and in need of assistance.

'Our radar shows a small vessel – perhaps a trawler. In the last hour we've been trying to establish radio contact with them. To no avail – they're not responding. Chances are that they have lost radio capacity. We are legally obliged to attempt a rescue operation.

'We have reported this to the nearest port, and they will be dispatching a search team in the morning. The weather conditions prevent them from sending helicopters right away. However, we are closer to that vessel than anyone else – we can't be more than two nautical miles away from where the flares were fired. That means we are now changing course to South-West with the objective to locate the vessel and render help to its passengers and crew.

'I can't answer any questions. Please remain calm. There is no cause for alarm. We will keep you informed. And, of course, we apologise for any inconvenience.'

Mr Hatton lowered his megaphone, turned on his heel briskly like a seasoned soldier, and marched out to attend to his urgent duties forthwith.

The hubbub of lively conversation followed his departure. The passengers seemed mainly excited. Not many were worried. It was an added bonus – a marine rescue operation – at no extra charge.

'Vincent has it under control,' Pi assured the table. He was still hanging around, a jar of cold coffee in hand.

'I bloody well hope so,' Hywel snorted. 'How old is that man? He looks like he should've retired years ago.'

'He did,' Pi confirmed, 'retire, but then he made an unwise investment – all his pension money went into a high-risk currency, and it all crashed.'

'Oh dear,' Barbara commiserated. 'I once was tempted to do something similar. My son stopped me just in the nick of time, as I was about to sign the paperwork on the dotted line. Ten years ago, but it feels like only yesterday.'

'About the same time as Vincent. It was ten years ago when he was forced to return to work. He was flat broke.'

'A cushy desk job or a village library would suit him better, surely!' Hywel pointed out.

'I wouldn't underestimate him, sir. He used to be in the Marines. Security business is what he does best. You can trust him.'

Despite being told to remain calm and below deck, a huge proportion of the passengers disobeyed the order and braved the elements to witness the rescue operation. The remaining portion were those who could watch the goings-on from their cabins on the starboard side where all the action was taking place. Everyone else put on hats and gloves, fetched their cameras, and hurried on deck. The wind was slapping them about their faces, the freezing rain lashing and soaking them to the bone, but curiosity was stronger than the adverse weather conditions.

Powerful search-lights were pointed at the small vessel wobbling haplessly on furious tides. The rescue craft from the cruise liner had reached the boat and four people had boarded it.

'Do you think they'll find them alive?' Maggie asked Sam.

'My guess is as good as yours. Though, on second thoughts, yours is possibly better.'

'Oh, is it?'

'Well, if you can't see any ghosts hovering over that boat, then maybe they're still alive.'

'Of course I can't see any ghosts, Samuel – it's way too far!' She pursed her lips, offended. 'I never know with you – if you're serious or taking the mickey.'

Sam put his arm around her. 'If I take the mickey, it is done with affection.'

People gasped and camera-phones started rolling when the first person emerged from the vessel, wrapped in a silver thermal blanket. He – or she – was led to the rescue craft, stumbling and leaning heavily on the crew member who had his arm hooked under their elbow. There were more gasps, more selfies, and a few exclamations, when another person – hopefully alive, but potentially dead – was carried out on a stretcher.

Once the person was safely transferred onto the craft, it shot through the waves towards the ship. Mr Hatton was overseeing the operation from the deck. As soon as the craft aligned with the pulleys, the person in the thermal blanket was lifted up onboard the ship. He – for it was a man – was instantly intercepted by a medic and led away. The harness was lowered to receive the person on the stretcher. Attaching the stretcher took no longer than two minutes, and it was up in the air, heading for the safety of the liner. Again, members of the medical team were on hand to swiftly carry the injured person away to the medical bay.

Meantime, the rescue craft was heading back towards the fishing vessel. Pixeled with the incessant icy rain, the search lights were crossing in front of the boat to guide it along the way.

'They found two more people!' Vincent Hatton shouted to the crowd by way of an explanation.

Indeed, two more stretchers were taken inside the boat and within ten minutes, they were returned to the rescue craft, laden with human cargo. The craft carried them to the cruise liner, and just like the other two, they were winched up onboard.

'They're dead,' Maggie told Sam.

'Both of them?'

'I think so. I can see two young women – their spirits, I mean. They're very unsettled, thrusting their arms in the air. They may be screaming – their mouths are wide open. No wonder – it's all new to them. Sudden death tends to throw people off balance.'

The spectacle was over. The search lights were turned off and the sea glared back at the onlookers, violent and black, like the gaping mouth of a leviathan threatening to swallow them. The storm wasn't relenting. The passengers were ordered inside.

CHAPTER 9

The storm was consigned to the past and the cruise liner was again on the straight and narrow course for Riga.

Sam's charm offensive was now in full swing. There were no more stops until they would arrive in the capital of Latvia, so he had to deploy his ingenuity within the confines of the ship. Maggie was resolutely refusing to attend any of the late-night shows, for which Sam was grateful. He too was wary of Count Dracula, or Maestro de Norte, or Benedict Rawbotham – whatever his name was. Although Sam wasn't a man given to superstition, in the case of Count Dracula, he succumbed to what one would call *a bad feeling*. Staying away from that man was in Sam's opinion a sensible thing to do – an extremely rare example of Maggie exercising common sense.

With the scheduled entertainment out of the equation, there was predictably little to do.

Left with limited choices, Sam contemplated a romantic star-lit dip in one of the outdoor swimming pools. It promised to be a respectable experience, almost skin-on-skin but not quite. It would be a small step in his and Maggie's courtship, but however small, it would be a step forward. He suggested that to Maggie (the swimming, not the courtship), assuring her that the pool was heated and therefore not likely to freeze over. Maggie politely declined the offer.

'Samuel, have you lost your mind? I'm not running half-naked in sub-zero temperatures. I don't care how hot the pool is.'

'It could be fun,' he persisted, unwilling to give up on the image of a half-naked Maggie.

'You go ahead, then. I'll watch.'

In the end, he had to content with speed-walking with Maggie the full length of all three decks every morning before breakfast. It was a small consolation, but a consolation nonetheless, especially because he was tailing Maggie. That meant enjoying the view of her wriggling rear as she marched in a fashion she believed could pass for speed-walking. In reality, it was something between a catwalk run and a duck-waddle. In Sam's eyes it was delightful.

Between lunch and dinner, they would have a session in the gym. Maggie was hellbent on eating her money's worth of cakes without putting on weight. Intense exercise was her solution to this conundrum. She would turn up on Sam's doorstep in her crushed velvet tracksuit, the colour of a fresh peach, at 3pm sharp, and lead him, jogging lightly along the way, to the top deck where the gym was. There she would embark on what she called her *routines.* Again, it was a rewarding experience for Sam even though he also had to work his backside off.

By the time Maggie was finished with her five miles on the treadmill, she would shed the top of her tracksuit, exposing her ample cleavage which was loosely and fluidly contained in her flimsy sports vest. When she was done with the rowing machine, her tracksuit bottoms would come off, leaving her tightly delineated in her Lycra shorts. Those left little to the imagination with every curve, fold and dimple of Maggie's behind duly accentuated.

When Maggie finally planted her bottom on a bicycle to complete the circuit, Sam just sat back and enjoyed the view. Those were the small blessings he was most grateful for. Still, this was as far as he was able to go simply because he did not know how to tell Maggie that he fancied the pants off her.

Two days after the rescue operation, at lunch, Vincent Hatton arrived in the restaurant to update the passengers about the people recovered from the fishing boat.

'I'm happy to report that our operation

was successful. The vessel in distress had lost function in its main engine and their radio had been damaged in the storm. We were able to rescue all of the crew: four men.'

Maggie leaned towards Sam to whisper into his ear, 'What about the two girls I saw?'

'You may've been mistaken, Maggie. It can happen to the best of spiritualists to see things that aren't there.'

Maggie issued a disgruntled humph.

Meantime, Mr Hatton continued, 'All four are recovering from their injuries in the sickbay.'

'I thought they had hypothermia, or something like that.'

Sam raised a querying eyebrow.

'From exposure to the elements, Samuel. Keep up!' Maggie scowled. 'Why would they be injured?' She clearly wasn't satisfied with Hatton's report. She couldn't get over the fact that she was wrong about those *dead girls.*

'We won't find out anything if we don't listen,' Sam hushed her.

'As soon as we arrive in Riga we will hand them into the care of the Latvian authorities. Two of them are Latvian and the other two, Swedes.' The Chief Security Officer concluded his briefing.

Maggie put her hand up, signalling to Mr Hatton that she had a question to ask. When he didn't get the message, she waved her arm vigorously in his face, literally squealing for attention. Mr Hatton could not miss that.

'Yes?'

'What were they doing in the open sea in the middle of that storm? Surely, they weren't fishing.'

'Apparently their radio had been playing up – they hadn't heard the severe weather warning.'

'And, just to be sure, Mr Hatton,' Maggie pressed on, 'are you positive that there were no women on that boat? Two young ladies, specifically.'

In reply she received a baffled frown from the man. 'Yes, madam, absolutely positive. We would've noticed if there were any, young or old.'

'Have you searched the whole boat?'

Hywel and Sidney looked to Sam for an explanation of Maggie's bizarre line of questioning. Sam compressed his lips and arched his eyebrows in an internationally recognised gesture of *I haven't got a clue.*

'Our rescue crew searched the vessel and satisfied themselves that there was no one else onboard before they abandoned it. There were certainly no women on that boat.'

'Well, that's very odd.' Maggie laced her fingers under her chin and fixed Vincent Hatton with a suspicious glare.

He cleared his throat, looking distinctly uncomfortable. 'Right then, that's all I wanted to say. There are no causes for concern, rest assured. We are continuing as per our itinerary, but we have had a five-hour delay. We are hoping to make up time with the fair wind behind us. Enjoy your meal, ladies and gentlemen.'

After he left, Barbara asked Maggie in astonishment, 'What on earth were you on about?'

Maggie seemed undeterred in her pursuit of that elusive truth she wanted to hear. 'Do you really believe his story? Four men fishing in the middle of a vicious storm. Fishing! And if that wasn't ridiculous in itself, just think of the international composition of that *fishing team*.' Maggie drew inverted commas in the air with her hooked fingers. 'Two Latvians and two Swedes joining forces to... fish. Come on! It simply isn't credible. Not to mention these two young women.'

'But there weren't any women – he just said.'

'He lied.'

Sam felt compelled to step in before Maggie inadvertently slipped into the realm of ghostly apparitions and was forced to join the two Latvians and two Swedes in the sickbay to treat her unexplained hallucinations.

'Maggie has a curious mind.' He smiled indulgently at her. 'She likes to sleuth and imagine things.'

'*Imagine things!*' Maggie puffed her cheeks with indignation.

'Different scenarios. Possibilities, I mean.' He was struggling to defuse the situation.

Defending his position to Maggie was a lost cause. He had to find a distraction. 'I mean, look at the time! We'll be late for the gym.'

When they left the gym, Maggie scampered to her cabin *to record her observations* in the travelogue she was writing for *Sexton's Herald*. She was still on about the *dead women* and the mystery of the fishing boat in the storm. She also threatened to carry out an online investigation into Mr Hatton*, who was lying blatantly about –* yes, you guessed it – *there not being any dead women.*

Sam stood no chance of talking her out of it and agreed that he would leave her to her own devices and pick her up for dinner at seven. He took a couple of hours to relax, read a book and indulge in wild fantasies about his and Maggie's bright future together.

At quarter-to-seven, he could no longer bear being parted from her, so he knocked on her door, let himself in on Maggie's invitation, and waited as she applied the final touches to her hair and makeup.

As usual, she looked gorgeous. She was wearing a sparkling silver dress with a thinly veiled décolletage, similar to the one worn by Marilyn Monroe in *Some Like It Hot.* Sam felt honoured to escort her to dinner.

CHAPTER 10

On their way to the restaurant they found themselves swept by the current of nervous commotion. Vincent Hatton ran past them – ran, at his age! – shoving Maggie out of the way without ceremony or apology. Sam felt like he should demand an explanation, but by the time he found his tongue, Hatton was gone. His voice could be heard, bellowing orders, telling his people to be careful and something else Sam couldn't make out.

The restaurant seemed to be running on skeleton staff. Pi was nowhere to be seen. Other waiters – few as they were – thrust and fussed about, red-faced and agitated. A couple of inevitable incidents of plates tumbling to the floor and drinks spilling on patrons' heads ensued.

Sam and Maggie joined Sidney, Barbara and Stacey at their regular table, and all shared their consternation about the state the ship was in.

'It's a calamity,' Maggie summed it up.

'I love your dress. You look glamorous, dear,' the lovely, kind-hearted and ever so diplomatic Barbara changed the subject. Being a woman of *her* generation, she was made of tougher stuff and didn't plan to fall apart because dinner wasn't served on time.

'Oh, do you like it? Really?' Maggie looked gratified. A big gloss-lipstick smile graced her face, producing two adorable dimples.

Sam kicked himself for not having made the dress comment himself, considering that he had thought it.

'I bought it in a charity shop. It cost peanuts.' Maggie ran her hands along her hips and thighs, smoothing non-existent wrinkles.

'You do look charming,' Sidney agreed. 'Your dress reminds me of someone – can't think of who. Damn memory! Oh, the joys of old age!'

'Marilyn Monroe – that's exactly what I thought when I saw you in it.' Sam had finally coughed it up. The compliment had sat in his throat like a furball, but now that it was out, he felt immeasurably better.

'Marilyn Monroe? Oh, get out of here, Sam! I know you're mocking me.'

'I'm not. You do look just like her – in that film—'

'Oh yes!' Barbara joined in, '*Some Like it Hot.* I loved that movie.'

Maggie lowered her eyes, modestly, one

would be tempted to presume, but then she said, 'That's what I thought when I tried it on. I do look like Sugar, don't I?'

Everyone agreed and the subject was closed. Pi appeared from nowhere, flushed and dishevelled, and prompted them for their orders. He looked rushed off his feet. It was then that Sam realised that Hywel was missing. 'Shouldn't we wait for Hywel?'

Stacey shook her head. 'There's no need. He wouldn't want to hold everyone back. Anyway, I can guess what he'd like. I will order for him.' Which she did.

Pi regained his breath listening to their orders. His eyes darted about anxiously.

'Are you all right, Pi? Is something the matter? You seem rather flustered,' Maggie narrowed her eyes.

'Everything is fine, madam... um, Maggie!' he added before she could remind him for the umpteenth time to remove *madam* from his vocabulary. He turned and hurried away, demonstrating how speed-walking was really done.

'Where's Hywel then?' Maggie redirected her curiosity elsewhere. 'Is he OK?'

'It's nothing really – his EFF work, the usual,' Stacey shrugged. 'He just can't leave the cause behind, even on holidays, I'm afraid. He's skyping with Mark. Won't be long, I shouldn't think.'

'Who's Mark?'

'Another wronged father. Hywel has been mentoring him. Mark's court case for shared custody went to appeal. He's been expecting the judge's decision today. I hope it went his way. He has a boy of five who doesn't even know what his – real – father looks like.

'It's a complete mess. The mother is divorcing the man the boy has known as his dad all of his life. In the first instance, the Court decided against Mark. The mother and the adopted father are fighting over the child – it's a bloody war. Adding Mark's claim into the mix would not be in the child's best interest – that was the rationale the Judge gave. The poor child is already confused about his mum and stepdad splitting up.'

'I can see that point,' Maggie's face dropped. 'Something similar happened to my brother, or should I say, my half-brother. Anyway, it didn't do him – any of us – any good to meet his biological father. Sometimes it may be too late to stir things up.'

'Hywel would disagree with you, Maggie.'

'I imagine he would.'

'His heart still bleeds for his boy. Twenty-odd years later.'

'It's never easy. For anyone.'

Pi returned balancing their starters on his left forearm, with one plate in his right hand. He looked even more flushed than before and forgot to proffer his customary *bon appétit.* Hywel joined the table just as they began eating.

'So, what's the news?' Stacey inquired.

Hywel shook his head, 'Not good.'

'How is Mark taking it?'

'Badly. As you would expect. Anyway, we'll be taking it to the European Court of Human Rights. We aren't giving up.'

'Good man!' Sidney gave Hywel a pat on the back.

'Look at them!' Maggie exclaimed, 'Mr and Mrs Lang have graced us with their presence.'

Indeed, Cordelia Conti Lang had entered the scene. Despite being indoors, she was wearing a white, faux fox-fur, ankle-long coat. It bristled in the light. One could be excused for thinking it was the real thing. It could well be. She paused impatiently in the middle of the restaurant, her chin up, her eyes scanning for service, her foot tapping the floor. A waiter approached her. She took off her coat and thrust it at him. Underneath she was wearing a figure-hugging white-pearl dress, pure satin. It was impressive, but not a patch on Maggie's Marilyn Monroe number, Sam assessed.

The woman was alone, and that fact was observed by Hywel. '*Look at her*, you mean to say, don't you, Maggie?'

Maggie peered at him, ready to elaborate, but quickly realised her mistake. 'Of course, to an untrained eye it's just her. Mr Lang, I understand, is long dead. He wouldn't be hanging around in his dated pinstriped suit and a silly hat, smoking a cigar, would he now?'

'She's usually accompanied by her son. I wonder where he is?'

'They had a fallout,' Maggie explained. 'Samuel and I heard them have a terrible argument, and we weren't even eavesdropping, were we Samuel?'

Sam briefly considered the differences between his and Maggie's definitions of eavesdropping. 'Erm…' he stammered.

'Well, it was out in the open, by the companionway between the top and middle decks, Maggie continued. 'A fallout over a girl.'

Mrs Conti Lang was shown to her table where she sat alone and bitter. Her eyes swooped over their table. A contemptuous snarl quivered on her lips. She whipped her head away and stared intently at the door, as if she were expecting company.

Sure enough, some ten minutes later the young Master Lang appeared. But unlike his mother, he was not alone. And although he clearly saw her as he entered, he chose not to join her. The air was thick with tension as he and his companion took a table in the corner of the restaurant, at the end diametrically opposite to where Mrs Conti Lang sat.

His companion was the lovely Mademoiselle

Coco, or as Samuel and Maggie had discovered earlier, Emilia. This time she wasn't dressed in ostrich feathers, but in a simple ensemble of a cashmere jumper and leggings. She looked like the prototype of a girl-next-door: young, pretty and sweet.

Cordelia had spotted them too. She shot daggers at them. If looks could kill, the lovely and innocent Emilia would be lying on the floor in a puddle of blood.

There was a moment of hesitation in the older woman's body language. She threw her napkin onto the table and rose to her feet, seemingly intent on either walking out or marching towards Ollie and Emilia to confront them. The storm was still brewing in her face, dark with anger, but she sat back down. She summoned a waiter and ordered a bottle of wine. It arrived on her table within seconds.

Meantime, Ollie and Emilia engaged in a cosy conversation, openly flaunting their mutual affection. Ollie was keeping a watchful eye on his mother, his eyes shifting constantly between her and his girlfriend. But it wasn't because he was in any doubt as to where his loyalties lay, that much was clear to Sam. The young man was just conducting a discreet surveillance of his volatile mother who could blow up at any minute. Other than that, his actions spoke louder than words: he had made his choice and he had chosen Emilia.

'They look a picture,' Stacey smiled at the young pair. Her smile travelled towards Hywel. It was filled with love. Their hands met on the table and interlocked.

Sam wished he could reach for Maggie's hand. It was so close to his that they were almost touching. Sidney was peering tenderly at Barbara, and Barbara tilted her head and peered back at him. It seemed like love was in the air. Butterflies were fluttering about, soap bubbles rising in a rainbow of colours, heavenly choirs singing—

And then suddenly, the bubbles burst. The butterflies dropped dead. And the vinyl playing the angelic music came to a screeching halt.

Count Dracula swooped down on the two young lovebirds.

Maggie was as unsettled by his arrival as Sam. Maestro de Norte wasn't fully in character. His eye makeup was missing and he was wearing civilian attire, but still it was black and he, being sinewy, carried it like a snake carries its new skin.

He joined the young couple at their table. They appeared comfortable in his company. They chatted and laughed. Count Dracula had charmed his way into their favours with jokes and the sort of easy joviality Sam would never suspect him of possessing. Watching him in action sent a chill down Sam's spine. The man was a master con artist.

Maggie too was watching him. Again she was spellbound, to the extent that she had abandoned her rum & raisin ice-cream. It had melted and turned into a milky puddle with a few raisins floating in it like flies in soup. Sam couldn't read her thoughts. Was she attracted to that evil vampire, or repelled by him? Her face was inscrutable.

In the hope that he could smuggle her out of the restaurant before the blood-sucker clocked her, he asked. 'Should we be going, Maggie?'

Too late!

Benedict-blinking-Rawbotham saw her. He sneered. Perhaps it was meant to be a smile, but it wouldn't fool Sam. The man was sneering at Maggie. He waved. She didn't respond, but was looking right at him. He got up from his table, kissed Emilia on the forehead in a paternal way, and made his way towards Maggie.

Grinning.

Sneering.

'Maggie! I never thought we'd meet again. After all those years!' He grabbed her hand, pulled it to his bloodthirsty lips, and kissed it. With great gallantry, Sam had to admit.

'Benedict,' Maggie mumbled. She had lost all her natural flair and gaped at the man like a halfwit.

'Are you going to introduce me to your friends?'

Maggie did the honours. Sam came last on

her list. 'And this is Samuel, my neighbour from Bishops, and my partner.'

'Partner?' Disappointment crept into Rawbotham's beady eyes.

'Business partner.'

He beamed, openly relieved. He extended his bony hand to Sam. 'Pleased to meet you, Samuel.'

Sam shook it reluctantly, and said nothing to him. He wished of course he could tell him to go back to hell where he belonged, but he held his tongue.

Rawbotham's attention returned to Maggie. 'We must get together for a drink, Maggie. For old times' sake.'

'Oh... I ... I don't really... I don't think so.'

Sam wanted to kiss her!

'Don't do that to me, Maggie,' The creature begged. 'Don't break my heart.'

'There's nothing to—'

'Oh, there is! We've plenty to talk about, Maggie. You know that. For one, I owe you an explanation.' He stopped fooling around and was now dead serious.

'I don't need to hear it.'

That's my girl, Sam triumphed.

'But I need to say it, Maggie. Please, let's talk. Later on, after the show. I will find you.'

Again, like the previous night, Maggie removed herself to her cabin on the pretext of writing her daily travelogue instalment for the *Sexton's*

Herald. Sam had his doubts. Whatever would she be writing about? She had already described the sea rescue operation. Nothing much had happened since. The cruise liner had been ploughing through the dull vastness of the Baltic Sea. The visibility was still poor. There was nothing to write home about. Who was she fooling? Sam was deeply disconcerted. Truth be told, he was plagued by suspicions, but he had no right to quiz Maggie about her plans, her whereabouts or the company she kept. He skulked to his cabin and sat there in stony silence, watching the wall.

CHAPTER 11

Maggie's Journal

I hadn't asked for this, and I wasn't enjoying it. It was late – well after my bedtime. I was still wearing the clingfilm of my Marilyn Monroe dress, which was bloody uncomfortable to put it mildly. I felt mummified. But I knew I looked good in it, and vanity made me take leave of my senses. For some unfathomable reason I wanted to look good for Benedict. I wanted him to lust after me. Idiocy, I know, after what he had done, but I am only human. Plus, I rarely hold grudges, and if I do, I can't sustain them for too long – certainly not as long as twenty-something years. I decided that if I were to have a drink with him for old times' sake, I may as well look smashing – make him regret what he had lost, or rather what he had thrown away.

We sat in a bar on the lower deck, the pianist

playing Gershwin on a grand piano, with a few other patrons chatting and laughing quietly so as not to disrupt the flow of music. I was so perturbed that I couldn't make up my mind about the drink I wanted. Benedict got me a cocktail of his choosing. I didn't listen carefully enough to register what it contained. I felt so awkward that I knocked the thing back like it was a shot of tequila. It didn't touch the sides. I wouldn't be able to tell what it tasted like and whether I liked it, but to occupy my hands with something I asked for another one.

'It's been a while,' Benedict observed.

'Twenty-three years, and counting.'

'How have you been?'

'Who? Me?' I blinked at him, still making up my mind whether I should be offended or amused.

He rubbed his chin and gave a remorseful look. 'I'm sorry. I just want to be sure you... you did well for yourself.'

'I survived – no thanks to you. And I am very happy. Life couldn't be better.'

'Glad to hear that, Maggie. It's a weight off my chest.'

'Bah!' I knocked back my second cocktail, and waved my empty glass at him. 'One more for the road.'

He ordered it. I noticed that it was just for me. He was still nursing his first drink. That wasn't the Benedict I knew. But when he peered at me in his trademark snake-charmer's way, it all came flooding back. This man could seduce a glass bead.

'You're as beautiful as ever, Maggie.'

Yes, I had heard that before, but these days I was too long in the tooth to fall for it again. I told him as much.

He chuckled, 'Touché! But I stand by what I said – you haven't aged at all.'

I haven't lived at all, I retorted inwardly, groaning at the realisation. I hadn't borne children, hadn't suffered from sleepless nights and sore nipples, or been abused by flights of raging puberty from my offspring. I hadn't allowed myself to fall in love again, hadn't had my heart broken along the same old scars and hadn't cried so many tears to make my eyes red and puffy. I hadn't struggled through the ups and downs of marriage, hadn't had to tolerate someone else's mother telling me where my place was. I hadn't calloused my hands cooking dinners, or washing up and scrubbing floors. I might have had a few drinks too many over the years and a few late nights watching horror movies, but such excesses don't age one as much as real living does. I didn't want to talk to Benedict about any of that. My life was none of his business.

'So,' I smoothly changed the subject before I wept my socks off, 'what was that commotion about at dinner time?'

'Commotion?'

'Half the waiters were missing. Pi – that's our waiter – was acting like the ship was on fire. In fact, the hullabaloo is still going on. I've noticed on our way here: people are dashing around with walkie-talkies to their mouths. What's up, Benedict?'

'You're quite the detective, aren't you, Maggie?'

'I am, as it happens. I dabble a bit.' I conceded the point. After all, it was true. 'So?'

Benedict leaned towards me and whispered, as if we were conspirators. 'I shouldn't be telling you this – we were told not to.'

'For old times' sake, come on!' I quoted him.

'Well, OK, I'll tell you. But don't get alarmed and please don't tell anyone else. Hatton doesn't think the safety of the passengers is compromised in any way. It's just an internal spat, between our – supposed – fishermen.'

I was intrigued, 'The people we rescued from that boat?'

'Yes, that lot. One of them is dead.'

At last, I was seeing a purpose to this tête-à-tête even if it wasn't the same one as Benedict's. 'Do tell!'

'We don't know what happened. The dead one can't tell us. The other two are heavily sedated and haven't got a clue what's going on around them. And the fourth one is missing.'

'Missing? You mean he's somewhere on this

ship?'

'Unless he jumped overboard.'

'So you can't find him? Is he hiding? Why?'

'Why do you think, Maggie?'

'He killed the other man...'

'It looks like there was a scuffle. They came to blows over something, and one of them grabbed a scalpel and slashed the other one's neck. And then he took off. He's gone into hiding somewhere on this ship.'

'And Mr Hatton doesn't deem it necessary to tell us!?' I must say I was appalled.

'It would only create panic. Tomorrow we'll be in Riga and their police will take charge of the situation. Hatton is sure that passengers' lives aren't at risk. The captain agrees. The man is hiding. He's scared. It was some unfinished business between the two of them. Alarming the passengers would do more harm than good.'

The pianist stopped playing and the barman told us the bar was now closed. I started thanking Benedict for the lovely evening, keen to run to Samuel and break the news to him, but Benny wouldn't have it.

'You promised you'd hear me out. I must clear my conscience, Maggie. Please let me. It's now or never. I won't bring myself to do it again. I owe you this much.'

His cabin was about the same size as mine, but it was well lived in. I suppose it was his home away from home. He worked on this cruise liner, and lived here. There were some family photos of him, a woman and a little girl – a toddler. I didn't nose about, didn't pause for long enough to take a good look. I didn't wish to know about his life after me. He had a bottle of whisky at the ready and poured us two generous glasses.

I downed mine, determined to have this over and done with quickly. 'OK then, tell me, Benedict – give me the short version: why did you have to steal from me? Was there no one else handy for you to take advantage of? Was I that stupid?'

'No, of course not, Maggie. Please…'

'It's just that I thought you cared for me – loved me. You swore at the time you did, remember? A ridiculous idea, I know now, but then… Then, it took me a little while to get over the bloody hurt. It wasn't the money. I found work, didn't even have to tell my parents – spared myself the shame of it. But the jewellery? It was my grandmother's, you pitiful bastard.'

'I'm so sorry, Maggie! But even if I could turn back time, I think I'd have to do it all over again.'

'Blimey! So what the hell was it that made you do it? Gambling debts?' I remembered Benedict being partial to a game of poker for high stakes. That was in his heyday when money was no object. 'Was someone going to knee-cap you, or sell you into slavery?'

'No, not exactly. It was something I couldn't

shake off without paying my way out. It was business.'

'Some business you had got yourself into!' I cried.

He poured us two more drinks and began telling me. I must confess by this time my brain was slightly pickled and not quite retentive of the finer detail. Benedict's soap story boiled down to some dodgy dealings which required regular investment injections from new clients in return for the dividends in the business that Benedict had received – and spent – well in advance.

Unbeknown to me, he had dropped out of RADA and embarked on a full-time career in finance. He was selling investment portfolios and making a fortune. To start with. Then it all dried up, but the cash injections had to keep coming. So it was my turn to make an involuntary investment. Behind my back, Benedict helped himself to my bank account: my student loan and the lifelong savings my parents had squirreled away for me. And while at it, my greedy Benny-boy decided to take the jewellery too. It was worth a few bob. It was for his fresh start – his new life as a respectable family man, and magician.

I was sipping my whisky, which had by then numbed my lips and cauterised my bleeding heart. My mind was numb, too.

'Please believe me, Maggie, I had no choice.

If I'd tried to run away, they would've found me and made an example of me so their other reps would sit down and take notice. I had to buy my way out.'

I mumbled something which I intended to have the effect of an absolution, but it didn't come out that way. It sounded muddled even to my own ears.

'I'm so sorry. I was going to repay you. That was the plan – I was going to reinvent myself, make a decent living, save up and come to you with all your money back.'

Again, I emitted a couple of mangled mutterings, which were meant to amount to a query about my grandmother's jewellery. And again, it didn't come out that way.

'But then life had different ideas, as it often does.' Benedict bit his lip, his eyes humble and penitent. 'It wasn't as easy as I thought to earn honest money, and on top of that I met someone... someone else.'

'Can... um... an... anothah dwink,' I managed. He refilled my glass. I drank it as an anaesthetic as I continued to listen to his confession about that *someone else*, his family, his duty as a father, a mortgage, something about the wife falling ill, dying.

My head wasn't spinning anymore. It was now so heavy that it weighed on my shoulders like a boulder. I could feel physical pain in my neck. My eyesight was blurred with that extra weight. It felt as if the veins were bursting in my eyes. I had to shut them. I could no longer hear anything he was saying to me. Not that I didn't want to listen – I just couldn't. Whatever sounds entered my ears, I couldn't make them out. My brain was unable to decipher them, and then it went on to block them altogether.

Ugly rubbery faces stretched, screamed and swore at me. I was experiencing a distorted, surreal world similar to that I had seen when I'd crossed over to the other side and started seeing the dead. Something black and impenetrable overcame me. Thick sticky liquid was flowing lazily in my skull, swelling until it had to come out somehow.

I felt it in my throat and I retched.

'Where's the loo?' I managed to ask but couldn't hear a reply. A high pitch sound was cursing through my ears.

I heaved myself to my feet – somehow – and staggered about the cabin in search of the toilet. I bumped into a piece of furniture. The pain seared through me and gave me an instantaneous moment of lucidity. In the dim light I found the loo and stumbled into it just in time to relieve myself of that thick sticky mucus.

I tried to pull the chain, but couldn't find it. My skull had a mind of its own and would not be kept in place. It was rolling from side to side. A voice of reason in my head told me that I had to get out of the bathroom before that skull of mine made lethal contact with the hard edge of the toilet or the sink. I staggered out of there. I collapsed, I think, on the bed where I passed out safely.

◆ ◆ ◆

'When Emilia left college, I sold out and we started cruising. It's not an easy life, but we're saving all we earn. It's a temporary solution.' Benedict's voice was droning, making it through to my brain and even beginning to make sense.

I was thirsty, but my tongue had calcified and I couldn't force it to form words to ask for a drink. A drink of water, I hasten to add. I could only peer haplessly at Benedict who was talking. At least, I could see him, and hear him, which was a marked improvement on my previous audio-visual impairment. His face wasn't even rubbery. It was perfectly human. His black hair seemed to cling to his forehead in heavy wisps, wet or sweaty.

The door was pushed open and Emilia's face appeared. It looked very white. 'Dad! It's Ollie's mother – she's dead! We don't know what to... Come with me. Hurry!'

Benedict jumped to his feet and walked slowly towards Emilia with his arms outstretched, as if he was approaching a dangerous animal. 'Now, now, calm down. Sit down and tell me from the beginning.'

'I can't be sitting down! We found her dead. She's dead! You must do something!'

'It can't be... What are you saying – *found her*?' Benedict asked a question that didn't make any more sense than Emilia's exclamations. I was of course more experienced in the art of witness interrogation, alas I still couldn't speak. However, I was now able to sit up and listen with understanding.

'We found her dead – in her room, on the floor. I think she was stabbed. There's blood. Come please, come now!'

'Are you sure? Have you checked? Did you get help?'

'Ollie's gone to fetch the doctor. I don't know why – she's dead. Cold. Please come, Dad!'

'Yes, yes, I'm coming. Calm down, darling.' Benedict embraced Emilia – his daughter – as I had succeeded at deducing. He stroked her hair with his eyes closed in some eerie trance.

I waited, unsure what to do with myself and how to fit into the private moment between father and daughter.

After a few seconds, he opened his eyes. He spoke to me from above her head which was pressed against his chest, 'Maggie, will you be able to make your way to your cabin on your own?'

I'll do my best, I thought and, still incapable

of articulating words, I nodded. I left them, letting Benedict focus his attention on his daughter and on verifying her outrageous story.

CHAPTER 12

Maggie's Journal

Murder was beckoning to me, begging to be solved, but it would have to wait until later. Walking – or rather tottering and zigzagging – back to my cabin, I quickly devised a plan of action. I would get out of the suffocating dress, shower and get some sleep. After breakfast, and only then, would I knuckle down to solving the mystery of Mrs Conti Lang's stabbing. That was on the proviso that I hadn't dreamt it all up in my alcohol-infused stupor.

I was shattered, but still I had enough sense to take off my shoes and tiptoe past Samuel's room. What would he think of me if he saw me returning home at this young hour after a night out with an old beau? He would jump to the wrong conclusions. I wanted to spare him –

and myself – the indignity of explanations. Or, to put it plainly, I was ashamed of myself. The cold, hard truth was that I had got drunk, passed out, thrown up like a sick puppy, and spent the night in another man's bedroom, getting up to – well, whatever I had got up to, I couldn't remember, but it can't have been good. In my defence, I hadn't enjoyed myself at all.

I hoped to return to my cabin undetected and to present myself for breakfast revived and exuding innocence. I didn't want Samuel to see me like this. I wouldn't be able to bear the disappointment in his eyes. In fact, I didn't deserve his, or anyone's, condemnation – the disastrous rendezvous with Benny hadn't been my idea and I only conceded to it in order not to appear rude.

My hopes were dashed, and my worst nightmare began, the moment I opened my door.

The first thing I saw was the gory apparitions of the two young women from the fishing boat – the same ones I had seen board our ship during the rescue operation. They still hadn't had the time or the presence of mind to restore their appearances to what one would consider *their best*. They were distressed, confused, wide-eyed, with their hair wet and stuck to their faces like seaweed. All in all, they resembled a pair of battered sirens, or two fish tossed out of water for long enough to be beyond resuscitation. I knew they were dead, naturally – no one else but me had seen them come onboard.

Of course those two weren't physically in my room, but someone else was: someone who was alive and to whom their spirits had become attached. That was all I had a chance to consider before a heavy blunt object landed on my head and rendered me unconscious.

When I regained consciousness, I found myself unable to sit up. I was slumped on my back. My hands rested on my stomach, tied together with rope. My head was exploding in blinding pain. From under my brow, I could see a patch of what seemed like blood – my blood – coagulating on the fibres of the silver-grey carpet in my room.

If I weren't so traumatised, I would have been pleasantly surprised that I was still alive. However, I was traumatised because a man with a crazed look in his eye and a small but vicious-looking axe in his hand was glaring at me from above. It was one of those fireman's axes that one would find next to a fire extinguisher, a fire blanket and a life belt on the top deck. I was in no doubt that that axe was no child's toy. I shut my eyes, bracing myself for the first blow.

It didn't come.

I squinted, allowing one of my eyes to open. The man was still there, but he lowered the axe. It was dangling loosely next to his knee. If I just heaved myself up a fraction, I could grab it. Except that my hands were tied. And the man, though currently inactive, bore signs of violence: his hospital gown (for that was what he was wearing, probably courtesy of the medics) was torn and covered in blood. I surmised that it was not only his own blood coming from the cuts and gashes on his face, but also the other man's blood – his victim's. The man's front was saturated in blackened crimson, from collar to hem.

Oh yes, I knew who he was and that he had slashed his fellow fisherman as well as Mrs Conti Lang with a scalpel. Only now he was holding his new choice of lethal weapon – the aforementioned axe – and I was trussed up on the floor, ready for chopping.

I contemplated screaming, and instantly gave up on the idea. My throat was still hoarse from my drinking excesses. My prospects of producing anything louder than a gravelly groan were slim. I would only provoke him. I couldn't bear the thought of another blow to my head. So I spoke softly to distract him from his murderous intentions.

'Could you help me up to the chair, please? I can't do you any harm whether I sit or lie on the floor, and I'd much rather be sitting up. My head, you see, is throbbing. I had one too many last night.'

He put away his axe and leaned over to lift me up by the elbows and help me to the chair. I hunched in it, feeling like I imagine a snail would feel when its shell had been torn from its back. Still, I thanked my captor for his gallantry and requested a glass of water. Again, he obliged. I held the glass with my tied-up hands and drank slowly whilst assessing the seriousness of the situation I was in. It didn't look good.

I was being held hostage in my room, and that was my own fault as I had failed to lock the door. Being his only hostage however, I could reasonably expect that he wouldn't dispatch me out of this world in a hurry. He couldn't afford to kill me. My confidence grew. I raked my memory for how to handle a hostage situation based on the Liam Neeson movies of the *Taken* franchise. I discarded the idea of direct combat and opted to simply talk the man into submission. I introduced myself and invited him to make himself comfortable. I told him calmly that there was no need to stand. He looked knackered; he could do with a lie-down. He took his axe and, gripping it firmly in his lap, sat on my bed.

'It's my first time on a cruise liner,' I was blathering. 'Come to think, it's my first time at sea. Not quite like you – you must be used to it, being a fisherman, and all. So, is it herring you fish for? I hear the Baltic is teeming with herring at this time of year. I can't say I've tried herring – to eat, I mean, not to fish for. Though I've never fished for it either. Or for any other fish, for that matter. Hm...yes, all that water...'

He wasn't engaging with me. He wasn't responding, wasn't even listening. He was rocking, forward and back – forward and back – on my bed, like an orphaned child. And he was crying. It wasn't a sobbing with all the sound effects that define it, but his face was contorted and there were tears. He let go of the axe and was frantically pushing the balls of his fists into his temples. For a moment, I feared that maybe he was listening to some internal voices telling him to kill me. Maybe he was mentally ill – after all, what reason would a rational man have to kill one of his mates and a middle-aged woman he had never met before? Not to mention holding captive another – younger – woman who didn't have two halfpennies to rub together. Let's face it, I would never be a model hostage for ransom. You could tell by just looking at me and my cheap accessories. Therefore, I concluded, the man had lost his mind.

I couldn't let him remain in this state of agitation for much longer if I valued my life. What if he succumbed to those voices? I had to change tack. Because he wouldn't listen to me, I would have to get him to talk – just talk until the cavalry arrived.

I chanced a tentative question, 'So, who are these two young women? They don't look like fishermen – fisherwomen – material to me? They're so young – can't be more than twenty. They're girls, really.'

He gaped at me, aghast, or shocked, and finally he spoke with a broad foreign accent I could safely guess was either Swedish or Latvian. His eyes lit up. 'Did you find them? They alive?'

'No, they're dead, I'm afraid.' I had to be honest with him.

He nodded, looking defeated. 'Yes, they are dead – they must be dead.' He inhaled with a sort of hiccup and cupped his mouth. I could read horror in his eyes.

'What happened to them? How did they die? Was it you? Did you kill them?'

'No!' he shouted, and then added quietly, 'No. I was trying to save us – save them – save all of us.' And without any further prompting from me, he told me the whole tragic story, and more. He went into every detail. I could tell the man was dying to get it off his chest and trusted me enough to make me his confessor. I was flattered by his confidence in me even though he still had me bound in ropes like a Christmas turkey.

Their story did not involve fishing for herring or any other sea-related pursuits.

They were drug couriers, my captor (his name was Alvar Olegin) and his accomplices: Ebbe Rasmussen (the leader of the pack), and two Swedes of Turkish origins - Nedim and his son, Utku. They had worked together for over a year. They transported drugs from Asia, mainly Afghanistan, via Turkey, the Ukraine and Latvia, and from there across the Baltic Sea to Sweden. They used an old Viking trading route between Scandinavia and Byzantium. They were part of a big organisation who controlled the suppliers, borders and customs officials as well as the end-user distribution. It was a formidable criminal enterprise with its tentacles spanning Europe and Asia. The four men were small fish in a deep blue sea, no pun intended. And the little fish I was talking to was definitely out of his depth.

From what I gathered, Alvar had no problem with smuggling heroine, which would end up in the veins of many young people some of whom it would kill, but he drew the line on human trafficking.

It was Nedim who had brought the two Armenian girls on that fateful crossing. They were sisters, one only seventeen and the other one, nineteen. Alvar didn't know their names. They were kept locked in the cabin. Nedim advised the crew that they were payment for their older brother's honour debt of some kind, though I couldn't think how honour came into this and neither could Alvar. The girls were to be taken to Stockholm and handed over to a man known to Ebbe as Erasmus. There was little doubt as to what fate awaited them. That didn't sit well with Alvar, or with Utku who argued violently with his father about the lines that they shouldn't have crossed. Unlike his father, Utku was a second-generation Swede and had a slightly different take on how to treat women, especially as they were just teenagers.

Despite the bitter arguments, the girls remained locked up and the voyage proceeded as planned.

Then came the storm and the damage to their main engine. Ebbe decided that they would wait the storm out and as soon as it blew over they'd continue on their planned route to Stockholm on the second engine. It would take longer, but they had no other options: the boat was stocked with drugs from bow to stern, and there were two female slaves onboard. But Alvar panicked.

It was he who sent the three flares up into the sky and alerted the cruise liner to their distress. Ebbe realised what he had done after they received the radio contact from our ship, which by then was on its way to rescue them.

That was when a decision was made to throw the illegal cargo overboard, and that included the girls. Nedim and Ebbe emptied the stock into the depths of the sea. Then they dragged the girls out on deck. Alvar stood in their way, but when he was threatened with being dispatched to the bottom of the sea with the girls, he hesitated. It was then that Utke took action. Wielding a knife, he went for Ebbe, trusting that his own father would ultimately take his side. But the old man did no such thing. Between Ebbe and Nedim, Utke was beaten to a pulp and left unconscious while the two men disposed of the girls. Alvar stepped in, but his hesitation had cost him his only ally, and he was on his own. They neutralised him quickly.

When he came to, the girls were gone. Utke was still unconscious and Ebbe was bleeding profusely and close to passing out. When the rescue boat arrived to save them, the only man standing was Nedim.

In the medical bay, their wounds had been inspected and taken care of. Utke was heavily concussed and confused. They were all given tranquilisers to help them sleep. Ebbe was put on a drip.

When Alvar woke up a day or two later (he had lost count of the time), he found himself eye to eye with Nedim. The old man was holding a scalpel to Alvar's throat. The sting of the first clumsy cut across Alavar's cheek had stirred him into alertness. He reacted quickly and threw Nedim off. A scuffle ensued.

Alvar was able to wrestle the scalpel out of Nedim's hand. He gave the Turk a chance to walk away, but Nedim was not prepared to leave behind a hostile witness. He thought he could succeed at silencing his son, but he wouldn't trust Alvar. He tried his luck again and took Alvar by surprise when Alvar turned his back on him.

Unfortunately for Nedim, Alvar had the

scalpel in his hand. The blade slashed across Nedim's neck as Alvar twisted his body and lifted his arm to defend himself. When he saw what he had done, he dropped the scalpel and ran.

'It was an accident,' he told me.

That depends on your definition of an accident, I didn't say it out loud, but instead I said, 'Even if it wasn't, you probably acted inside the boundaries of self-defence. My good friend Samuel is a barrister. He could help you. As it happens, he is on this ship, in the cabin next door. We could ask him, if you like. Anyway, you can't stay here hiding indefinitely. You'll have to come out at some point.'

'Where's this ship heading?'

'Riga, I think that's our next port. But, honestly Alvar, you can't possibly think you could sneak out unnoticed. Shall I give my friend a call?'

'No!' He snapped, but he was beginning to lean towards my way of thinking, I could tell. His fists tightened and he pressed them hard against his cheekbones. That had caused the slash on his cheek to reopen. Blood trickled between his knuckles. His lips were trembling as he mumbled something to himself in his own language. He was hesitating and debating the matter with himself. I prayed that reason would triumph in the end. And it did because he said, 'It was – that's what it was. It was self-defence.'

'I'm sure it was, though Mrs Conti Lang wasn't. Why on earth did you kill that woman?' I heard myself shrill with indignation. One glance at his face and I quickly abandoned the high moral ground and offered him a way out: 'I'm guessing she was the head of the whole drug smuggling operation, wasn't she? I've heard things about her, you know. She was a nasty piece of work. I can totally see where you're coming from.'

He blinked at me and furrowed his blood-smeared forehead.

I proceeded with my hypothesis, 'So when you saw her on this ship, you lost control, your emotions got out of hand, and Bob's your uncle!

'You were so charged – two innocent girls dead, you on the run, and there she was – basking in luxury. You lost it, didn't you?' I quipped without thinking. Whatever possessed me to start this thread of conversation, I will never know.

He was still frowning and staring blankly when he asked, 'Who?'

'I know about her. She's dead, in case you were wondering. Cordelia Conti Lang is very much dead, Alvar. Her son and his girlfriend found her in her room. Stabbed, I believe, just like Nedim.'

Alvar cocked his head, possibly contemplating doing away with me the same way he had done away with her. I heard his jaw grind. He rose to his feet, gripping his axe rather purposefully. 'What are you saying to me?!'

I was saved by a knock at my door. The cavalry had arrived. And it wasn't any odd horseman. It was my knight in shining armour.

'Maggie? I need to come in – I've something to tell you. Are you decent? I'm coming in!'

CHAPTER 13

Sam was seething with impotent jealousy. If he could get away with it, he would have wrung Rawbotham's neck there and then, and spared himself the torturous night that followed. He never doubted that Maggie would in the end accept the bastard's invitation. Firstly, because she could rarely say no to a drink. In fact, in all the time that he had known Maggie, Sam couldn't recall an occasion when she had declined an alcoholic beverage. Or a piece of cake. Maggie was addicted to self-indulgence. The second reason was that, like most people from Bishops Well, Maggie would find it hard to be overtly impolite. She would rather suffer a minor – or major – inconvenience than make someone feel bad about themselves.

After saying goodnight to her, Sam sat in his cabin with his ear to the wall. He didn't have to wait long. At a quarter to ten, he heard someone knock on Maggie's door to which she responded in her customary, 'Come in! The door is open.'

Sam's heart bled. He liked to think that those words were reserved for him only, be it at Priest's Hole in their home town or on this ship. He fancied Maggie's door being always open – for him, and no one else. Yet, she had uttered those very sacred words, addressing them with equal ease to Count Dracula. Sam couldn't blame Maggie, but he considered sharpening a few stakes to plunge into the man's chest at the earliest opportunity.

Meantime, he strained his ears to tune into the conversation next door. It was a quiet and seemingly intimate one – only a soft murmur made it through the wall. Were they whispering sweet-nothings into each other ears? If they didn't stop soon, if Count Dracula didn't leave Maggie's cabin in the next five minutes and alone, Sam would go mad. He pushed his fist into his mouth to stifle a scream.

Five minutes later, give or take, Rawbotham left Maggie's cabin.

And so did Maggie.

Their steps and soft voices passed by Sam's door and dissipated further along the corridor. Sam set off in pursuit.

Following their scent like a bloodhound, he tried to maintain a disinterested, man-about-his-own-business deportment. It wasn't easy to behave casually while every fibre of his body was frayed with anxiety and his thoughts oscillated between killing the bastard and throwing himself on one knee before Maggie to claim her for himself once and for bloody all. If only he had done it earlier, she would be wearing his ring on her fourth finger and telling Maestro de Norte to get a life. As it were, the blood-thirsty leech was free to help himself to Maggie and all Sam could do was watch.

They went to the bar with the grand piano on the lower deck. Straightaway, Maggie began knocking back cocktails as if they were smarties. Her eyes were fixed on Rawbotham. Sam could swear the bastard had hypnotised her – he was bound to know how to do that in his line of work. Sam wished he could hear what they were saying, but he didn't dare enter the bar for fear of being spotted. There were only a few couples drinking there, and the piano player. He was making such a racket that Sam would have to stand right next to Maggie and Rawbotham to hear what they were saying. As it was, he positioned himself in a foyer just outside the bar from where he could observe them but without hearing a sausage.

There was a lot of commotion around him. People were running up and down, looking distressed. Vincent Hatton flew by, shouting orders. He even bumped into Sam and instead of apologising looked him up and down as if Sam was an illegal stowaway. As if that wasn't unpleasant enough, Hatton glanced over his shoulder and shouted, 'You're best advised to stay in your cabin, sir!'

Bizarre!

Still, the man had a point. What on earth was Sam doing hiding behind a pot plant, spying on his neighbour? This was juvenile behaviour. There was no point in torturing himself. If, God forbid, he was to be found out he would be exposed to ridicule. It bore no contemplation. Sam took Hatton's advice and retreated to his cabin.

But he couldn't sleep. He sat in the dark, waiting for Maggie to return, listening to every sound, hoping she would come back soon, and come back alone. But she did not.

Hours went by so slowly that Sam was sure time had turned tail and started running backwards. All noises died out. Pickled in darkness and desolation, Sam must have nodded off.

He was awakened by a thud in Maggie's cabin. Sam sat up and checked the time on his mobile. It was almost six in the morning. She had been gone the whole night.

He pressed his ear against the wall to discover that she wasn't alone either. She was speaking to someone. After a while that someone responded. It was a male voice. Sam's heart sank to the pit of his stomach. It could only be Benedict Raw-blinking-botham. He was with Maggie, in her room, after a whole night together. They couldn't get enough of each other.

Sam gave in to despair. He was losing the will to live. Rawbotham had snatched Maggie from under his nose. It was his own fault: his inaction, his doubts, his stupidity. There was no fight left in him (not that he had put up much of a fight in the first place).

He again checked the time on his mobile. It was twenty past six. In ten minutes, Maggie would normally be emerging from her room, wearing her peachy tracksuit and trainers, ready for their joint power-walk on the decks. Hoping against hope that she would do that this morning, he put on his sports gear and waited. On the dot of six-thirty nothing happened. Maggie did not come out.

He dragged himself out of his cabin, primarily to get some air on the promenade. He felt like he would suffocate if he stayed indoors. He didn't intend to power-walk or run, or do anything other than breathe. There was no point. Without Maggie wiggling ardently in front of him and leading the way, he had no motivation to put one foot in front of the other. It was a cold and dark December morning at sea. Sam was a defeated man. His heart was broken. He felt unloved and useless – all alone in this world. In other words, he was wallowing in self-pity.

He used the metal staircase and the fire exit on the stern to avoid human contact, though that wasn't likely at this hour. How surprised he was to run into Vincent Hatton!

The Chief Security Officer emerged from the companionway coming from the lower deck. He looked as if he, too, had never gone to bed last night. He was wearing the same crumpled uniform. His eyes were bloodshot and sported dark circles. Streaks of his grey hair were tossed in the wet wind. He clutched Sam's top and pulled him forcefully towards himself. Sam body stiffened. Baring his teeth, Hatton shook him. It was a disturbingly violent act. He assessed Sam and, realising who he was, relaxed his hold on Sam's hoodie.

'Sorry, sir,' he breathed stale air into his face. 'I was expecting someone else. I'd like you to return to your cabin, please, and stay there.'

'I was just coming to get some air, if you don't mind,' Sam protested.

'For God's sake, man! Why can't you people just mind your own business! I told you to go. It's an order.'

That was a bit rough. Sam felt rebellion rising in his chest. 'I beg your pardon! I don't take orders from you, Mr Hatton.'

Hatton inhaled deeply to calm himself. 'This is an emergency, sir. We've a dangerous man on the loose. He has killed twice already. One of his victims was a passenger. We're looking for him and need you out of the way. You will be safe in your cabin. Lock the door.'

Two staff walked hurriedly towards them. One of them reported, 'We checked the upper deck – no sign of him.'

'Where the hell is he? He's injured. He can't run forever!' Hatton was frustrated.

'It's not hard to find a good hiding place on a ship this size.'

'I suppose not. We'll be in Riga in an hour. Their Special Security squad is waiting for us. I just got the call. Mr Muir, commence the evacuation protocol.'

'Sir!'

'Once we've evacuated the passengers, they'll go through every nook and cranny with a fine-tooth comb. But,' Hatton cracked his knuckles, 'I bloody well wish I could get my hands on him before they do. Otherwise it's my head on the chopping block!'

He looked at Sam and realised that he was still there. 'I thought I asked you, sir, to go back to your cabin and lock the door.'

Sam didn't have to be told twice now that he knew the seriousness of the situation. He negotiated the metal stairwell and ran down the corridor at breakneck speed. All he could think of was Maggie's irritating habit of leaving her doors unlocked. He knocked and tried the handle.

'Maggie? I need to come in – I've something to tell you. Are you decent? I'm coming in!'

CHAPTER 14

He was too late.

Maggie was slumped awkwardly in a chair, her hands bound with rope. She looked ashen and drained, but enormously pleased to see him. A man with a long and deep cut across his face, wearing a bloodied hospital gown, stood next to her. He was wielding an axe. He looked poised to charge at Sam.

'Okay, gentlemen,' Maggie spoke with astounding calm, 'can we all take a breath, please? And a step back.'

She peered at the nutter with the axe and added, 'Alvar, darling, this is the man I told you about – my neighbour, the barrister. His name is Samuel Dee. He'll be only too happy to help. If you just stop waving that axe.'

'Samuel Dee?' the individual referred to as Alvar gawped at Maggie with little comprehension. He sounded foreign.

'That's right – Samuel Dee.' Maggie

confirmed emphatically. 'Samuel, this is Alvar. He is one of the men we rescued the other day.'

'I see...' Sam could see it right from the moment he opened the door. Maggie was casually harbouring the killer that everyone was looking for. And she seemed to have made some outrageous commitments to him on Sam's behalf. What was the *only too happy to help* all about?

'Unfortunately, he got himself into a spot of bother, and he needs a lawyer. I recommended you, Samuel.'

'Right...'

'I know what you're going to say – you're retired, and all that. But these are exceptional circumstances and Alvar isn't spoilt for choice. It's you or no one, as matters stand. Now, come in, sit down and I will explain it all to you from the beginning.'

Sam was instructed to take a seat next to Alvar (still possessed of the axe) on Maggie's bed while she appraised him of Alvar's story and the predicament he was in. While listening to her, Sam experienced the most inappropriate sense of relief: at least she wasn't with Benedict Raw-sodding-botham – at least she was being held hostage by a total stranger! And she didn't appear that much inconvenienced.

'... so, you see, Samuel, Alvar will need a good lawyer. The best he can find. It is short notice, I admit, but he's in real trouble and we could do with a miracle-maker. To cut a long story short, we need you. Can you see that?' Maggie blabbered on. It was nervous talk, something she would deny later and claim that she had the situation under control. But Sam could see the fear in her eyes. Putting a brave face to a bad game was Maggie's forte, but her eyes were betraying her.

Sam briefly considered taking on this dangerous killer, for that's what this Alvar character was, mitigating circumstances and fantastical tales notwithstanding. Sam took quick stock of the situation. The man was armed. He was dangerous. He had frightened Maggie, trussed her up at axe-point and held her prisoner. The woman Sam loved dearly was in lethal danger, whether she realised it or not. And she didn't know half of the story!

She clearly didn't know about the murder of one of the passengers. Sam had only just found that out himself. He had the full picture of what Alvar was capable of. Killing a hapless passenger was inexcusable. It couldn't have been self-defence. It was cold-blooded execution of an unarmed witness – a bystander who had randomly crossed the man's path.

And now that was precisely what Maggie had done too by leaving her door unlocked. To make matters worse, she seemed to have already developed the Stockholm syndrome and was liaising with her captor on getting him out of trouble. But the man was unhinged. He was still holding the axe and kept Maggie tied. With her big mouth, she could easily make a mistake and end up with that axe wedged into her head.

Sam had to tread carefully. His only option was to collaborate, acting on the principle of *if you can't beat them, join them.*

'Okay, I see. I understand what happened.' He nodded slowly but assertively, pretending to be mulling over the facts that Maggie had presented, and agreeing with them. Whether he actually agreed or not was irrelevant. Being happily retired, he would – could – not intervene to represent the man. Besides, as the crime was committed in Latvian territorial waters, it would fall under their jurisdiction. British law wouldn't apply. Nevertheless, Sam had to play his part in order to protect Maggie.

It wouldn't be for much longer. He had heard Hatton say that soon the ship would be docking at Riga where the Latvian police awaited them. The trick was not to aggravate the man in the meantime.

'Yes, Maggie is right. There are reasonable grounds on which to cite self-defence. Your life was in danger and your attacker was holding a lethal weapon to your throat. Was it a scalpel, you say?'

Alvar nodded.

'Yes, I see. You acted out of necessity and that point can be argued, I daresay, with good prospects of success. And to your further advantage you have the extenuating context of you trying to save the girls' lives. Hopefully, the other young man – what was his name?'

'Utke?'

'Yes, Utke. If he backs up your story he can be subpoenaed as witness for the Defence – you may even escape a custodial sentence altogether.'

'I told you Samuel would help!' Maggie exclaimed. She would clap her hands if they weren't tied together.

Alvar rounded his lips and exhaled. 'Okay, that's good.'

Having gained his confidence, Sam was ready to state his terms and conditions of engagement, which he did: 'But, before we go any further, you must untie Maggie and let her go. You will have to come out with me and hand yourself in to the Latvian police. You must demonstrate goodwill. Holding Maggie hostage makes you look guilty as hell. From now on, full co-operation with the authorities is the name of the game, are we clear?'

The Latvian police had an easy job of apprehending the dangerous criminal, courtesy of Samuel Dee. As soon as they boarded the cruise liner, Alvar was waiting under the watchful eye of Vincent Hatton, ready to surrender himself into their custody.

Maggie gave him a hearty hug and repeated

for the umpteenth time, 'Don't worry, Alvar, you've done the right thing.' She repeatedly assured him that Sam was a great barrister and would *do his best for him.*

Sam was tempted to smack her. For the danger she had got herself into. For her gullibility. For the unwise kindness of her heart. For nearly losing her precious life through her own fault. And most of all, for making promises on his behalf that he could not possibly keep!

He held back his despair and, as soon as Alvar was out of sight, spoke with as much calm as he could muster, 'You don't know the half of it, Maggie. I can't possibly help him, and I wouldn't want to. He didn't tell you the whole story, did he now? Did he tell you that he had also killed one of the passengers? I don't know who but it could be someone we know.'

'He didn't have to tell me.' Maggie shrugged. 'I already knew, though I didn't really get a chance to quiz him on that. As it happens, you interrupted me with your ill-timed arrival.'

Sam's jaw fell out of joint and hit the deck. The cheek of that woman! 'So you knew everything before everyone else?'

'I did – I do. It's Cordelia Conti Lang, right? She's the dead passenger. She's been stabbed.'

Sam blinked at her for he was gobsmacked by Maggie's revelation.

'Oh, Sam, don't get any ideas if I tell you this,' Maggie peered into his eyes pleadingly, 'but

I found out when I was with Benedict. If you really must know every detail! Emilia – that's Benedict's daughter – and Cordelia's son had found her body. So, of course, I knew.' She sighed. 'But I'm not sure that it was Alvar who killed her. In fact, I am sure that he didn't.'

Sam had to roll his eyes. 'You've become his greatest fan, Maggie. You can't be that naïve! You know what this is called? The Stockholm syndrome.'

'I don't care what it's called. And I am not naïve. I just have this feeling. And I am also very observant, and a good judge of character. So, when I mentioned Conti Lang to him, he was genuinely puzzled. He doesn't know her and I really don't think he would've killed her. And for what purpose, you tell me!'

'He didn't have to know her to kill her. It could've been an accident. He may have run into her, weapon in hand, and—'

'No, no, no... No, Samuel! He couldn't have *run into her.* They found her in her cabin, not on deck or in any public space. And anyway, he didn't know she was dead – he just didn't know. Trust me on that.'

'You can't believe everything a hardened criminal tells you.'

'He may be a, sort of, criminal, I can see your point there, but he is not that *hardened,*' Maggie drew indignant inverted commas with her fingers, 'plus, I gave him my word. Please don't make me go back on my word. How could I explain it to him? He trusted me. He trusted you!' She stabbed her finger at Sam's chest. 'You made a deal with him.'

'We don't have to explain ourselves to him, Maggie. We won't be seeing him ever again. For crying out loud, the man held you hostage!'

'But I have a good feeling about him. And I'm never wrong about people.'

'Bah!'

'You will help him, won't you, Samuel?' Her lower lip quivered. She was close to tears – her world and her word were about to be compromised for ever. Sam couldn't let that happen. He pulled her into his arms and felt the warmth of her body melt his heart.

'I'll do what I can. I'm just so, so relieved that you're okay.'

She peered at him from under her furrowed brow, presenting an impish grin. 'Have I told you lately that you are my knight—'

'In shining armour? Only a hundred times.' His spirit travelled to the dizzy heights of the stratosphere. At this point he would do anything for this woman. Anything she asked! And that state of total intoxication led him to kiss her – to really kiss her.

CHAPTER 15

Maggie's Journal

I don't believe Mr Hatton approved of that kiss. He scowled. Kissing in public wasn't something he was accustomed to. He clearly didn't know how to respond to it with grace by, for example, smiling indulgently or simply turning a blind eye. I, on the other hand, responded with fervour. I reciprocated Sam's kiss, and I made it last. Frankly, I could have done with another one had Samuel not pulled away from me, looking aghast and ashamed of himself. He groaned and then muttered something contrite under his breath. I licked my lips with relish, just as one would lick one's favourite ice cream. And, just like ice cream, that kiss had the sweet flavour of my youth. That should give you some idea how bloody long it had been since my last one.

Unlike the other passengers who were confined to their cabins and second-guessing the goings-on, we were given the privilege of staying on deck and watching the Latvian police clear the crime scene. After they led Alvar away, they wheeled off two corpses in body bags, those being Nedim and Cordelia Conti Lang, and removed a shedload of material evidence, including Alvar's axe. Only when I looked at it bagged in a transparent pouch did I realise that it was spotless; it couldn't have been used for the commission of violent crime that involved blood-letting.

I wondered if they had found the scalpel. Alvar had dropped it in the sick bay before he ran out.

The paramedics carried out our remaining house-guests: Ebbe and Utke. Both were on stretchers and seemingly out of action. I don't think either of them was in a fit state to commit any crimes, such as murdering Mrs Conti Lang.

I was delighted to see Ebbe unconscious, but I rooted for Utke to get better soon so that he could testify in Alvar's defence. A lot was hanging on Utke's goodwill. How he would react to Alvar killing his father, was anyone's guess. He could easily turn against Alvar and refuse to corroborate his story. If it was true in the first place. Personally, I didn't think Alvar had made it up, but it was the Latvian police he had to convince.

Detective Smilga shook hands with Mr Hatton and thanked him for apprehending Alvar. He was a large man with a squarish head which seemed too big even for his large frame. His chin was long and his square jaw overlapped slightly, giving him the grumpy appearance of Gruffalo. He had short-cropped, blond hair which made me think that the top of his head was covered in frost. His complexion was baby-pink, so much so that I felt like pinching his cheek or playing peek-a-boo with him.

'I will need to formally interview the witnesses.' He spoke to Hatton but gave a short nod towards Samuel and me. 'I'm sorry about the inconvenience, but it will have to be conducted at the station. Miss Kaye and Mr Dee, and the two passengers who found Mrs Conti Lang.'

'Emilia and Ollie,' I elucidated helpfully.

Hatton gave me a startled look. He was probably dying to find out how I knew. I gathered Benedict hadn't told him how I came into possession of those facts. It was considerate of him to keep me out of it.

Detective Smilga added, 'Would they all, including yourself, Mr Hatton, be able to accompany me now?'

'Could they at least have breakfast?' Hatton replied.

I beamed at him my gratitude. My stomach was rumbling, playing a gutsy version of a loud and disorderly march punctuated with lively drum sections. It was after 10am, and I didn't have anything inside me (having discarded my undigested dinner in my puking episode in the night).

Hatton added, 'I will also have to update the passengers on the current situation and sort a few things out before I can come down to the station. If you could give me a couple of hours, I'd be obliged. Is that all right?'

'Yes, of course. My driver will wait for you. I'll be ready at the station whenever you are. Shall we say, not later than noon?' It was a question but it sounded final. Gruffalo Smilga departed.

Our very belated breakfast that day felt like a royal feast. Only once you've been denied something do you really come to appreciate it. That goes for food, too. I, for one, appreciated my salmon and scrambled egg croissant no end. I was devouring it and paying little attention to what went on. Then again, I didn't have to pay any attention. I already knew everything.

Mr Hatton entered the restaurant appearing oddly rejuvenated and buoyant despite his whole night long hunt for Alvar and the stress that was bound to be crushing his chest. After all, nasty things had happened on his watch. Nevertheless, he was glowing as he appraised us of the double murder and the successful capture of the killer.

'I wouldn't be so sure of that,' I muttered

under my breath before being fussily hushed by everyone at my table. They were intent on hearing what the Chief Security man had to say, even though it was I – with some help from Samuel – who had actually apprehended the culprit. And I had the inside knowledge of his motives.

Hatton asked us to join him in remembering our tragically departed *friend*, Mrs Cordelia Conti Lang, who – he said with little conviction – had been brutally and senselessly murdered by a man to whom we had provided a safe haven.

I noted that neither Mr Hatton nor anybody in the room looked particularly distraught. Admittedly, Barbara gravitated closer towards Sidney, and he put his arm around her. His right hand was on hers, stroking it absent-mindedly. Those two, I surmised, had grown very close indeed since I introduced them to each other. Well done, Maggie! I gave myself a virtual pat on the back. But, going back to Hatton's shocking announcement, literally nobody seemed to be grieving the loss of one of us.

Hatton himself was unmoved. Maybe it was his ex-soldier's training that helped him control the adrenaline rush better than your average civvy. He said his piece and asked for a moment of reflection on Mrs Conti Lang's sudden and violent death. The passengers obliged him with a few seconds of silence to show a modicum of respect for the woman, but there was no empathy in anyone's eyes. The woman had comprehensively failed to make a good impression on any of us.

After those few seconds of our truncated minute of silence, the buzz around the tables resumed with boosted merriment and animation. After all, the double-murder on top of the dramatic rescue mission earlier were thrilling and unique additions to the cruise entertainment programme. None of us would forget this voyage in a hurry. You could feel the electricity of excitement cursing through the air.

Even Cordelia's son appeared eerily joyous.

Ollie was seated at the same table as he had been last night, and in the same company. Both he and Emilia were at ease. Their heads were inclined towards each other and, believe it or not, they were giggling. Under any other circumstances, that would be perfectly normal: two young people in the bloom of first love – naturally they had a lot to smile about. But it was only five hours ago that they had found his mother's dead body in a puddle of blood. Their conduct wasn't what I would call *befitting*.

Hywel was also watching them, I noticed. I said to him, 'Quite remarkable, don't you think?'

'What is?'

'Well, he's Mrs Conti Lang's son. Having just lost his mother, he's acting... hm... unnaturally cool, almost blasé, I'd say.'

Hywel shrugged. 'I don't suppose she was his

favourite person. They'd been rowing over that girl. You yourself told us the other day.'

'Yes, I know, but I mean – the shock! Why isn't he at least a tad shaken?'

'Maybe because she had it coming, don't you think?' Hywel sounded callous.

'But still!' I argued. 'They actually found her body. Ollie and Emilia, I mean. Did you know that? The shock of it! Whoever's body it was, even a stranger's, it should have some effect on them, don't you think? They should be lying in bed, packed with tranquilisers.'

'And you were held hostage by a killer wielding an axe, Maggie,' Samuel chipped in, uninvited. 'You're not in bed, packed full of tranquilisers – you're chomping on your toast with marmalade.'

'It's a croissant, actually, with salmon and egg, both poached,' I corrected him for the record.

Hywel and Stacey chuckled. I shot them a warning glance. It wasn't funny and I wasn't going to be distracted. 'You can all laugh, but you know what they say – it's often the person who discovers the body that turns out to be the killer. Or a close family member. In this case, Ollie is both.'

'Don't be ridiculous, Maggie!'

'*Ridiculous*, really? You should've heard him issuing threats to his mother. It was vicious. No love lost! He as much as accused her of killing his father. Remember, Samuel?'

Samuel frowned at me.

'He said Cordelia killed his father?' Hywel asked. At long last, someone was taking me seriously. 'Did she actually tell the boy his father was dead?'

'No, Hywel, not that. Of course, he knew his father was dead. He didn't have to be told. Pay attention. What he said was that she killed him. He said she had, well, in essence... sort of wormed her way into his father's favours, stolen his fortune and... well, got rid of him – killed him, yes.'

'He didn't say that.' Samuel was being insufferable.

'He implied it.'

'I see,' Hywel said.

'No, you don't. He expressly and to her face blamed her for his father's death. He accused her outright. It took some guts, I can tell you. And he rebelled against her after she forbade him from seeing Emilia. He had a motive – a double motive. He and Emilia. Maybe they did it together? They found the body – together. It's often the person – or persons – who find the body.'

'Yes, you did say.'

Stacey bestowed upon me a patronising and very irritating smile, and said, 'The problem with your story is that the police already have the killer in custody. Mr Hatton just told us it was one of those men rescued from the fishing boat.'

'Ha! I don't think so.'

'Maggie, let it rest,' Samuel warned me as if I were a five-year-old. 'You can't accuse people at a whim.'

I was livid. I was just about to retort when my attention was snatched by the arrival of Benedict. He joined Ollie and Emilia at their table. He too looked unbothered. His quick eyes caught me staring at him. He had always been like a bird of prey on the prowl, and it seemed he had not lost that quality. He waved at me, smiling. I had to take a moment to compose myself. I reflected. There was no point in holding grudges over a few pieces of jewellery and the historical theft of my savings. I decided to be magnanimous. I beamed and waved back at him.

Encouraged by my benevolence, Benedict approached our table and greeted everyone affably. Everyone but Samuel responded. He purposefully ignored the man. His petulant conduct was embarrassing.

'What do you say to us joining tables for tonight's Christmas dinner? Me, Emilia and Ollie would love some company,' Benedict offered.

In all the rumpus of the last few days, Christmas had somehow managed to sneak under my radar. But it was Christmas indeed in its full wintry bloom at sea. I peered gingerly at Samuel. I knew he had a problem with Benny – he couldn't hide it. His expression was crestfallen. He looked up and glared mulishly at poor Benny.

I feared he was going to decline his offer. I couldn't let him do that just to pander to his ego. I had bigger fish to fry. I would explain it to him later.

For the time being, I struck while the iron was hot, and chimed, 'What a wonderful idea! The more the merrier. Let's get together.'

Barbara added, 'That's so lovely of you, Benedict.'

Hywel was positively elated and sporting a big grin, but Samuel looked as if he had been hit by a bus. I felt for him.

CHAPTER 16

Maggie insisted that her lawyer was present during the police interview. By her lawyer she meant Sam. Detective Smilga patiently pointed out that she wasn't under arrest and wasn't even being interviewed under caution, so there was no need for a lawyer. She was just giving a witness statement.

'I may not need a lawyer, but I would like one,' Maggie countered. 'Surely, I'm entitled?'

'Of course, ma'am, if you wish.' The burly Viking submitted to the little plump woman, instinctively recognising her bloody-mindedness.

Maggie arched her eyebrow pointedly at Sam. He could venture a couple of guesses as to why she wanted him by her side. She may have wanted him to hold her hand, which would be awfully flattering. But that wasn't her most likely reason. Sam's best bet was that she had a cunning plan, such as keeping an eye on him to ensure he delivered on his – and her – promise to Alvar. Under all that airy-fairy lightweight silliness lay Maggie Kaye's unrelenting shrewdness.

They were offered coffee. When it arrived and Maggie took a sip, she screwed her face in disgust. 'Would you have tea? Builder's tea, any tea?' she inquired.

Detective Smilga sent his officer out to organise tea. That would probably involve a samovar – after all, Latvia was almost Russia. Sam reconciled himself with the instant coffee and for the second time settled down to listen to Maggie relaying Alvar's story. This time, he found it even more embellished with dramatic pauses and shrills of exclamation. It was abundantly clear that Maggie was on Alvar's side, body and soul. When she reached the crescendo of Nedim's tragic end, she offered Smilga her interpretation, 'So, any half-intelligent person can see it plain as day – it was a classic case of self-defence. Wasn't it, Samuel?'

Caught unawares, Sam winced behind his cup of bad coffee.

'Samuel is an eminent barrister in England. He's already concluded – unreservedly – that Alvar acted in self-defence, and no court would convict him of murder. But why am I telling you this? Silly me! Samuel can tell you himself. Go on, Samuel.' She fluttered her eyelashes at him.

'Well, hmm…' Sam floundered.

'Our courts will take everything into account, Miss Kaye,' Smilga assured her while Sam was still trying to verbalise his position without making a fool of himself.

'Tell him, Samuel. You did say it, didn't you?' Maggie pinned Sam to the wall with a razor-sharp scowl. You could not mistake the warning in her tone.

'From what Alvar told you, and then you told me second-hand, as it were, well, of course, it seems like he had no choice but to defend his life. He acted out of necessity.'

'Didn't I say!' Maggie triumphed.

'But that applies only to Nedim. As for Cordelia Conti Lang, I can see no extenuating circumstances whatsoever.'

'Alvar didn't kill her! He had no idea who she was, and no idea that she was dead,' Maggie protested. Feeling let down by Sam, she quickly turned against him, 'I told you that already, Samuel Dee. You promised to help him!'

'I'm trying my best, Maggie, but this isn't how it works. We can't tell Detective Smilga how to do his job. He needs to investigate and come to his own conclusions, not be told what they are.'

She snorted in reply and turned to the big Latvian, 'I'm telling you, Detective, Alvar had nothing to do with Cordelia's death.'

Detective Smilga nodded to pacify her. 'Yes, I can hear you, but Mr Olegin will be given every chance to tell us his version of events himself.

What I'd like you to tell us is what happened to you. Let's start with this: how did Mr Olegin gain entry to your room?'

That was the point when Maggie's unbridled charge came to a screeching halt. She now had to explain herself, and in particular her all-night cavorting with Count Dracula. She probably no longer wished for Sam to be present to witness this part of the interview. She threw him a semi-furtive, semi-apologetic glance. He looked into his coffee mug, purporting huge preoccupation with its contents.

'Well, he just walked in, I suppose.'

'When? Could you tell me what time – approximately?'

'That's the problem. I really can't help you there. I don't know.'

'You don't know when the man burst into your cabin. It'd be hard to miss.'

'I wasn't there.'

'But there were no signs of a break-in. I had assumed that he either followed you inside as you opened the door, or knocked and you inadvertently opened the door, thinking it was a friend – Mr Dee, for example.'

'Well, no. He was there when I got back.' Another guilty glance at Sam. He couldn't miss that.

'And what time did you get back to your cabin?'

'I'd say, um...' She was trapped in a corner

of her own making. No amount of squirming would get her out of it so she blurted out, 'Around 6am.'

'You were out all night?'

'As it happens, I was. It's not a crime. I was... I was catching up with, erm, an old friend of mine, Mr Rawbotham. We bumped into each other. He's a magician.'

'A magician?'

'Yes, onboard entertainment, magicians, stand-up comedians and so on.'

'I see. So, you spent the night with him?'

'*Talking to him*, yes.'

'And you two were *talking* in his cabin?'

'Yes.' Maggie was blushing. That could mean anything. Sam did not wish to contemplate the possibilities. He downed the rest of his dreadful coffee. At least he could use that to justify the bitter grimace twisting his face.

Tea was served at last. The poor officer tasked with getting it must have travelled to India and back to fetch it. Maggie took her time to fluff around with the milk and brown sugar. Sam didn't know her to take sugar with her tea – any type of sugar. Smilga waited, tapping his fingers on the table. Finally, when she took her first sip and smiled her satisfaction, he continued with the interview.

'So, at around 6am you discovered Alvar Olegin in your cabin?'

'He discovered me before I discovered him. I

knew someone was there. You see, I saw the girls first—'

'Girls? What girls?' Smilga looked intrigued.

'Two Armenian girls died on that fishing boat, detective. They were thrown overboard like worthless ballast. Alvar did his best to save their lives, but the others,' Maggie gave a heavy sigh, 'well, Elbe and Nadim, that is, ganged up on him and beat him up. He stood no chance. He'll tell you all about it, and then you'll know that Alvar is a decent man. He just got mixed up with the wrong crowd. Ask him, detective. Don't ask me. Coming from me, it'll be inadmissible. It's hearsay, isn't it, Samuel?' Maggie fixed Sam with a superior gaze. He raised his eyebrows, suitably impressed with her legal expertise, and nodded.

'Going back to those two girls,' Smilga pressed on with his line of inquiry, 'you say you saw them first. What do you mean by that?'

'Never mind those girls – they're dead,' Maggie retorted. 'I just sensed someone was in my cabin, but didn't see him at first. He must have whacked me on the head and I passed out. He had an axe. He could've used it and killed me, but he didn't.'

'Yes, he could have done that, but he could also find use for a hostage. It wasn't out of the kindness of his heart that he chose to spare you.'

Sam was glad he wasn't the one to point that out.

'Personally, if you ask me... If you care to

know what I observed being there with him in that room,' Maggie paused to demand silence and their undivided attention. Smilga and Sam sat up and listened. Maggie went on, 'He didn't look like a man who had the presence of mind to consider hostage-taking or his next step. He was frightened, thoroughly shaken, and he cried. Yes, he wept like a baby. Alvar is not a cold-blooded murderer, if you want my opinion.'

'OK,' Smilga conceded the point even though he had never asked Maggie for her opinion. 'But he had the presence of mind to identify your room as a potential hideaway, and he broke in without damaging the lock.'

'He didn't have to break in. I don't lock my door. I forever misplace the blinking key card so I just leave it on the latch, so to speak – slightly ajar. I don't have any valuables anyway.'

'I did warn her about it,' Sam couldn't help himself. Maggie drove him to despair with her recklessness.

'You did, yes,' she sighed. 'But that's beside the point. My door was open and Alvar just walked in. You'll have to ask him exactly when. When I got there, he settled me down in a chair.'

'Roped her to it, to be precise.'

'Please, don't interrupt, Samuel. This is *my* witness statement. So, we sat down and he told me what happened. And I believed him. I still do. He could've used the axe to silence me, but he didn't. Did you notice that the axe was as clean as a whistle? There was no blood on it, not a drop.'

'Yes, we did notice. But that wasn't the murder weapon. A sharp blade was used to slash both victims' throats, and in a very similar fashion.'

'A scalpel,' Maggie elaborated. 'Alvar told me he'd wrestled a scalpel out of Nedim's hand and, as I told you already, he used it in self-defence. But then, he said, he had dropped it and he'd run. He picked up the axe from the Fire Point on the top deck. What I would like to know is if you found the scalpel. Did you?'

'We can't divulge that information.'

'Course, you can't.'

'Where did he say he dropped it?'

'So, you didn't find it. I knew it!'

Sam smiled under his breath. That was trademark Maggie. She picked up the faintest of clues as she blundered about. She was a canny operator.

Maggie took the last sip of her tea and leaned over the table to fix Detective Smilga with her all-knowing eyes. She said, 'He dropped it in the medical bay. Someone else found it and killed Cordelia Conti Lang. Someone else has it. You find that scalpel, you will find her killer.'

'The scalpel may be languishing at the bottom of the sea.' Sam speculated.

'It may be, or it may not. If I were you,' Maggie was still fixed on Smilga, 'I'd be searching everyone's cabin.'

'You can't do that without a warrant, and you won't get one without just cause.'

'Oh, Samuel, these are just technicalities! I can't be bothered with such things. I'm going to find that scalpel, and I am going to find the killer.'

'Leave the investigation to us, madam.'

'But you won't be investigating anything, will you? You think you have your man. Our ship travels onwards tomorrow, with the real killer onboard. Someone has to find the bugger and bring him to justice. I guess, it will have to be me.'

Detective Smilga cocked his eyebrow and looked to Sam for an explanation, or at least some form of moral support. Sam shrugged. 'Maggie will be Maggie,' he said. 'She has a penchant for sleuthing, I'm afraid. Forever getting in harm's way. It's a compulsion. I will keep an eye on her.'

Maggie shot him a dirty look, and she had one too for Smilga.

'Are we done here?' she asked. 'I've nothing else to add to my witness statement.'

He thanked her for her time and cooperation and confirmed that the interview was at an end. Maggie retorted that she didn't mind giving her time to the police while everyone else was enjoying the jewels of Riga's medieval architecture, but that she expected him to take her seriously. Then she demanded his business card. He gave it to her.

'I'll call you as soon as I have something.'

Smilga thanked her with all the seriousness he could muster. Then it was Sam's turn to give his – short – account of the events he had witnessed, starting with finding Maggie trussed up in a chair like a Christmas turkey.

CHAPTER 17

Maggie's Journal

I n the true spirit of Christmas, I wore my prehistoric woolly dress featuring Rudolph the Red-nosed Reindeer. If I am not mistaken, it dates back to the mid-nineties. It had occurred to me that Benedict may remember it, but I no longer cared to impress him. We had cleared the air between us. As soon as all the cobwebs were removed, I was able to see him in the cold light of day. He was just a small-time crook who had made a few bad decisions and couldn't afford the price-tag they attracted. Being a crook, he had swindled me into paying his debt. I was over him. Subject closed.

Normally, I wouldn't spare him a second thought, and most certainly wouldn't have agreed to suffer his company at Christmas. But I had an ulterior motive. His invitation to join tables was a one in a million opportunity to interrogate my prime suspect: Oliver Conti Lang. Or perhaps even my two prime suspects, because Emilia was also topping the list, sitting firmly on Ollie's right-hand side.

The giant Norwegian fir in the restaurant was twinkling with lights and smelling as if we had sailed into the heart of a conifer forest. That scent alone brought Christmas to me on a golden platter. My mood received an instant facelift.

Everyone at our table had gone to the trouble of looking festive, though it was rather hit-and-miss for most of us. Stacey and Hywel wore matching elf outfits, complete with bells attached to the noses of their slippers. If I had seen them dressed as they were at any other time outside the Christmas season, I would have reported them to the police. They looked suspicious. Barbara didn't fare any better with her gigantic Christmas lantern earrings which lit up and shot out laser beams each time she shook her head. Sidney, sadly, resembled a psychotic clown. He was wearing a jester's hat. I feared he had confused Christmas with Halloween. Samuel managed a thick jumper with the Nordic motif of white reindeers pulling sleighs. He fidgeted constantly as if he couldn't wait to take it off. It still had the price tag attached at the back. I pulled it off for him. Benedict, who in his day job fashioned himself as a macabre Maestro de Norte clad in black from head to toe, went to the trouble of sporting a red-and-white scarf (I noted that it featured the emblem of Liverpool FC so technically it wasn't seasonal). Only Ollie and Emilia looked comfortable yet suitably Christmassy, he in a smart shirt with a print of tiny snowflakes and she in a gorgeous dress with a white collar of frost-patterned lace and matching gloves. But then again, those two were young and beautiful and they would look dapper in brown paper bags.

We also had the pleasure of both Mr and Mrs Lang's ghostly company. She was glamorous in a sparkling body-glove dress. Without her numerous Botox injections and a couple of decades lighter, she was simply stunning. It was no wonder that the most powerful mobster in London had fallen for her. He wore his immortal pinstriped suit, wide-brimmed hat and sported a cigar between his teeth. In my experience, it was unorthodox for two spirits to populate the same space simultaneously, but I guess, they came as a package. After all, it was Christmas – a family time. Having said that, I must add that there was zero intimacy between them. They just sat with us at the table like two pillars of salt, as if they themselves didn't realise they were here.

Frankly, I could do with a little nod in the right direction or a spot of finger-pointing. Assuming that Cordelia had stayed on this earth to haunt her killer, she was doing a poor job of it by showing herself only to me. I certainly didn't murder her so haunting me was a waste of effort. However, I could do with some help finding her killer. I tried sending her a telepathic message: *Come on, Cordelia, give us a hint.* My message didn't seem to reach her for she didn't as much as twitch a muscle. A pillar of salt, like I said.

The chef had prepared a feast. Our roast turkey graced our table, accompanied by all the usual trimmings. Pi carved it for us and slapped generous portions of white meat onto our plates. Magnanimous in his Santa hat, he acted as if he had paid for the roast out of his own pocket. We helped ourselves to Yorkshires and vegetables. A bottle of Australian chardonnay accompanied the meal.

I had neither much appetite nor could I stomach the wine. I was still in a mental recovery position from my alcohol-drenched night with Benedict and the police interrogation that I had endured only six hours earlier. A feeling of tiredness had come over me. I couldn't shake myself awake. I pushed my unloved Christmas dinner around the plate and listened idly as Stacey and Barbara extolled the charms of Riga. Apparently, it had a quaint Old Town. Samuel and I had missed it as we had been busy giving witness statements, and so had Ollie and Emilia, for the same reason.

'I was looking forward to seeing Riga,' Emilia said, 'but it was dark by the time we left the police station and all I could think about was cuddling up in my bed.'

'The police station?' Hywel inquired. I realised, he didn't know that Ollie and Emilia had found Cordelia's body.

Ollie enlightened him to that effect.

'It must've been awful for you,' Barbara commiserated.

'It wasn't pleasant, no,' Ollie said.

It struck me how little emotion he had put into that statement. My suspicions about his part in his mother's death were reignited. I knew I may not get a better opportunity than this to interrogate him close up and personal. Perhaps doing it over the Christmas dinner wasn't exactly in good taste and my timing was off, but as the saying goes, there's no time like the present.

I started diplomatically, 'I'm ever so sorry about your mother, Ollie. Please accept my condolences.'

'Thank you.' He peered at me dolefully.

'I've seen you and your mum around Bishops Well. We met once at The Old Stables Café. Not that long - a couple of years ago, just as you and your mum moved into Forget-Me-Not. You didn't look your best at that time, as I recall.' I was of course referring to his dilated irises, gaunt and patchy skin and skinny frame – all symptoms of drug abuse.

'Oh?' His expression changed to slightly alarmed.

'We're virtually neighbours. Samuel and I live in Priest's Hole, by the church – St John's.'

'Oh yes, I know that church. Small world!' I could sense his discomfort.

'How are you enjoying Bishops Well?'

'Yeah, it's a nice village,' he mumbled. I let the label of *village* pass unchallenged. I had a bigger fish to fry. 'And no, I wasn't in the best of places when we moved in. I was... Well, I was a crackhead at the time. But no longer. Thanks to this beautiful woman.' He reached out for Emilia's hand and smiled. In that smile and in the way he looked at her I could easily see the love that I couldn't see when he spoke of his late mother. So, since he had already opened up about his addiction, I decided to pursue the anomaly without beating about the bush.

'Forgive me for saying this, I realise I may be out of line, but you don't seem very affected by your mother's death.'

I felt a sharp pain in my ankle. Samuel had kicked me under the table. I glanced at him, surprised. He glared. I decided to do some emergency back-peddling. 'I'm sorry, I didn't express myself well. What I meant—'

But I didn't have to take anything back, because Ollie looked me straight in the eye and confessed, 'You're right. I don't feel her loss. I know she's gone, but I don't miss her.'

'It may be too early for that,' Sidney interjected.

'People react differently to grief,' Barbara added.

'I don't think I am grieving. I'm not even sorry,' Ollie admitted. 'My mother and I – we've always had our differences, but recently it got to a point where – I don't know... There were times I just wanted her out of my life.'

A shocked silence fell on our table like a brick.

Neither I nor Samuel should have been startled after what we had overheard the other day on the top deck. Ollie's sentiments were consistent.

I said, 'I'm not surprised. I heard you and your mother argue over Emilia. No holds barred...'

'Good. Then I don't have to explain,' he said, and instantly went on to do exactly that: 'She did everything she could to separate us. She controlled me, my whole life, every smallest detail. She was suffocating me. I'd had enough. You heard me say it to her face. And I won't pretend I'm sorry that she's dead. She was my mother and I know I should mourn, and all that lark,' he sighed, 'but she was impossible to live with.'

'I understand,' I offered him a warm, indulgent smile. Then I drilled into him, 'But there's something you said to her that puzzled me. I can't stop thinking about it.'

'What about?'

'Your father. Did I get it wrong – I might have misunderstood – did you say she killed him?'

Samuel jumped in, 'Maggie, stop battering him. He's in no state.'

'That's a ridiculous allegation to make, Maggie. Come on!' Hywel sided with Samuel. I was on my own and had to defend myself against their twinned alpha-male assault.

'I'm only asking! If I misunderstood, well, I apologise.'

'No, you didn't misunderstand.' Even I was taken aback when Ollie said that. He squared his shoulders and proceeded to tell us what had happened.

CHAPTER 18

He had only been seven when his father had died. His memory of that day was hazy, but as the years went by he started making sense of what he had witnessed as a child.

Something had woken him up in the night.

They lived in a big house in South Kensington. His father was on his deathbed, fighting a losing battle against pancreatic cancer which had returned after he had briefly gone into remission. That was Cordelia's official version. But he couldn't have been dying if he needed Cordelia's help to do so – that's what Ollie had been mulling over for many years, trying to understand what he had seen that night. Was it a mercy killing or murder?

Lenny Lang wasn't that old when he died: seventy-two. He had been diagnosed at sixty-nine and got an all-clear two years later. Since his first diagnosis, he had been looking after himself punctiliously. He had engaged a private nurse, who lived in the house. He was receiving regular blood transfusions, boosters and meds intravenously, through a drip in the night. For that reason, he and Cordelia had stopped sharing their marital bed. Cordelia moved to the smaller bedroom next door to her husband's. There was a connecting bathroom between them. Ollie's bedroom was opposite his parents'. The nurse slept in the room on the other side of the master bedroom.

What had awoken Ollie could have been a noise: something being dropped, a door or a floorboard creaking. It was an old Georgian house with many authentic features which regularly scraped and rasped.

Young Ollie sat up in his bed and listened. He wasn't satisfied with the silence that had followed the noise. Whoever had made that noise was being extra-quiet, concealing themselves in the shadows. Ollie was frightened and wanted his mum.

He swung his feet off the bed and slid them into his slippers. It was winter and the floors were cold. His eyes adjusted to the dark – he neither needed to switch on the lights nor wanted to. He was afraid of what he may see. He shuffled gingerly to his mother's bedroom and pushed the door open. He whispered, 'Mummy?'

There was no answer. He hurried towards the bed, intent on jumping in and hiding under the duvet, next to her. But she wasn't there. The bed was empty. Ollie's heart was pounding. His small child's logic told him that the best hiding place for him would be back in his own bed. He could hide there until the morning when he expected everything would be back to normal. But as he was tiptoeing soundlessly back to his room, that noise had returned. It had come from his father's bedroom. Ollie didn't think it was wise, but he couldn't help himself: he went to check.

He didn't enter. He only looked through a gap in the door. And that was when he saw his mother. It was a relief to discover that she hadn't been kidnapped in the night by a bogeyman – she was just visiting Dad. Except that it was an odd time for a visit and they weren't even talking.

Some instinct told Ollie to stay hidden, breathe silently and say nothing. He wasn't scared anymore, just curious. He watched his Mum as she injected something into the tube leading from the drip bag to his Dad's arm. She then slid the syringe into the pocket of her dressing gown and stood over Dad's bed. She didn't say anything, not even when Dad's body went into a jerky spasm, and shuddered, and then went limp.

Ollie expected Mum to call the nurse, but she didn't, so he assumed that Dad must have had a bad dream, and that all was well now. Mum wiped Dad's mouth with a hanky, and that seemed to be a loving, caring gesture in Ollie's view. She then said, 'Cheerio, love,' turned and went back to her bedroom via the connecting door. She did not see Ollie.

He stayed in the corridor for a bit. He wasn't sure what to do – whether to do anything. He waited for Dad to turn in his bed or to make a snoring sound, but nothing happened. On tiptoe, Ollie ventured into the room. He craned his neck over the side of his father's bed to look at his face. Dad's eyes were open and they were staring into the ceiling. They didn't blink when Ollie touched Dad's hand. Admittedly, it was a very light touch. Dad may not have felt it. Ollie prodded again and that was when Dad's hand rolled off the bed and rested palm up, with his fingers curled like a bird's claws. The sight of those curled, yellow talons scared Ollie. He ran to his bedroom and hid under his pillows. Something told him running to Mum wasn't a good idea. She would be angry if she knew he'd gone to bother Dad in the night.

The next day his father was found dead. The family doctor's verdict was that Dad died peacefully in his sleep. It was the deadly cancer that had finally claimed him. That was what Ollie's mother told him. She never mentioned her visit to Dad's bedroom and Ollie never asked. But it troubled him and with time he drew his own conclusions.

He had investigated all the possibilities:

his mother could have injected Lenny with something like insulin – undetectable if not specifically tested for. Or with a small bubble of air. That was all it took to kill a man: a bubble of air.

His father's death had been expected for some time. Lenny was packed full of drugs as it were. Nobody would suspect foul play. Except for a little boy who had witnessed something out of the ordinary the night before his dad's death.

'Good Lord, it must've been torture living with a secret like that!' Barbara exclaimed.

'Not being able to tell anyone, because after all she was your mother. And you loved her.' Emilia added. She lowered her head onto Ollie's shoulder, but he was still too charged to respond in kind.

'And what if you were wrong?' Samuel speculated, always the lawyer cross-examining witnesses and sowing seeds of doubt into their minds. 'What if you had misinterpreted her actions? What if there was a logical explanation? You would've accused an innocent woman – you own mother, at that. Your faith in her stopped you from questioning her intentions, which makes perfect sense.'

'I didn't feel any loyalty towards her,' Ollie argued. 'I just wasn't sure.'

'She was an evil witch,' Hywel presented his total stranger's take on the matter. 'She killed Lang, no doubt about that.'

'Yes, I know that now for certain: she killed him. The cancer probably hadn't come back, contrary to what she had told everyone, and she decided not to wait any longer for Dad to die naturally.

'He was much older than her, and frail, he would go sooner rather than later, but that wasn't enough for her. She was greedy – always wanting more. She was my mother, I know, but sometimes... Sometimes I hated her.' Ollie stared intently into the space across the table from him, where nobody was seated. Nobody alive, that is, because if he could see his dead father he would be looking right at him. For a moment, I thought he was seeing him, but I quickly realised that wasn't the case. Because Lenny Lang rose to his feet, and left, but Ollie's gaze was still fixed on the same spot.

As soon as Lenny's pinstriped silhouette vanished from sight – *my* sight – I looked at Cordelia to see her reaction. After all, her crime had finally come to light and it was her own son who had exposed her.

One would expect a modicum of guilt, or at least a level of discomfort. But not from Cordelia. She offered no reaction whatsoever. She barely noticed her husband's departure. She was still glowing in her ethereal ghostly light, beautiful, cold and unresponsive. And she was still amongst us. The mystery of her death weighed heavily on my shoulders. That dreadful woman would be knocking around, troubling me, until such time as I handed her killer to the police. I didn't think she deserved justice, but Alvar did.

I turned to Ollie and shot from the hip, 'So, if anyone had a motive to kill your mother, it was you. You held her responsible for your father's death. She threatened to disinherit you if you pursued your relationship with Emilia. She controlled your life, made it hell. Do I need to go on?'

He looked bemused, but agreed, 'You're right. She'd made my life hell – that's exactly it. I became so rotten in here,' he tapped his chest, '– a moral bankrupt. Like mother, like son.' He smiled wryly. 'I started dabbling in drugs – the harder, the better. If you have a rich mother, you're never short of suppliers. They're falling over themselves to get you hooked. I don't think I stood a chance.'

'You poor, poor boy,' Barbara whimpered.

'It's fine, Barbara. No need to be sorry for me. I got clean. And no, not thanks to my mother. Thanks to Emilia. She saved my life. She gave me reason to live.'

The two young lovers peered at each other tenderly. There was no dry eye around our table, apart from mine.

'And your mother forbade you from seeing

her,' I pointed out. 'She called her nasty names. That must've made you angry.'

'It did,' he agreed. 'You heard me – I told her to go to hell. I was bloody angry.'

'Angry enough to kill her?'

'Yes, but I didn't do it, tempting as it was.'

'Maggie, you're being unfair,' Samuel rebuked me, and Barbara gave me a pleading look, begging me to stop.

'She's talking nonsense,' Hywel was speaking to Ollie. 'Don't listen to her. You don't have to explain yourself to her, son.'

I wouldn't be bullied into silence because what I was saying may sound insensitive. Evil as Cordelia Conti Lang may have been, she was dead and Alvar was accused of her murder. I knew it wasn't him and I had made a promise that I would find the real killer. I was doing just that. I pointed this out to them, 'Ollie had a strong motive for killing Cordelia. She had murdered his father before his eyes—'

'Not true.' Hywel tried to shut me up, but I wouldn't let him.

'He had an opportunity. His cabin is next door to his mother's—'

'You're forgetting, Maggie, that he was with Emilia,' Samuel reminded me. *Thank you, Samuel!*

'True. That's why I think they did it together.'

'Utter bollocks! Take it back, you stupid,

stupid woman!' Benedict, who had so far sat quietly, erupted with outrage. I understood his outburst and forgave him for calling me stupid. His paternal instincts were too strong to let him take my accusation against his daughter without protest.

'It's all right, Dad. Maggie is just sharing her thoughts.' Emilia spoke calmly. She was remarkably composed, considering the accusation I had just levelled against her. The only sign of her uneasiness was in her fingers which were wrapped around a silver locket she was wearing. The chain holding the locket was taut against her neck. She was pulling it, and mechanically pressing and releasing the clasp on the locket, as she spoke, 'But I can assure you, Miss Kaye, we didn't kill Ollie's mother. By the time we found her, she was already dead.'

That locket seemed eerily familiar. I focussed on it. When her fingers momentarily opened, I could inspect the elaborate poison-ivy carving on the lid. I recognised it. That locker used to belong to my grandmother! Grandpa Bernie had gifted it to me when I left Bishops to study in London. Benedict had stolen it. The swine! He had said that he sold all my jewellery to pay his debts, but he had lied yet again. I felt sick.

CHAPTER 19

Maggie pushed back her chair, and fled. No explanation. No apology.

Sam excused himself from the table and ran after her. He caught her by the lift.

'Maggie, stop! Wait, please!'

She turned. She was as pale as a sheet, as if she had seen a ghost, which in all probability she had.

'It's me, Maggie. You can talk to me. What's wrong? What happened?'

She didn't answer. Her eyes sailed over him without recognising his face. She abandoned the lift and took the stairs. Sam followed.

He wanted to grab her and hold her in place until he shook some sense into her, but he didn't dare. She reached her room and tried to push the door open. It wouldn't shift. Since her hostage scare, she had learned to lock it. Exasperated, she fumbled in her clutch bag. It fell out of her hands. Its incongruous contents spilled on the floor: the large iron key to her house in Bishops, a small bag of jelly babies, her mobile phone – switched off, a wrist band promoting Red Nose Day, and the key card to her cabin.

Sam picked it up and handed it to her. He said, 'You're under great stress, Maggie. I can't leave you when you're like this. Can we talk?'

She snatched the card. Her eyes shifted away from him guiltily and somewhat shamefully. She unlocked her door.

'No, I can't. I'm sorry, Samuel. I want to be on my own.' She darted in and shut the door in his face.

He had wrapped the small box in shiny paper with red hearts. He had been planning to give it to her as a Christmas present. He would wait for her to unwrap it and lift the lid open. She would find the ring and her eyes would light. She'd gasp and ask if it was really for her. She'd insist he shouldn't have gone to all that trouble and expense just for her. That's when he would go down on one knee and propose to her the way Maggie would have liked it: with splendour and solemnity, and with the fervour of a man in love.

She would have to say *yes.*

She would remove the ring from the box and slip it onto her finger. It would be a perfect fit. He knew that for a fact. His mother Deirdre had secretly borrowed one of Maggie's rings and they had taken it to the jeweller to resize the ring Sam had chosen. His mother had been in on the subterfuge from the start – in fact, she had come up with the idea.

'How much longer will you be torturing yourself, huh?' Deirdre had demanded in a fit of impatience. 'Maggie is the best thing that has happened to you since Alice. When are you going to make a decent woman of her? God knows, she needs a man to take her in hand!'

So, the idea of a Christmas proposal had been contrived. Sadly, Sam had failed to deliver on it.

He was sitting in his cabin, loosely holding the little shiny box in his lap. He was wallowing in self-pity. It had gone past midnight. Christmas was over. The plan had fallen through. Maggie had slipped through his fingers and rejected him before he had even opened his mouth to declare his love. Had she sensed it coming and run away to spare him outright rejection? Could it be that bumping into Rawbotham had reignited her feelings for the bastard? Had Sam already lost Maggie? He was devasted and raw with pain, but it would only get worse: he would never hear the end of it from his mother.

He swore piquantly and hurled the stupid box across the room. It bounced from the wall and landed back under his feet. He picked it up and put it in his pocket. He would return it to the jeweller and tell his mother to mind her own business. He would do things his way, and even though that meant inaction and self-flagellation, at least he wouldn't have to deal with rejection. He might yet move out of Priest's Hole. He would definitely move out of Priest's Hole if Count Dracula moved in.

'Samuel? Are you awake?' Maggie's trembling voice asked from the corridor.

Sam leapt to his feet. 'Maggie?'

'Can I come in?'

He hurtled towards the door and swung it open. Maggie's pyjama-clad person stood in a wedge of bright light. He pulled her inside. 'Are you okay?'

Her eyes were already red and puffy, but she broke into more tears. 'No, not okay! I'm not... I'd rather be home. This cruise was such a bad idea, Samuel. Whose idea was it in the first place?'

Samuel passed her a paper tissue. She blew her nose loudly. It turned as red as her eyes. She looked tormented.

Sam put his arm around her and led her to the armchair. She flopped in it and dropped her chin onto her chest.

'You've been through a lot in the last twenty-four hours, Maggie. It's no wonder you're unsettled. The trauma of being held hostage would've thrown anyone off kilter.'

'It's not that, Samuel. I really didn't mind that so much. I knew Alvar wouldn't hurt me. It's not that.'

'What is it then?'

'It's Benedict.'

'Benedict Raw-bloody-botham?!' He heard himself holler. He always knew that man was nothing but trouble. What had he done to Maggie, the scoundrel!

'What has he done to you? I swear to God, I'll wring his neck.'

'No, please don't! I know what you're capable of.' Maggie peered at him, genuinely horrified, the shooting of Wayne Kew never too far away from her mind. 'He isn't worth it, Samuel – not worth the trouble. Can I just sit here with you for a little?'

'No! I mean, yes – stay here as long as you like, but you must tell me what the bastard has done to upset you.' Sam wouldn't let it go – not this time.

She pinched her lips and shook her head, tears streaming down her cheeks. She reminded Sam of a little girl trying to be brave after grazing her knee. 'I can't tell you. It's too embarrassing. I can't!'

He cupped her cheeks in his hand and forced her to look at him. 'It's me, Maggie – Samuel. You know you can tell me anything. I'm here for you. To help you, or just to listen if that's what you prefer, but you must talk to me. Please.'

'I've been so, so stupid! It's beyond laughable. I can't.'

'I'd never laugh at you. A problem shared is

a problem halved,' he used one of his mother's readymade wisdoms.

'Turn off the lights then,' she whispered.

'Lights off?'

'I can't tell you with the lights on.'

He did as she bid him and sat on the bed, looking vaguely in the direction of the armchair, getting his eyes adjusted to the darkness. 'Is that better?'

'Yes. Thank you, Samuel.' She sniffled.

'So?'

There was a moment of hesitant silence, but then a torrent of anguish and fury poured from Maggie lips, 'He stole my money – everything... I don't know how he knew my PIN, I didn't give it to him, I swear! But he took it all. Day after day, out of my account, in small steps until there was nothing left. But I don't care! I don't care about that. I stopped caring. I, I...' He heard her blow her nose.

'I see. You're doing well, Maggie. It's awful what he's done to you – it's criminal. But I won't do anything about it if you don't want me to. Unless—'

'Don't! Please don't. I forgave him.'

Perhaps it wasn't such a good idea to forgive Rawbotham so quickly, or at all, Sam reflected. Maggie was too soft-hearted and too easy to take advantage of, but things had changed. She now had Sam and he wouldn't let the bastard off so lightly.

'It's not about the money. I said, I don't care. But my grandma's locket! I can't—' Maggie surrendered to violent sobs.

'Grandma's locket? Tell me about the locket.'

'When I saw Emilia wearing it, I... Something just crushed my chest. I could feel the pain – I could hear my ribcage crack.'

Sam ground his teeth, impotent to do anything.

Maggie snivelled. 'It was my grandma's. She wore it all the time, Grandpa Bernie told me when he gave it to me. I never knew her, you see. That locket was all I had of her.' Another loud sob shook her body in the darkness. 'I couldn't forgive myself when I lost it. But I didn't lose it, did I? Benedict stole it. And then he gave it to his daughter. It was my grandma's!'

Wringing the bastard's neck would be too kind. Sam would later consider slower and more painful ways of killing him. For the time being, he calmed Maggie down and obtained a detailed description of the locket. It was a small, white-gold locket with poison-ivy leaves carved on the lid. Emilia had worn it to the Christmas dinner. Sam couldn't remember seeing it but then he wasn't in the habit of noticing ladies' trinkets.

He rose from the bed and felt his way towards Maggie. He found her curled in the armchair, shaking with emotion and shame. He placed his hands on her shoulders and looked firmly into her eyes whose puffiness and redness were mercifully veiled by the dark.

'Leave it to me. I'll get your locket back.'

'You will?' Maggie's voice twinkled faintly.

'Of course, I will.'

'But you mustn't shoot anyone, or … you know, harm people.'

'I wouldn't dream of it!' He lied. Oh, how he longed to harm Rawbotham!

'Thank you, Samuel,' she whispered. 'You're always so … so wonderful. I don't know what I'd do without you!'

'You can thank me when I give you the locket back. You can even call me your knight in shining armour.'

She chuckled, then sniffled.

'Can I put the lights back on?'

'No! I don't want you to see me in this state. I look awful.'

'You never do.'

'Still, I'd better go back to my room. It was good to talk.'

She headed for the door. There were a couple of thuds and yelps along the way, signifying her bumping into furniture, but she found her way. She opened the door and the light from the corridor sneaked back in.

'Thank you, Samuel.'

'Goodnight, Maggie.'

The door was shut and the beam of light cut off. Samuel felt reinvigorated by his newly found sense of purpose. He flew onto his bed, keen to catch up on some sleep before he confronted Count Dracula in the morning holding a well-sharpened wooden stake.

Before he closed his eyes, the busy door swung open again. It was Maggie. Her head with the halo of her curls popped in.

'Sorry, Samuel, I've locked myself out of my cabin. Can I stay at yours?'

There was a first time for everything in life and, for the first time, Sam was grateful for Maggie's recklessness with keys.

'Come in, make yourself comfortable on the bed. I'll sleep in the chair.'

'No, certainly not. It's your bed! Stay where you are – I'll just perch on the edge,' and she lay next to him, and within minutes was cradled in his armpit, snoring softly.

CHAPTER 20

Sam couldn't sleep. That was his second sleepless night in a row. He should be dog-tired, and he probably was, but adrenalin was pumping through his veins and his brain was doing overtime in heavy-duty thinking. Having Maggie sprawled over him, warm and trusting, didn't help matters. For one, it felt so good that it would be sinful to sleep through it. Mainly though it was because she had pinned him down with the full weight of her ample body and he simply couldn't move. He lay stiff as a plank of wood, killing time by planning his next step. Ultimately, it was Sam's arm that had gone to sleep while Sam stayed wide awake.

At five in the morning he'd had enough. His whole body was numb and bruised in places. Maggie had had a fitful night, muttering in her sleep, tossing and turning, and on a few occasions jabbing her knee into Sam's groin and her elbow at his jaw. She had slept right through her assaults.

Gently, Sam lifted her arm, holding it by the wrist, and placed it on her chest. That enabled him to sit up. From there, it was just a small nudge against Maggie's knee and her leg obligingly swung away, taking Maggie with it as she turned. Sam was free to go.

He spent a few minutes limping the length of his room to restore blood circulation to his limbs. When he was at last in full control of his extremities, he changed from his Christmas evening wear into his tracksuit, ready for his morning power walk with Maggie. But before that, he had a visit to pay to Benedict Raw-stinking-botham.

The ungodly hour of five o'clock in the morning didn't matter. This wouldn't be a social call. It'd be a dawn raid. Sam was looking forward to it.

He knew exactly where to find Count Dracula's sarcophagus – his cabin was on level 2, where most of the crew and entertainers lodged. Sam had located it on one of his earlier recces when he had gone exploring the man's unhealthy interest in Maggie. He had conducted his operation the day after the scoundrel had given Maggie the roses. A cheap tokenistic gesture, without a doubt. Sam was glad he hadn't resorted to such tacky exploits himself. And he never would. Actions spoke louder than flowers.

He hammered on the bastard's door – no

half-measures, no small pleasantries. 'Open up, Benedict! I need a word!'

A sleep-muffled voice responded from within, 'Who the hell is that?'

'It's Samuel Dee!'

'Who?'

'Maggie's friend – Samuel!' Sam kicked the door in sheer frustration. 'Open the damned door or everyone will hear what I have to say!'

Expletives and rushed movement ensued inside the room, and promptly Maestro de Norte presented himself in the doorway, bleary eyed and scowling. He was clad in a pair of pathetic greyed long johns with stretched knees and a hanging crotch. His naked chest looked scrawny with a few strays of white hair sprouting from his breastbone. It was clear that the man's raven-black head was just an illusion perpetrated with the aid of a bottle of hair-dye. Sam took it all in with a great sense of gratification, assured of his own physical superiority. He was fitter, hairier and au naturel from the top of his head to the bottom of his chin. He pushed his way inside.

Rawbotham recovered his wits. He put on his dressing gown and sat on his bed, crossing his legs with the flourish of a natural-born artiste. He addressed Sam sardonically, 'Lovely to see you. It's a bit early, but I appreciate your keenness. So, what is so important that it can't wait until sunrise?'

'Your daughter is wearing a stolen locket.'

Sam didn't waste any time. 'You took it from Maggie. I want it back. Now.'

Even though Sam hadn't been invited to take a seat, he made himself comfortable in a chair in front of a mirror. In his black hooded tracksuit, he looked like Batman himself, and that was exactly what Sam was: a vigilante on the mission of saving a damsel in distress. He was rather pleased with his image.

'A what? Are you referring to Emilia's locket?'

'No, not Emilia's – it was Maggie's grandmother's locket. But I don't have to tell you that. You know because you stole it.'

'I found it.'

Sam laughed. 'Together with Maggie's PIN and all of her savings? We'll leave the money aside. For now, I just want that locket. I thought it'd be decent if I asked you first, before going directly to Emilia. Something tells me she doesn't know how you got that locket.'

Rawbotham's demeanour changed in an instant. He jumped to his feet, panicked. He thrust his hands up in the air, palms out. 'Okay, okay, calm yourself! I'll get you the sodding locket. Just leave my daughter out of it.'

'Great. I will wait here.'

A fleeting stare of incomprehension flashed in Dracula's eyes, but he soon got Sam's drift: he had to go and get the locket now. Or else.

'Wait here.' He growled.

He tied the cords of his dressing gown round his stomach and, looking moderately modest, left the room. While he was gone Sam took the liberty of searching through the boxes and drawers in Maestro's boudoir on the off chance of finding ladies' jewellery stashed away where it didn't belong. He didn't find anything of interest other than several bottles of multivitamins which could potentially contain something not mentioned on the label, but he wouldn't dream of testing the tablets on himself. Rawbotham was back within five minutes. He thrust a chain with the locket attached to it at Sam.

'Here! It was just a misunderstanding. I'll explain it to Maggie.'

'I wouldn't if I were you.'

'She'll understand when I—'

Sam drilled into him with his eyes, 'Stay away from her.'

Back in his cabin, Sam found Maggie in a deep slumber, an image which brought to mind Goldilocks in Papa Bear's bed. She looked angelic with her eyes closed, her locks tangled around her face, her mouth wide-open, catching flies and emitting gurgling grunts. Picture perfect.

Lightly, like a thief in the night but with the best of intentions, Sam managed to wrap the chain around Maggie's neck and closed the clasp securely in place. Then he sat back and waited for her to wake up.

It was a long wait so, after some twenty minutes of listening to her snoring, he produced a discreet cough. Maggie's eyelids flickered. After a short battle to keep her eyes closed, she opened them. They were still swollen from last night's crying.

'What time is it?'

He didn't have to look at his watch. 'It's ten past six – time for our morning exercise.'

She sat up in bed. Rudolph the Red-Nosed Reindeer on her woolly dress woke up too and flashed his lights.

'I need to pee.' She hurried towards the door but quickly realised that she had no key to her room. 'I'll need to use your toilet, if you don't mind.'

'Not at all. Be my guest.'

She turned on her heel and dashed to the loo.

A few moments later, Sam heard her exhilarated cries. She was invoking God's divine intervention and enthusiastically chanting Sam's name. She burst out of the bathroom, clutching the locket. Like an unstoppable steam train, she threw the whole weight of her body at Sam.

'You got Grandma's locket! You got it back for me!'

'I told you I would.'

She sobered up for a split second. 'But you didn't kill anyone, I hope?'

'Maestro de Norte was alive when I left him.'

Maggie sighed with relief and beamed at Sam, 'You are my hero!'

If I can't be your husband, I'll have to settle for that, Sam mused ruefully.

'Right then, should we go power-walking?' He suggested. He was looking forward to letting Maggie take the lead and for him to close their two-person peloton so that he could admire her shapely backside at his leisure.

CHAPTER 21

Maggie's Journal

I had to telephone Detective Smilga. We were due to arrive in St Petersburg the next day but my call could not wait that long. It had to be made urgently. Unfortunately, sailing in the easternmost confines of the Baltic Sea meant that I had no mobile signal. Neither did Samuel – I asked. First, he tried to dissuade me from making that call altogether. When I refused to follow his advice, he pleaded with me to wait. That couldn't be done either.

'Samuel, I – both of us – we have a duty to report our findings to the police. This is a murder investigation and poor Alvar is rotting in jail for something he didn't do. You promised—'

'I don't think they'll be executing him at dawn,' he countered brusquely. 'He's probably quite comfortable in his cell and one day won't make that much difference.'

'But it will – to me. I told Smilga I'd contact him the moment I thought of anything else – and I have thought of it!'

'You mean you thought of Oliver Lang killing his own mother?'

'You know as much as I do – he has a lot to answer for: he had a motive, an opportunity and … what's that third thing?'

Unhelpfully, Samuel raised and dropped his shoulders, claiming ignorance. He was clearly trying to obstruct the course of justice every step of the way.

'Never mind. It's for the police to worry about details. All I'm saying is that he should be apprehended and interviewed without delay. We must inform Smilga now – that way we'll give him time to organise an arrest warrant with the Russians. By the time we dock in St Petersburg tomorrow, the police will be waiting.' I had it all sussed out.

Samuel scratched his head and sighed wearily. He did seem drawn and tired, and utterly unenthusiastic, but this wasn't the time to ask him what the matter was. Anyway, it was probably nothing other than male obstinacy. He was an open book. I could read the defiance loud and clear in his body language, and the same was evident from the way he spoke to me, 'So what do you propose we do, Maggie? I was hoping for a nice, peaceful cruise. No dramas, no deaths, no witness harassment, and no Alec Scarfe or DI Marsh telling us off for interfering with police business. Just a couple of weeks to catch our breaths and relax away from it all. Just you and me, and the deep blue sea...'

I cringed at his poor attempt at lyricism. Lawyers and poetry just don't mix.

'What do you say, Maggie? Let's stop playing detective just this once?'

'I didn't ask for people to go around killing one another in my presence!' I protested (though deep down, I have to admit, I embraced the challenge of multiple homicides). 'But it's our civic duty to cooperate—'

'To cooperate – yes. To meddle – an emphatic no! What you're doing smacks of meddling.'

That hurt. I had to pause to get a grip on myself. I didn't dignify his assault on my character with a comment.

We stood silently for a while, watching the grey sky laden with clouds and the expanse of fog rising from the sea ahead of the sun which would be too weak to break through it anyway. We had a whole day of greyness to look forward to. This was supposed to be our morning walk, but we had only managed the top deck and run out of steam because of this argument. It was my turn to sigh – repeatedly. I sighed and sighed as I was contemplating my limited options.

As much as I didn't come up with any miraculous solutions, I managed to wear Samuel down. He sighed over me and said, 'We could speak to Vincent Hatton. He could facilitate contact with the Latvian authorities. The ship will have radio channels open with or without a mobile signal.'

And he was right.

All it took was a touch of goodwill. We explained to Mr Hatton the emergency and, just in case he didn't see it himself, that he had a duty to keep the passengers safe from a killer who could be running free aboard his ship.

He set us up with Detective Smilga on a conference call in his quarters. I conveyed to the good Detective my suspicions and the evidence I had gathered against Oliver Conti Lang and his likely accomplice, Emilia Rawbotham.

Smilga listened without interrupting (how refreshing!) as I told him the story of Lenny Lang's death. He agreed by way of a short but affirmative grunt that it gave Oliver a motive to murder Cordelia. He also conceded on the point of opportunity and the weak alibi that the young couple provided for each other. But that was where he parted ways with me.

'Thank you for that, Miss Kaye. We'll certainly share this historical information about Mr Lang's death with Scotland Yard.'

'But this is about Mrs Conti's death,' I objected. '*You* are investigating it, not Scotland Yard, and I've just given you a strong lead. You can't ignore it!'

He assured me that he wasn't ignoring any leads and was very grateful for my efforts, but that he had to be guided by evidence.

'What evidence?' I couldn't hold back my frustration. 'You've got your scapegoat in custody – poor, innocent Alvar – and you don't care about anything else. Anything that could contradict your premature conclusions about his guilt.'

That was when Detective Smilga made a number of revelations. I suppose he wanted to pacify me so that he could return to his police tasks. I do have this talent for grinding people's resistance to dust.

Firstly, he told me Alvar was now held solely in connection with Nedim's killing. He was no longer linked to Cordelia's death. There was no forensic evidence to place Alvar in Cordelia's cabin at the time of her murder – or at any time. If that wasn't sufficient, no traces of Cordelia's DNA could be found on Alvar's person. He had arrived in my cabin wearing the same clothing he had worn when he had killed Nedim. Nedim's blood was all over it. But there were no traces of Cordelia's blood. She had been killed in the same way as Nedim and with the same weapon: the artery on her neck had been stabbed with a sharp surgical instrument such as a scalpel. That would have produced a pattern of blood spatter with a fair amount of her blood landing on the perpetrator. Alvar had no time and no opportunity to wash or to change into something else before he entered my room.

'Ha!' I exclaimed, victorious. 'I could've told you all of that – in fact, I did tell you!'

'Not exactly,' Samuel interjected, and I glared at him. Mr Hatton pressed his lips together and looked away, which was the right thing to do.

'No, not precisely word for word, but I did tell you Alvar did not kill that woman. And now I am telling you that it was Oliver.'

The second revelation came at that point. So, Ollie and Emilia had entered Cordelia's cabin directly from his room, via the interconnecting door. Their fingerprints could be found there, as expected. The killer however had entered from the corridor. He, or she, must have been let in by Cordelia as there were no signs of a break-in (though one could argue that Cordelia had left the door open. Some people do just that, but I didn't raise that point). According to Detective Smilga, Cordelia either knew her killer, or may have been led to believe that it was someone with a legitimate reason seeking entry. After the deed was done, the killer had gone to the trouble of wiping clean all the surfaces, including the door. However, he – or she – had left a partial fingerprint in the bathroom. That fingerprint had traces of Cordelia's blood and therefore, in all probability, belonged to the killer. And that print wasn't Oliver's or Emilia's. Their fingerprints had been taken for elimination purposes and they didn't match.

'So, it was neither Alvar nor Oliver,' I said as soon as I recovered my wherewithal. 'So the murderer is somewhere on this ship and they could kill again?'

'We are running the print through all the databases, Europol, Interpol, you name it,' Detective Smilga attempted to sound confident, but he wasn't fooling me. 'But in the meantime, I urge you to—'

I knew what he was going to tell me not to do. I didn't have time for idle chit-chat.

'What about the scalpel? Shouldn't we be looking for it on the ship?'

'The murder weapon was indeed, in all probability, a scalpel.'

'You're not telling us anything new. Of course, it was a scalpel. We knew that all along, the crew knew that all along. Anyway, Alvar would've already told you that he'd used the scalpel to kill Nedim. The question is: does the killer still have it and should we be searching for it before he or she gets rid of it. Or, worse yet, uses it again to kill someone else.'

'No, Miss Kaye. You cannot put yourself in harm's way.'

Samuel barged in again, going all godfather-paternal on me, 'I won't let her.'

We'll see about that, I mused within the confines of my head but held my tongue. I wasn't going to surrender to male dominance. I wasn't about to give up on an investigation that had just become very interesting indeed.

Dinner time was painful. My head was buzzing: I was glad Alvar was off the hook, surprised that I had been wrong about Oliver, none the wiser about who the murderer was and worried because, whoever he was, he was walking amongst us. Possibly with a sharp scalpel in his pocket. Or hers. There was nothing to suggest that it couldn't have been a woman.

Samuel had been preaching to me the whole day about the virtues of minding my own business and the importance of staying alive. I think he was trying to tell me how much he cared about me. I cared about him too, and that was why I had to identify, capture and neutralise that mystery killer lurking in our midst. God knows, Samuel could be his next victim. How would I explain it to Deirdre if something happened to him? He didn't seem to understand any of that and went on and on about keeping my beak out of it. And something about having a good time instead. I was having a grand time tracking down the killer, thank you very much.

Heading for our table, we walked past Oliver and Emilia. Cordelia was there too. They saw us but looked the other way. That didn't upset me. After all, I had accused them of murder. I would have to clear the air with them, possibly apologise and definitely explain myself.

The lot at our table weren't any friendlier. They too muttered reluctant hellos. Even though prior to our arrival the conversation at the table appeared quite lively from a distance, the moment we sat down it died a sudden death. An awkward silence fell upon us and upon our lamb chops with mint sauce.

In the end, Barbara couldn't hold herself back and gave me a piece of her mind, 'I hope you can take it from an old lady, Maggie, but your behaviour at the Christmas dinner was ...Well, your accusations against that poor boy were inexcusable.'

'Hear, hear!' Hywel bellowed. He glared at me resentfully. 'You put him off our table and all of us. I, for one, was glad of his company.'

'And I thought he was glad of ours,' Stacey added, eyeing me with equal vituperation. 'The young man needs all the support he can get right now. Not to mention that he trusted us, to talk to, and to share that dreadful secret. That took some guts.'

'It must've weighed heavily on his mind. Can you imagine suspecting your own mother - *knowing* that your own mother killed your dad? It must've been eating him inside.' Barbara speculated, wringing her hands and shaking her head in a display of fervent compassion.

Only Sidney and Samuel sat without condemning me to hell, though it was anyone's guess what they were thinking. I have to confess I didn't feel very good about myself.

'Yes, I know,' I mumbled under my breath. 'I wasn't very... nice. I'll apologise to Ollie, and to Emilia.'

'There you go. That's all it takes.' Samuel regained his power of speech. 'Problem solved.'

Not entirely, I begged to disagree. I wouldn't be gagged and, let's face it, *the problem* was far from being solved. We were all in danger. I said, 'I have it on good authority that Alvar – that's the man who kept me hostage – did not kill Cordelia. You know what that means, don't you?'

They gaped at me. That included Pi who happened to be floating around, checking if we had finished our mains.

'There is a cold-blooded killer on this ship. And I intend to find him,' I declared.

'Maggie—' Samuel began, but I didn't want to receive any more of his sermons.

I looked right through him and reached for my cutlery.

'That's it. I said it. Let's eat. I'm starved.'

CHAPTER 22

Maggie's Journal

S t Petersburg in winter is a dream come
true. It is better than anything I have ever
seen – better than Narnia. It is glamorous,
shackled in ice and gold, exquisitely cold and
filled with a strange yearning for its former
glory. I loved it.

I can't say what was going through Samuel's
head because he was behaving bizarrely. He kept
peering at me with mawkish eyes, smiling a lot
for no discernible reason and insisting I held his
hand when crossing the road or when navigating
perfectly safe pavements. I feared that he had
taken way too seriously the threat of a murderer
skulking in the shadows. There was a murderer
among us, that much was obvious, but I wasn't
convinced that tripping me up in an icy Russian
street or pushing me under a passing tram

featured prominently on his *To Do* list.

I attempted to locate Oliver and Emilia to offer my apologies as promised, but Samuel dragged me away, claiming that those two could wait. He apparently couldn't. He was particularly insistent that we enjoyed St Petersburg, and pretty much the rest of our lives, in each other's exclusive company. His intense, if awkward, attention was rather flattering. Was the great, heroic Samuel Dee, the destroyer of all evil, feeling marginally possessive over yours truly? I swear I would have blushed red-hot if it hadn't been so cold.

And it was freezing! We were subsisting in the sub-zero temperature of minus 18 centigrade.

We had to keep moving. We had become painfully conscious of that fact after we had sat down on a bench in the Summer Garden. It may be called the *Summer* garden, but believe you me, in winter there is nothing summery about it.

We had been ambling around the garden for an hour, traversing the snow-padded and tree-lined alleyways, and watching our misty breaths form icicles on our scarves. That was fun. As was the brief snowball battle we fought in a small square featuring an ice-fettered fountain. I won the battle, based on the number of hits I landed on Samuel (though he is still disputing it).

When we tired of fighting and ambling, we swept what snow we could from a bench, and sat down. It was no more than half an hour that we were seated there. Samuel was waffling on about the joys of appreciating the small things in life which were *just there, over the fence* as he had phrased it. Or perhaps it was something about the inferiority of grass on the other side of the fence, I couldn't quite figure him out that day. It was an unusually high-brow theme to ponder for Samuel – he is normally a very pragmatic man. He went on and on, and I was getting colder and colder. In the end, before my lips turned blue and I lost the power of speech, I interrupted his soliloquy.

'Better one bird in the hand than two in the bush,' I elucidated on his ramblings.

'Precisely! And you are—'

'And I am blinking cold. Should we find somewhere indoors to thaw?'

Easier said than done. I couldn't get up. The layer of snow on the bench which at first had melted on contact with my backside, had cooled down over the thirty minutes of my inactivity and frozen again. As a result, my trousers were stuck to the bench. I cried in horror, unable to tear myself away. My whole back was paralysed with the chill and I feared the frostbite would take away a chunk of my bum.

'Friction!' Samuel declared enigmatically.

I gaped at him.

'We need to apply friction – to warm you up. If you don't mind, I'll have to vigorously rub your bottom.'

'Why don't you!' I cried.

Samuel commenced the rubbing and the occasional spanking of my backside in order to generate enough heat to defrost my bum and free it from the shackles of ice. A couple of passers-by laughed and taunted us loudly in Russian. I was glad I couldn't understand what they were saying. Probably something demeaning.

At last, I was detached from the bench and we rushed towards the Winter Palace to seek warmth (and a touch of cultural experience). My distress wasn't over though. Upon thawing, I was now sporting a big wet patch on my trousers in the shape of my buttocks. Samuel said it wasn't that bad, looking at it from behind, but I didn't believe him.

The touch of cultural experience was electrifying. Luckily for us, the Winter Palace wasn't as wintry as the Summer Garden, so we could enjoy the gold-crusted interior without worrying about freezing to death. Traversing one magical hall after another, I found myself submerged in amazing and beautiful things. Hermitage is one of those few places on earth that can swallow you whole. And that's just the building: the crystal chandeliers dripping from ornamental ceilings, the white marble staircases and gold-framed columns, the glittering mirrors and the abundance of gilded motifs catching the eye and holding it hostage. And then there is the Art – the whole world encapsulated in one place.

I gaped and I gasped, and soon I was too knackered to take another look, never mind another step. All that gold was pouring out of my ears. We decided to find a quiet café – the smaller and quieter, the better – and try the famous Russian tea. And cake. At that point, I fully embraced Samuel's idea of appreciating the small things in life. I told him so and that made him smile.

He said, 'That's not what I meant, but I'll go with whatever makes you happy, Maggie.'

We toasted that thought with our tea cups.

I had one heavy burden weighing on my conscience: I had to deliver my unconditional apology to the people I had accused of murder. I promised I'd do it, and I would. Apologising to Ollie wasn't a problem, but I had to find him alone – without Emilia. I just couldn't bring myself to seek her forgiveness after everything that her father had done to me. My rational brain lobe (is that the left or the right one? Not that it makes much difference to me. I can't tell them apart), so my rational thought was that the girl was innocent of any wrongdoing. Wearing my grandmother's locket without knowing where it came from was not a crime. Yet, I struggled to say sorry to her. Her tugging on that locket in front of me felt like sacrilege and an insult. I should really be blaming Benedict, but his daughter got the blame by association. So, I looked the other way whenever I happened to bump into the two of them, which was an unsettlingly frequent occurrence.

At long last I spotted Ollie unaccompanied. Of course, Cordelia's apparition was clinging on to him, but she didn't qualify as *company*. That was my moment. Samuel and I were having afternoon tea (you can never have too many of those), and Ollie was just passing through the lounge. I asked Samuel not to follow me. I didn't need witnesses to my capitulation. I flitted after Ollie and caught up with him on the staircase.

'Ollie! May I have a word? Please.'

He paused and gazed at me with a scowl and narrowed eyes. 'I'm in a hurry.'

That wasn't polite or gracious, considering I was just about to prostrate myself before him and beg his forgiveness. I swallowed my pride.

'I won't take a second of your time. I just want to apologise. You know, the accusation I made against you?'

He snorted. 'I do know.'

'It wasn't fair, or … Anyway, it turns out I was wrong. You couldn't have,' my voice faltered to an inaudible *killed your mother*, and rose again to stress the next bit, 'but truth be told, you had the motive and the opp—' I bit my tongue. Rehashing my accusation would take me back to square one. 'So, what I'm trying to say is—'

'You're sorry?'

'Yes, that.'

Cordelia arched her immaculately plucked eyebrows, contemptuous of my efforts. Then again, that self-aggrandising expression was how she usually looked at people when she was alive – it seemed to have followed her into the afterlife.

Ollie said, 'Apology accepted. After what I told you, I'd have probably jumped to the same conclusion...'

I exhaled with relief – rather prematurely, as I was about to discover. For Oliver Conti Lang had learned a few things from his mother and he had not quite finished his sentence.

'... only I'm not given to sticking my nose into other people's lives and passing judgments on them.' He cocked his head in a confrontational fashion. I gawked, wide-mouthed. He concluded with the final touch of: 'Right now I've got better things to do. Must dash! Ta-ra!'

That was me put in my place. I scuttled back to Samuel and asked him to get me a brandy. I needed it to take the edge off my embarrassment and to nurse my bruised ego. I downed the brandy and slammed the glass on the table. Samuel knew better than to ask me what the matter was.

CHAPTER 23

Maggie's Journal

With the unpleasant task of saying sorry out of the way and my ego resuscitated with the help of two brandies and a chocolate éclair, I was ready to party.

We were having a New Year's Eve ball. It was to be held on dry land, at a mystery venue in St Petersburg. Formal dress code applied: evening gowns for the ladies, and a jacket and tie for the gentlemen. Since I had run out of funds at the point of purchasing my trunk, I had to resort to hiring a dress. That had its advantages. For one, price was no object. I had chosen a white-satin, ostrich-feather floor-length gown – a faithful replica of the one Ginger Rogers wore in *Top Hat*, when she danced Cheek-to-Cheek with Fred Astaire. I love pre-war musicals, and that dress had always been my childhood dream. The moment I saw it, I had to have it. Even if only on loan and only for a couple of weeks. I was planning to dance my socks off in that dress.

Even Samuel made an effort and shed his threadbare jumper in favour of a tailcoat. He looked handsome in his special way, almost like Fred Astaire, though he still had a long way to go before he started moving like him. He became cutely tongue-tied when he beheld me in my ostrich feather dress. I had to fill his silence. I grabbed his arm and pulled him towards the mirror.

'Can you believe it? We look just like Fred and Ginger! I can't wait to hit the dance floor.'

'I can't dance, Maggie.'

I didn't want to hear that. I refused to acknowledge that with an answer. I threw my white stole over my shoulders and hooked my arm over his. 'Let's dance the night away!'

'Right,' said he.

A coach was taking us to the venue. Samuel and I found our table companions at the back. They were happy to see us. I was relieved that they had forgotten about my unfortunate run-in with Oliver and Emilia over the Christmas dinner. I didn't feel the need to tell them I had made good on my promise to apologise. All seemed well.

The coach brought us to an outwardly unremarkable place hidden within large grounds. It was one of the many smaller palaces in St Petersburg, dating back to Tsar Peter I (who I understand was a keen property developer).

As soon as we entered the building, we were overwhelmed by a multitude of bright lights reflected in a multitude of polished mirrors. The ballroom had a wooden parquet floor with crystal chandeliers suspended above it. A live band of tail-coated musicians occupied a small stage next to a grand piano. They were tuning their instruments, chatting amongst themselves and laughing. I felt like blinking Cinderella. And I do mean *blinking* because I was dazzled.

Everyone observed the dress code. Hywel and Stacey looked glamorous, she in a flowing silk dress with diamond-studded straps and he in his cobalt-blue tuxedo. Sidney was dapper in a jacket with a pink rose in the buttonhole. Pink roses were his late wife Eleanor's favourites, he told us with a hint of a tear in his eyes. Keeping up a brave face, Barbara tilted her head wistfully. Those two had become very close during this cruise, courtesy of yours truly. It was a sad moment when Eleanor, who was the reason for Sidney being on this ship, suddenly came between them. But not for long, I hasten to add, for Sidney presented Barbara with his arm and asked her in the most gallant way if she would do him the honour of being his companion for the night. Barbara glowed.

Dinner was served by the radiant Pi.

I didn't eat much. I was too excited, not to mention that I wished to stay light on my feet and wide awake until midnight. Rich food makes me sleepy.

Vincent Hatton joined us when pudding was served. He, too, looked amazing in his ceremonial uniform. I nearly swooned over him.

Having warmed up their instruments and their fingers, the musicians began to play. Magic descended upon the ballroom. Only I had the privilege of seeing it in its full glory. A few brave couples trickled onto the dance floor, but I saw dozens of revellers: both the living and the dead. The dead were in high spirits. They twirled and hopped, bowed and brandished their lace handkerchiefs. Some men in fancy wigs and white stockings tapped their ruby-buckled slippers and strutted around flirty ladies in low-cut, tight-bodice gowns. There were men with bushy beards and traditional boyar hats and capes trying to maintain dignified poses but even their feet twitched to the music. I wondered which one of them was the great Tsar.

Sidney asked Barbara to dance. They entered the floor and he took her in his arms. As they waltzed, a young woman appeared and began circling around them. She was laughing, her arms flung out, her feet hardly touching the floor. In fact, they weren't touching the floor at all. She was a ghost. Her white dress with full skirts and her waist-long veil seemed familiar.

Another ghostly pair swirled past her: a handsome man with impressive sideburns and a young lady wearing a tiara. It hit me that the two women looked uncannily alike, except that the style of their attire was separated by a few centuries. That was when I realised who they were: Eleanor and her many times removed Russian-countess grandmother. I recognised Eleanor's wedding dress from the photograph Sidney had shown me. She had been here all along, waiting for him to arrive. And she had clearly found her long lost family. They had been keeping her entertained while she waited for Sidney to turn up. She was pirouetting close to him, basking in his proximity, happy. Barbara's presence in Sidney's arms didn't seem to trouble her.

I tugged on Samuel's sleeve. 'Sidney's wife is here.'

'His dead wife?'

'Yes, dead – what else? Unless it's her Second Coming, she's been dead for a while.' Samuel still struggled with accepting the reality of the dead mingling with us on this earth on a whim.

'How's she taking Barbara?'

'She likes her, I can tell. I think she just wants Sidney to be happy. If only you could see her. She's having a ball, literally!'

A shadow crossed Samuel's face. He said, 'I hope Alice is happy – wherever she is.'

I squeezed his arm. 'Of course, she's

happy. She knows I'm taking good care of you. Otherwise, she'd still be hanging around, breathing down your neck. Though, of course, breathing as such may not come into it.' I winked at him. I was joking, but I was also dead serious. I do think Alice had finally left as soon as she realised that Samuel wouldn't be alone on this earth. He had a friend in me, always. I was terrifyingly fond of him, so fond that I feared to admit it even to myself. He was my hero.

If only he could dance!

The music was sweeping across the floor and I just couldn't resist it any longer. I jumped to my feet and grabbed Samuel's hand. 'Enough brooding. Let's dance!'

He fought back, the silly oaf. 'I can't, Maggie. I told you, I can't dance. I'd only make a fool of myself.'

'Come on! Just once!' I wasn't giving up.

Neither was he. He dug his heels in. I felt like smacking some sense into him. Nobody can dance these days. We all just improvise based on what we see on *Strictly Come Dancing.* But not the distinguished Samuel Dee QC! He wouldn't shift.

'May I have this dance, Miss Kaye?'

It was Vincent Hatton, who now insisted on being called *Vince.* I might have mentioned this before but I have to say it again: he was irresistible in his dashing ceremonial uniform. I wouldn't dream of saying no.

He whisked me out onto the dance floor.

Forget his age, he was a formidable dancer. We whizzed and whirled until my head started spinning and my mouth turned as dry as pepper. We stopped for a drink, at my request. He could probably go through the night without breaking sweat. There is a lot to be said for the stamina of a seasoned soldier.

We sat in a bar, just off the main ballroom. From there I could see the people and ghosts on the dance floor. Benedict was dancing with his daughter. He presented well: elegant and graceful. I remembered him being a good dancer from our days in London nightclubs.

I wondered where Ollie was. He wouldn't be too far from Emilia. I searched for him. I found him chatting with Hywel of all people. Seated at a corner table, they were engrossed in conversation, leaning towards each other. Ollie looked distraught. A couple of times he tussled his hair and cupped his face in his hands. At one point, Hywel put his hand on Ollie's shoulder and shook it, speaking animatedly. I guessed he was offering him moral support. Maybe the loss of his mother had finally hit home.

Vince bought me a gin-and-tonic. It wasn't exactly a thirst quencher so I asked the barman for a glass of water. I downed it first before tackling the alcohol – in small sips.

'So, how's the investigation going?' Vince inquired. 'Any progress?'

'I've suspended it for the time being,' I said,

mindful of Detective Smilga's request to keep my nose out of his investigation. Hatton had been in the room and heard him say that. Maybe he would report me to Smilga if he found me to be – meddling.

'I'm glad to hear that. I wouldn't like any of my passengers to put themselves in unnecessary danger, especially not lovely young ladies such as yourself.'

'But the danger is there – we both know that,' I reposted, resentful of his patronising tone. 'The killer is on your ship. Maybe there is more than one. Have you thought of that?'

He stiffened a little. I noticed his jaw twitch.

Hywel pushed his way to the bar to buy drinks. He only noticed me when I said hi.

'Oh, Maggie!' He looked at me somewhat reluctantly, as if I had waded into some intensely private moment. 'Sorry, didn't see you. I was deep in thought.'

'How's Ollie?' I inquired, gesturing to the young man. 'He looks upset.'

'Dealing with his mother's death. It can't be easy.' Hywel shrugged.

'I'm glad he can talk to someone about it.'

'Yeah, I suppose I'm a good listener. I've mentored many men about – you know. It's what I do.'

He left. I watched him give Ollie his drink. Something bothered me about those two, but I couldn't figure out what it was.

I didn't have the chance to think about it because suddenly I was accosted by Benedict. He appeared from nowhere, a bit short of breath, with Emilia on his arm.

'There you are! Having a good time?' He sat on a stool next to me. His breath ruffled the ostrich feathers of my dress and they tickled my neck.

Emilia nodded at me pleasantly enough. I assumed Ollie must have told her that I had made my peace with him, and perhaps that was enough for her. She stood with us for a few minutes, smiling uncomfortably at Vince Hatton's compliments.

'There's Ollie,' she said and fled.

'Looks like I've been abandoned,' Benedict grinned. 'You don't mind if I join you? Another drink? What're you having?'

Vince Hatton grabbed the opportunity to avoid my question which remained hanging between us unanswered, and made himself scarce. 'Nothing for me, thanks. I'm on duty even off the ship.' He shot me an evasive glance, 'It was a pleasure dancing with you, Miss Kaye.'

I was left alone with Benedict. I didn't like that. I wondered where the hell Samuel was. I had lost him since I hit the dance floor with Hatton.

'I'd better find Samuel,' I said. 'I don't want to miss the countdown to midnight.'

'It's only a few minutes past eleven. What are

you drinking?' Benedict sniffed my empty glass. 'Gin and tonic, right?'

He summoned the waiter.

'I shouldn't, really,' I tried to protest.

'Please, Maggie. Let me explain. About your grandmother's locket.'

Not again! I was tired of him and his endless explanations. That man was beyond redemption and I was beyond putting up with his porky-pies. 'You don't have to, you really don't.'

'But I must.' He pinned my hand down. 'You see, Emilia doesn't know anything. She must never find out.'

'She won't find out from me,' I assured him and pulled my hand away. I took a swig of my G&T. I may as well, I thought.

'Thank you. You're a saint, Maggie.'

'I'd better go now and find Samuel.'

'Emilia believes that locket belonged to her mother.' He was telling me even though he knew I didn't want to hear it. 'But there's nothing of her mother's that I could give her. Her mother was a junkie. She had nothing to her name. Towards the end, she was just a bad memory, a thief and a whore. She was pathetic, Maggie. Not the sort of mother you'd want a child to know. She'd lost access to Emilia soon after Emilia turned three. She went back to her old habit and was dead within a year. An overdose. Emilia doesn't know. I wanted her to believe that her mother was a lovely person – like you, Maggie ... I told her that her mother had died in a car crash and left her the locket that belonged to her grandmother. I lied to spare my daughter's feelings. Surely, you can understand?' He squeezed my hand way too hard. 'How I wished it was you who was Emilia's mother! I interposed you – the idea of you – on her.'

That was rich! I had somehow become the girl's surrogate mother. I drank more of my G&T, but that was where I decided to stop, conscious of my previous drunken night with Benedict.

'Okay,' I said. 'You've told me. You've got it off your chest. I must go, find Samuel.'

He didn't object and let go off my hand. I got up, glad to be rid of him at last.

'You do understand, Maggie, don't you?' I heard him grovel behind me.

I shot him one fiery glare. I couldn't make out his expression. His face was bleary. I stepped off the stool and nearly fell. My legs felt like they were made of jelly. I pushed through the crowd, away from him, by my sheer willpower. I couldn't be that drunk, I thought. I'd only had one drink, and a bit.

My brain wasn't functioning quite as it should. My eyes were deceiving me. Glancing towards Ollie and Hywel, I saw their heads melt into each other and become one – one man with two pairs of hands and throbbing eyes, as if they were moulded from wet clay. I blinked and their heads momentarily separated, but they still appeared to be one and the same person. I shifted my gaze towards Emilia. Her mouth was stretching as if made from rubber – maybe she was talking to me, but I couldn't hear her. Something was pounding in my ears.

I dragged myself towards the dance floor. I was gasping for air. It had to be the stuffy bar that had rendered me light-headed. But the ballroom wasn't any better. The music was a cacophony. It hurt my ears. The dancers – the ghosts and the real people – had turned into vile corpses. They were reaching out to me, eager to catch me and tear out my limbs. I evaded a couple of them, but my legs got stuck to the floor, smeared with something gluey. I shouted, calling for Samuel, but I don't think that his name left my lips. Not a single articulate sound was coming out of my mouth. And my legs stopped working. That was the last thing I remember.

CHAPTER 24

'**A**n overdose?!'

Sam exclaimed fractionally too loud, for the good doctor flinched and screwed his lips. He looked exhausted after a night shift at the St Petersburg's A&E. And it wasn't any old night – it was New Year's Eve. That meant all sorts of health and safety hazards on a mass scale: drinking, brawls, assaults and car crashes. And to top it all, Maggie Kaye happened to be visiting the city.

'But Maggie doesn't take drugs! She may drink a little too much. On occasion, but no drugs! Never drugs!'

'It was not alcohol poisoning.' The Russian doctor shook his bald head, and winced again. Maybe he was having a headache or was hung over. The Russians are famous for their drinking.

'Could it be some other … poison?' Sam found it hard to squeeze that word through his throat. He dreaded admitting the possibility that

Maggie – his Maggie, his dearest sweet Maggie next door – may have been poisoned.

'We sent her blood sample for testing, but you have to understand, Meester Dee, this is the New Year's Day in Russia – all services are on holiday. Things won't get done until we will have sobered up. That may take a couple of days. When is your boat leaving?'

'Tomorrow evening.' Sam was exasperated.

'Oh well … At least, Mees Kaye will be joining you.'

'But, will she be safe aboard the ship? If what you're saying is true she may be in danger.'

'That's not for me to tell. I can only tell you what I know about her condition. Miss Kaye took an overdose of a powerful depressant, probably opiate or benzodiazepine. Without the naloxone administered on the spot by our paramedics, she would be dead, and we wouldn't be having this conversation. You'd be talking to our pathologist, and it wouldn't be today – he's on vacation. That's what I do know.'

Sam could only gasp in response. He sank into his chair. His heart sank into his stomach. He had almost lost Maggie. He was supposed to look after her – to marry her, for God's sake! The blinking engagement ring was burning a hole in his pocket. His revised plan had been to give it to her on the last strike of midnight, but he had taken his eyes off her for one second and in that time she had managed to get herself poisoned.

What sort of an excuse for her knight in shining armour was he?

Numbed by shock, he could not get up to leave. His legs felt leaden.

'You can see her now. She's awake.' The doctor rose from his chair. He was well over 6ft tall and thick-necked. He extended the spade of his hand to Sam. 'That's all. I've got other patients. Miss Kaye isn't my only case.'

'Yes, yes, sorry. Thank you,' Sam mumbled and, by his sheer willpower, took himself out of the man's office before he was thrown out.

Maggie appeared groggy, but she was awake and half-reclined in her bed. Her usually rosy cheeks looked pale and gaunt, and even her curls had lost their bounce and sat lank on her shoulders.

'Oh, Samuel, I swear I've no idea what happened!' She blinked at him guiltily. 'I couldn't have had more than a couple of drinks. It must be some Russian super-bug.'

Swallowing his anxieties, Sam grinned gawkily, braced himself and bellowed, 'Happy New Year, Maggie!' He could not resist the urge to pull her into his arms and cling onto her, feeling the small of her neck under his chin and inhaling her scent while at the same time blinking away tears.

'I missed the countdown, didn't I? Oh, what a mess!' Her voice was muffled by his shoulder. She pulled away from him. 'But, really Samuel, what happened? Did I pass out?'

He couldn't bring himself to tell her the truth. Instead he said, 'They don't know yet. They sent your blood samples for testing. You may've ingested something, or—' His voice trailed off. She had almost died.

Maggie wriggled on her bed, screwed her face anxiously and said, 'I've been worried, Samuel.'

'So have I!'

'You thought about it too?'

'About what?'

'About my dress! Where is it? Is it damaged?'

'Your dress?'

'Yes! The ostrich feather dress! Catch up – look at this,' she tugged at her hospital gown, 'this isn't my dress. Where is it? I have it on loan. I'll lose my deposit if it's damaged.'

Sam looked around him hopelessly. 'Well, it's not here.'

'I can tell that. But where is it?'

'I'll ask. I'm sure it's somewhere safe.'

'Please do! Now, if you don't mind. I'm worried sick.'

So Sam found himself hunting for an ostrich-feather dress, interrogating bleary-eyed hospital porters and quizzing the staff on the reception desk. Finally, he was directed to the Personal Effects department in the basement of the hospital. There, with the help of a skinny man with stale beer breath, he located Maggie's gown.

It wasn't in the best of shape: it had been slit open across the front and some of the feathers were saturated in some oily substance and looking sorry for themselves. Sam carried the dress to Maggie's bedside.

'Oh my!' she cried.

'We'll have it mended, all right? Leave it with me.' Sam was hellbent on taking Maggie in hand and getting to the bottom of what on earth had happened to her. 'But for now, tell me everything you remember from the moment you went off to dance with Hatton.'

Maggie was fuzzy on the actual points of interest to Sam, but she waffled on about things that didn't matter. Sam had to arm himself with patience and skilfully deploy his well-practised witness interrogation techniques.

'Yes, I'm glad to hear Vince Hatton is an amazing dancer – some people are.'

'You're not one of them,' Maggie chortled.

Sam let the slight go over his head. He pressed on, 'So then you both went for a drink?'

'One G&T,' Maggie nodded contritely. 'Plus a huge glass of water.'

'He bought it for you?'

'He's one of those old-time gentlemen. You know the sort? You could be one of them too if you learned to dance.'

'I'll add it to my *To Do* list,' he conceded.

'Who else was there – in the bar?'

'Actually, I wanted to talk to you about this, Samuel. Something rather interesting.' Maggie wiggled in her bed and heaved herself up on her pillows. 'I saw Hywel and Ollie jabbering away. There was something about that – I couldn't quite nail it, but there was something off. You know what I mean?'

Sam didn't. Maggie had entered the alien sphere of woman's intuition and all matters irrational, none of which was Sam's forte.

'Oh, you do know! Well, there was something – odd – between them. Ollie looked upset, like brimming with emotions. Hywel said, when I asked him, that it was about Ollie's mother. But, you see, I didn't see Ollie that much shaken when her body was found.' Maggie raised a forbidding finger at Sam. 'Don't you start now, Samuel! I know what you're going to say.'

'You do?'

'That people grieve in different ways, sometimes things catch up with us later, and so on. And maybe you're right. Maybe I'm imagining it.' She shook her head, and a couple of her curls bounced back up. 'No, I'm not. Something was definitely off with those two. I just don't know what.'

Sam patiently redirected her back to the matter at hand – establishing who was anywhere near Maggie's food and drink that night. 'So, you say you spoke to Hywel in the bar. Did he join you and Hatton for a drink?'

'Not quite. He just came over to get drinks for himself and Ollie. We chatted. He scarpered.'

'Who else was there?'

'Let me think.' Maggie raked through her fuzzy memories of the night. 'Oh yes! Benedict and Emilia. They'd been dancing. I saw them. He's always been a smooth mover.'

A sharp object pricked Sam's gut. Perhaps it wasn't an object – more like a feeling: jealousy.

Maggie continued, oblivious to Sam's inner demons forking his stomach lining. 'They popped over for a drink. Emilia didn't stay that long. Benedict insisted on explaining to me about the locket. Dreary! And he bought me another G&T. I bloody well deserved that, having to listen to his lame stories.'

Sam had to push aside his petty envies and concentrate on his mental note-taking. He had a list of – hopefully – all the individuals who could have put something into Maggie's drink: Vincent Hatton, Benedict Rawbotham, Emilia Rawbotham and Hywel Edwards. There could have been others that Maggie had missed in her daze, but he had to start somewhere. He had to identify the killer before Maggie was back onboard the ship. He had twenty-four hours.

CHAPTER 25

Forsaking the sight-seeing opportunities in the beautiful city of St Petersburg, Sam spent the rest of the day in his cabin, thinking. He had four suspects. Each had had the opportunity to slip something into Maggie's drink. The question was who had a motive: a motive to kill Cordelia Conti Lang in the first place, and subsequently to make an attempt on Maggie's life. This was the premise of Sam's reasoning: the attack on Maggie was linked to the killing of Cordelia. Was it because Maggie had come too close to unmasking the murderer, or because she was just snooping about and making him nervous? Him, or her.

Emilia was the most likely candidate. Cordelia stood in the way of her union with Ollie. She had denounced her as a gold-digger and threatened to end their relationship, even if it meant cutting Oliver out of her Will. Ollie would have chosen Emilia over his inheritance (or so he had told his mother), but was Emilia prepared to do the same? Ollie's future inheritance sounded like a cosmic amount of money. The temptation would be huge for a girl who came from nothing. Perhaps, Emilia Rawbotham was her father's daughter in more ways than one, Sam pondered savagely. Perhaps she was as greedy and unscrupulous as her daddy.

There was however the problem of her alibi. She was with Ollie all night and the bloody fingerprint found in Cordelia's bathroom was conclusively not hers. And neither did it belong to Ollie. The two of them had to be eliminated from Sam's investigation on the basis of straightforward forensic evidence.

That fingerprint could however belong to any one of his other three suspects: Hatton, Rawbotham or Edwards.

As much as Sam would relish Rawbotham committing murder with all the consequences that it entailed, including a long period of incarceration, he couldn't think of a valid motive. Yes, Rawbotham had a motive to get rid of Maggie – the fear of being exposed for stealing her money and jewellery had to weigh heavily on his mind – but he didn't have one for killing Cordelia Conti Lang. Not to mention that Maggie was his alibi. She was with him on the night of Cordelia's death, a fact that Sam had to accept even though he strongly resented it.

Sam's least likely murderer was Hywel

Edwards. Firstly, he wasn't connected to Cordelia Conti Lang. He was a man who happened to choose a cruise into the Baltics to celebrate his wedding anniversary with his wife. A random bystander. Even his potential for spiking Maggie's drink in the bar was slim. Like many other patrons that night, he bought a couple of drinks at the same time as Maggie was gulping down her G&T. They spoke in passing. He didn't buy her a drink and may have not even come near the one she was having. In addition, he wasn't on Maggie's investigative radar and had nothing to fear from her. She had made a few strong enemies in her short, but prolific, detective career on this ship, but Hywel was not one of them.

Finally, there was Vincent Hatton. He had deliberately hijacked Maggie away from Sam. At face value, it was with the innocent intention of dancing with her, but Sam was bitter about it and therefore suspicious. He had good reason to be. Hatton didn't return Maggie to Sam's side after the dance. That wasn't the conduct of an old-time gentleman, no matter what Maggie thought. A true gentleman would have escorted the lady back to her companion. Why didn't Hatton do that? Why did he monopolise Maggie that night? He knew she was with Sam.

Bitterness and etiquette aside, Hatton was best placed to spike Maggie's drink. They spent a long time together in the bar, with Maggie

– by her own admission – distracted by Hywel and Ollie. Hatton had every opportunity to slip something into Maggie's glass behind her back. He also knew of Maggie's sleuthing. He had heard her reporting her findings to Detective Smilga. Perhaps something she said had hit a nerve? Perhaps she was getting too close to the real killer for his liking? And that thought took Sam to the question of motive.

Sam remembered Pi telling them that Hatton had lost his savings to a fraudster or some dodgy financial scheme that quickly folded. Sam wasn't clear about that – his recollection was hazy. He would have to speak to Pi to investigate this link further. There was a chance – slim perhaps, but still a chance – that the dodgy financial scheme led to Cordelia Conti Lang. After all, wasn't she and her mobster-hubby, into ripping people off for profit?

Sam was late for dinner. He had been so engrossed in his musings that he'd lost track of time. He hurried to the restaurant. He would grab something quick to eat and then pin down Pi for a chat about Hatton. To use Maggie's imprecise expression: *Sam had a strange feeling about Vince Hatton.*

He was dismayed to discover that Oliver, Emilia and even Raw-blinking-botham had once again joined his table. The company looked comfortable, laughing heartily. All his suspects, bar one, sat there together, carefree and enjoying themselves, while Maggie was confined to a hospital bed, fed intravenously with an awful mixture of liquid nutrients, all alone and stranded in a foreign city. She was not allowed visitors until tomorrow morning. She was probably frightened out of her wit and wouldn't sleep a wink all night.

Instantaneously, Sam lost both his appetite and the ability to socialise. He turned tail and set off towards the exit. He didn't get far.

'Samuel!' Barbara spotted him.

He pretended not to hear her, but it was no good because Sidney was on his way to get him.

'Samuel!' the old chap called out, panting behind him. 'Over here! We've moved to a bigger table – over here!'

He caught up with Sam and gripped his arm. 'Come, please. We're all dying to know how Maggie's faring. We've been worried about the poor lass.'

Indeed, as soon as he sat down, they all swooped on him to inquire after Maggie. Genuine concern rang in their voices. Pi dashed over to take Sam's order, but mainly to listen to his account of Maggie's hospital recovery. Sam felt better. They cared. He explained at length about the suspected poisoning – he refused to use the word *overdose* – to which they gasped in collective horror. He assured them that Maggie was out of danger and would be joining them tomorrow evening before the ship sailed out of St Petersburg. That was received with a group sigh of relief.

'Good Lord!' Barbara squeezed her chest. 'When I booked this cruise I never dreamt it'd be so eventful. It's more drama than I've seen in my whole life: sinking boats, murder, poison. What else?'

'All's well that ends well,' Sidney said.

Pi departed to place Sam's order with the cook and the diners returned to more savoury conversation about the joys of St Petersburg. Sam didn't take part – he couldn't. He had missed all of it, sitting at Maggie's bedside. Truth be told, he was shell-shocked. He withdrew into himself, nodding absent-mindedly. His eyes shifted from one face to the next around the table as he pretended to listen.

Until it hit him.

As his gaze moved from Hywel to Ollie, he paused and looked again – really looked at the two men seated side by side, in a well-lit restaurant. At last he knew what Maggie meant. Her odd feeling that *something was wrong* made sense. Everything made sense: that Hywel was an activist for fathers' rights, that he had links to Conti Lang after all, and most of all, that he had a compelling motive to kill Cordelia.

Sam addressed Hywel, 'You are Oliver's father, aren't you, Hywel?' and the whole table fell silent.

◆ ◆ ◆

Hywel Edwards and Cordelia Conti Lang met for the first time in 1995. He was a young, up-and-coming estate agent in the affluent suburb of South Kensington. She was looking for a home that would take her and her husband out of East London. She wanted to leave it behind, as well as Lenny's wider family and criminal associates. She was keen to swap it for the status and prestige that South Kensington could offer, its eye-watering house prices being no object. The new respectable post code was part and parcel of Cordelia's plan to switch from violent to white-collar crime.

By the time of their first encounter, Cordelia had been married to Lenny for a few years but their union had produced no offspring. Cordelia was desperate for a child and heir apparent to Lenny's ill-gained fortune. Hywel knew nothing about that when he fell head-over-heels for her after her short but effective charm offensive. The day they sealed the deal on the property, they also consummated their illicit affair. It didn't last long – only as long as it took Cordelia to fall pregnant. As soon as that happened, she terminated their relationship without any explanation. She informed Hywel that if he tried to contact her, she would complain to Lenny, and Lenny would cut off his balls and feed them to his dog; and that was just for starters. That was more than enough to convince Hywel to stay away from her, heartbroken though he was.

Seven years later and by then already married to Stacey, Hywel came across a newspaper article about the death of Lenny Lang. It was a sympathetic piece which only touched lightly upon the subject of Lenny's illustrious criminal career, but focussed more on his philanthropies and his family life. There was a photograph of Lenny's son, Oliver – a six-year-old boy with a mop of red hair and a freckled nose. It didn't take Hywel long to do the maths and work out the boy's true parentage. Just looking at the boy, Hywel saw the inescapable similarities to his own junior school photos. Oliver was his child. He contacted Cordelia.

She neither confirmed nor denied his fatherhood, but in her customary blunt fashion told him to stay away from her and *her* son. Again, she threatened to destroy Hywel, his career and his family if he pursued this matter. Hywel was in no doubt that she meant what she said. Despite that, he challenged her in court, and lost. He discovered that he had no leg to stand on to claim any rights to his son. Following the court case Cordelia obtained an injunction prohibiting him from approaching Oliver for as long as Oliver was a minor. As a result of that crushing defeat, Hywel threw himself into championing the cause of biological fathers. He set up Equality for Fathers, an organisation that had gone from strength to strength over the years. He retired from his day job and devoted himself to the cause.

The moment Oliver turned eighteen, Hywel went looking for him, but by then Cordelia had sold their South Kensington residence and moved out without leaving a forwarding dress, taking Oliver with her. It took Hywel three years and a legion of private detectives to locate the boy – a man of twenty-one by then.

'So, Oliver knows you're his father?' Sam inquired.

'Yes,' Ollie spoke. 'It wasn't plain sailing to start with. I was in a bad place when Hywel got in touch – I was popping drugs like smarties and couldn't care less. I told him to go to hell.'

'And I did. I gave you space. Though I lost the will to live when you rejected me.' Hywel's voice trailed off.

'I'm sorry. My head was in the wrong place.'

'I know, and I couldn't do anything to help you.' Hywel gazed tenderly at his son. There was a great unresolved regret in his eyes.

'I wouldn't have it – wouldn't accept help from anyone. It wasn't your fault.'

Silence fell between father and son. Stacey filled it, 'Ollie got in touch last year. He'd put the drugs behind him – with Emilia's help.' Stacey smiled at Emilia. 'He wanted to see evidence of Hywel's paternity.'

'Which we had from the days of the court case.'

'It felt great,' Oliver said. 'It felt like I'd got a second chance at having a dad, especially after ...' He didn't finish that thought but everyone guessed what he had in mind. 'I wanted to get to know Hywel. I wanted him and Stacey to meet Emilia. It just felt so normal. I'd been craving normality.'

That may have been so, Sam mused, but the reality was that they could all have planned the murder together. Hywel hadn't come on this cruise just to celebrate his wedding anniversary. He could have chosen many other cruises, but he chose this one. Was it because he knew Cordelia would be here?

'Did you kill her, Hywel?' Sam fixed him with a probing eye. 'I don't think anyone would blame you. I wouldn't. The woman had stolen your son, threatened you, deprived you of the chance to see him grow up. You must have hated her.'

'Oh, I did!'

Barbara released a staggered whimper. Her eyes rounded with dread.

Ollie gaped too. 'You didn't kill Mother! Did you?'

Stacey stepped in, 'No, of course he didn't kill her. You misunderstood. Tell them, Hywel.'

He smiled ruefully. 'So many times I wished I could get my hands on her! But no, of course I didn't kill her. What I was saying was that yes, I hated the bitch. But no, I didn't kill her. All clear?'

'Not quite.' Sam had to follow this through. Hywel had the motive to murder Cordelia. With that, there was a link to Maggie's impromptu investigation which may have unsettled him. In the bar last night, he'd had the opportunity to spike her drink. Sam had to pursue this further. He said, 'You came on this cruise because you knew she'd be here.'

'Not exactly. It was mainly because Ollie was here.'

'If that's the case, why did you hide your relationship with him? He's an adult. You're not breaking any court orders fraternising with your son. And yet you acted as if he was a stranger. Why?'

'We agreed,' Ollie said, 'that Mother wouldn't be told about Hywel getting in touch with me. You know what she was like – you met her. She would've cut me off. She would've forced me to choose. Just like she tried to do with Emilia. She may have even delivered on her old threat to destroy Hywel. My mother was an evil woman. And she was as powerful as she was evil.'

'So we kept it secret, for the sake of peace. I came on this cruise to spend some quiet time with my son, not to kill his mother. She didn't mean anything to me.'

'Anyway, that night when she was killed, we were playing bridge,' Stacey pointed out. 'Well into the night. It must've been five in the morning when we came back to our cabin.'

'That's right,' Sidney added. 'They were playing us, in my room.'

'All night,' Barbara confirmed.

'There goes your theory, Samuel,' Hywel offered Sam a glib shrug.

CHAPTER 26

The revelations of last night left Sam with just one viable suspect: Vincent Hatton, the cruise liner's Chief Security Officer. His position meant that he knew the location of the CCTV cameras on the ship and could easily navigate the decks and passenger quarters without leaving a trace. He was also one of the first people to know of the fatal fight between Nedim and Alvar. He had made the unorthodox decision to keep the fact of Nedim's death secret from the passengers. His motivation may have been to avoid panic, but on the other hand it could have been to buy time. He'd given himself twenty-four hours to plan Cordelia's murder and to frame Alvar.

Sam had to find Pi. It was imperative that Hatton's hypothetical motive was explored as quickly as possible. If Sam's suspicions were confirmed, that man had to be arrested and removed from the ship before it sailed. And before Maggie was back on board – and in direct danger once again.

The latest from the hospital was that she was recovering so well that they would be releasing her after lunch. She would be back onboard sometime between two and four, and at five pm the cruise liner was set to depart. Sam didn't have much time left.

Pi was nowhere to be found at breakfast. Sod's law! Sam despaired. He hardly touched his food and exchanged nothing but a few fleeting pleasantries with the people on his table. He excused himself, citing urgent business. It didn't escape him when Stacey and Emilia rolled their eyes. Let them, he thought. He would make no excuses for doing his best to protect Maggie.

Sidney gave him a pleading look. 'Are you off now? What about your breakfast?'

'I'm not hungry. Things to do, I'm afraid. Must go.' Sam was already on his way out.

'That's a pity. I wanted to talk to you about something. I have to run it by you, I feel. If you have a minute.'

'The thing is I don't. Maggie's due back soon, and I have some pressing business to sort out quickly. Can it not wait?'

'I suppose it can. It's just a ...' Sidney mumbled the rest of the sentence inaudibly. 'But yes, it can wait. It's probably nothing.'

'I'll catch you later.'

Sam set off on his search for Pi. He scoured

the restaurants and inquired with other waiters, but none of them could stop to talk to him. They were all darting about, balancing pots of hot tea and racks of toast and serving breakfast to demanding clientele. Sam ended up with scrambled egg on the sleeve of his jumper after he inadvertently entered the path of a waiter who was juggling three dinner plates on his forearm. The waiter's face grew red with frustration and an unspoken curse quivered on his lips, but he was professional enough to apologise to Sam and offered to have his jumper dry-cleaned overnight.

'No, of course not. It was my fault,' Sam protested.

He abandoned his search for the time being and scampered below deck to his room. He would wait until breakfast was over. They stopped serving at ten. Meantime, he would make the necessary preparations to accommodate Maggie in his cabin. It was auspicious that his room featured two single beds joined into one double. They could be easily separated. He requested fresh sheets from Housekeeping, advising them that Maggie would be sharing his cabin. He was determined to keep an eye on her twenty-four-seven from now on. It was primarily because she required round the clock care while convalescing, but also because there was a murderer on board who had unfinished business with her. Until Sam identified him,

Maggie wasn't safe alone in her cabin, especially considering her recklessness around locking doors. He didn't share that latter reason with the obliging Housekeeping lady who brought the fresh sheets and, with a suggestive wink, inquired whether he was absolutely sure the beds were to be pushed apart.

I wish they could stay as they were! Sam exclaimed inwardly, but told the obliging lady to get on with separating them. He even offered her help.

At ten-thirty Sam resumed his search for Pi. Bounced from one person to another, he was finally directed to another Vietnamese man who worked in the kitchens and was Pi's second cousin. He had very little English – not that one needs much of it to wash dishes – but with the aid of vivid gesticulations was able to inform Sam that Pi was having his half-day off; he was out on the town, buying presents for his kids. One could always score cheap knock-offs of famous brands in Russia, and that was a well-known fact. Sam was impressed with how much information could be conveyed via hand gestures and facial contortion. But he wasn't impressed that he had to wait for Pi until after Maggie was back.

Maggie arrived at two-thirty. Sam was waiting at the quay. The ambulance pulled over and when the back door flew open, Maggie could be seen laughing and cracking jokes with a good-looking young paramedic. She had transformed remarkably from the previous day: her cheeks were rosy again and her eyes sparkling and quick. She spotted Sam instantly and waved. Sam raised his hand in an awkward salute. He himself wondered what the hell that was about.

The handsome paramedic helped Maggie into a wheelchair. Sam felt a cold current travel down his spine. Why the wheelchair? Was something wrong with her mobility? Some form of paralysis from the poisoning? He watched in horror, his own power of speech in a state of paralysis.

The wheelchair with Maggie in it was lowered to the ground on a pneumatic platform, and Maggie set the wheels in motion with a shrill of excitement. She was pushing herself vigorously towards the ship, gathering speed. The paramedic jogged by her side. Sam dashed after them.

'Maggie!'

'Look Samuel! I always wanted to have a ride on one of those. Yuri promised he'd let me have a go.'

Yuri had to be the paramedic. He peered at Sam over his shoulder and flashed his square, white teeth in a wicked grin. He gestured to Sam to keep up, '*Davay*, Samuel! *Bistrah!* Come on, Samuel!'

Approaching the gangway to the cruise liner

with alarming speed, Maggie squealed, 'How do I stop this thing? Where are the brakes!'

Yuri didn't try to educate her. Instead, he grabbed hold of the handles and brought Maggie to a screeching halt. The wheelchair executed a wobbly half-turn and stopped, aligning itself with the quayside, precariously close to its edge.

Sam halted and doubled-up, his hands on his knees, catching his breath and recovering his wits. Maggie got out of the wheelchair with no trouble whatsoever. In fact, there was a distinct spring to her step as she threw her arms around Yuri. He reciprocated in one of those unmistakable Russian bearhugs.

'*Spasibah Yuri!*' Had she learned Russian during her short hospital stint? Sam marvelled. 'That was fun!'

'No problem,' Yuri flashed his teeth again. 'Thank you for your invitation. I visit you in summer in Bishops Well.'

'You must!'

'Have a good sailing!'

'Oh, I intend to, Yuri. I certainly intend to.'

Sam gawped as the two of them finalised their summer holiday plans to which he wasn't privy. Yuri grabbed the empty wheelchair and pushed it away, slaloming between bollards. Maggie rested her hands on her hips and declared, 'Come on, Samuel, I'm famished.'

Sam took Maggie to his cabin and explained that

she would be staying with him for the rest of the voyage. When she protested, he gave her his reasons: he was gravely concerned for her safety; until he had the suspect in custody, he was taking no further chances with her life. Maggie peered at him, gratified.

'Oh dear, Samuel, you really don't have to. It's too much trouble.'

'No, it isn't too much of anything, and that's final.'

'I am touched. I really am!'

'Good.' Sam rubbed his hands together. 'I shall go quickly and organise you something to eat?'

'I thought you'd never ask!'

'Just don't leave the cabin or answer the door. Promise me!'

'Cross my heart and hope to die,' Maggie grinned.

Invigorated, Sam headed for the restaurant to hopefully order room service. There was still no sign of Pi, which was disappointing, but he found another waiter. He led Sam to the kitchen where Sam was invited by a formidably tall chef to choose *whatever the lady would like, no problem.* When Sam queried what the choices were, he was told *cheese and pickle sandwich, sir – on white or brown bread?* Sam surmised that the choice lay between the types of bread. He selected the white option. To compensate for the paucity of the main course, he was presented with a selection of freshly-baked cakes. Maggie would be happy after all.

She was. After the hospital diet of thin cabbage soup and dumplings, she welcomed cheese and cakes with open arms, or mouth to be exact. Sitting on her new bed in his cabin, she was feasting on the sandwiches and listening to Sam's account of his sleuthing manoeuvres in her absence. She had a Eureka moment when he told her about Ollie and Hywel.

'I knew there was something there! I just couldn't put my finger on it. Well done, Samuel!'

'It was staring me in the face when I saw those two next to each other at our table. They were like two peas in a pod but for the age difference.'

Maggie moved on to the cakes. 'So, if the murderer wasn't Hywel, who was it?'

Sam shared with her his theories about Vincent Hatton. She listened fascinated, her eyes growing wider and wider.

'Well, I never!' she commented.

'It is a possibility, Maggie. The only possibility we're left with. You know what Sherlock Holmes would say, and all that.'

'I've no idea. What would he say?'

'When you have eliminated the impossible, whatever remains, however improbable, must be the truth.'

'But Vince? He's the loveliest, sweetest gentleman—'

'Appearances can be deceiving,' Sam interrupted her sharply. 'I just need to get hold of Pi.'

'Yes, you're a bit thin on the motive.'

Having gobbled up her last cake, Maggie licked her fingers. 'Shall we have a nice cup of tea? I'd kill for one.'

'I think we've had enough killing for one holiday.'

Just as the cruise ship set sail, Sidney intercepted Sam on the stairs and reiterated his desire to have a word. Sam saw no reason to delay the chat and Sidney didn't want to wait until dinner time. He wanted to talk in private so they went to the bar with the grand piano. They each ordered a beer.

'Hywel being Oliver's father – that was quite a shock,' Sidney started.

Sam raised his eyebrows emphatically and nodded, wondering where Sidney was going with this chinwag.

'I've been thinking about it all night,' Sidney went on. 'And there's something that bothers me. I don't believe for one minute that Hywel would be capable of murder. Well, as much as I've got to know the man … in recent days, that is.'

Sam sipped his beer.

Sidney rubbed his chin, sighing heavily.

'It's best just to get it off your chest, Sid. Whatever it is.'

'I wouldn't want to accuse an innocent man,

but … Well, like you said *off my chest.* So, this is my dilemma: We were playing bridge in my cabin, the four of us, all night, really, but of course one can't keep an eye on all the players at all times. Why would one anyway? I hope you know the game – somebody has to be a dummy. Each of us was at some point. And so was Hywel, four or five times. And on a couple of occasions, I recall, he left the cabin and went out for some fresh air. I did it once, too.'

'How long was he gone?'

'I can't tell you that with certainty, but there's something else that's troubling me. I only remembered it in the night when I couldn't sleep and was doing too much thinking, as you do. Well, it came to me that Hywel had changed his shirt. He came back wearing a sweatshirt. You see, I didn't make much of it at the time – I guess he was more comfortable wearing something more casual, but now … well, I don't know what to make of it, if anything.'

Sam jumped to his feet. 'You did the right thing, Sidney. We've got to find Vincent Hatton.'

'Hatton?'

'He's the chief security man. We need him to make a citizen's arrest. And he may yet turn the ship around.'

CHAPTER 27

Hatton knocked on the door of the cabin occupied by the Edwards. 'It's Vincent Hatton, Chief Security Officer.'

Stacey's anxious face appeared in a small gap when she opened the door gingerly. 'Mr Hatton? Has something happened?'

'We need to talk to your husband.'

'What about?' It was Hywel's voice. He sounded wary.

'Can we please come in.'

Hatton pushed his way past Stacey. Sam and Sidney followed. Sidney muttered, 'I am ever so sorry. I couldn't … I, I …'

'What's this all about?'

'Hywel Edwards, I have reasonable grounds to believe that you are implicated in Mrs Conti Lang's murder. I'd like to ask you to accompany me.'

'Hang on a second!' Stacey recovered her wits. 'You can't barge in and make accusations like that without any proof. It's preposterous! On the night of Conti Lang's death we were playing cards all night with Barbara and Sidney.' She sent Sidney an imploring look. 'Go on Sid, say something!'

'I'm ever so sorry,' Sidney repeated his mantra.

'Whatever do you mean: you're sorry?'

'Hywel wasn't there all the time. He left the cabin a couple of times,' Sam helped Sidney.

'As did you!' Hywel rounded on Sidney with a bellicose stare. 'As did all of us!'

'That's true, but ... You see, Hywel, I'm sure there's a logical explanation, and you can, you know – explain ... Oh dear, it's harder than I thought.'

To take the heat off Sidney, as transparently he was just about to roll over and give in to Hywel's intimidation tactics, Sam stepped in, 'Could we see the shirt you wore that night?'

'What does Hywel's shirt have to do with anything?' Stacey asked.

'Can we see it, please?' Hatton backed Sam up.

'Why?'

'You changed into a jumper that night. If you killed Mrs Conti Lang, there is a good chance that your shirt would be splattered with her blood in a particular pattern. The detective in Riga explained that to us – his forensics team looked into it. A bloodied shirt would give you a reason to change mid-evening, in the middle of a game of cards. Otherwise, it doesn't make sense – you changing your clothes,' Sam clarified calmly. 'So if you can show us the shirt then you'll prove us wrong and we'll leave you in peace.'

Stacey stomped to the wardrobe and flung the door open. 'I'll get you the damned shirt and then, kindly, get out of here. We've had enough of yours and Maggie's meddling.' She furiously shoved the hangers and they grated against the pole.

After she'd gone through all the items, she appeared momentarily baffled. It wasn't an emotion she could hide – Sam was watching her like a hawk. Judging by her initial reactions, he had already gathered that Stacey was not in on the deed. Hywel had acted alone. Sam observed her puzzlement, hesitation, dismay and finally: her resolve to save face. She bit her lower lip and pulled out a shirt with subtle, white and pale blue stripes. She threw the shirt at Hatton.

'Here! Happy?'

'This shirt hasn't been worn.' Hatton turned it in his hands.

'And it isn't the same shirt, I'm afraid. The one on the night was also light blue, but it was plain. I remember distinctly.' Sidney spoke confidently. Polite as he was, he wouldn't have the wool pulled over his eyes.

'I … I may be mistaken. Hold on, I'll find the plain one – it's somewhere here.' Stacey began a frenzied search through the drawers.

Sam was sure she wouldn't find the shirt. It was probably at the bottom of the sea. Hywel knew that too, naturally. Sam could see it in his body language: he had slumped in the chair, his shoulders folded in, his head low. Whatever miracle he was waiting for wasn't coming. Sam decided to stop wasting time. 'Look, there's a simple way of out of this. The police in Riga have a partial fingerprint from Cordelia's bathroom. The murderer wiped all the surfaces clean, but he missed that one print – no one could do a thorough job when in such a hurry. And you were in a hurry, weren't you Hywel?'

Hywel didn't answer.

'It is the murderer's fingerprint because there are traces of Cordelia's blood on it. We can resolve this quickly: Hywel provides us with his fingerprints, we wire them to Riga for comparison, and we will know. This shouldn't take longer than a couple of hours. It's a very straightforward procedure these days. A computer programme does all the work in a matter of seconds. So—'

'It's mine. The fingerprint is mine.' Hywel spoke without lifting his head.

'I was there, I admit it, but I didn't kill her. I know how it looks. I went to see her in her cabin in the middle of the night. Frankly, the thought of killing the bitch had crossed my mind. But I didn't have to do it. She was already dead.

'Ollie had told me about her threats over Emilia. We both knew she was serious, but so was Ollie when the girl he loved was threatened. I wanted to tell her that, to warn her off. I was going to blackmail her. If there was anything she was scared of, it was losing her son. If I threatened her with telling him the truth about me and how she'd erased me from his life, she would cave in. She'd be afraid that he'd walk away from her. He was already on edge over Emilia. All he needed was another nudge and he'd disown her. Finding out about me might send Ollie over the edge – she could believe that. Of course, she didn't know me and Ollie had already found each other and that he knew everything anyway. It was just an idea to help my son.

'And yes, as I was slinking along the corridor on my way to confront her, it did occur to me that the easiest way to save Ollie, his relationship with Emilia and his inheritance would be just to throttle the bitch. And maybe I'd have done it, but like I said, she was already dead when I got there.

'I didn't knock on the door. It stood ajar. I pushed it and walked in. I saw her on the floor. I didn't see the blood, not at first. My first instinct was to run to her, to check on her. She was lying on her stomach. I turned her over – I saw ...' He ran his tongue over his dry lips.

'I saw the blood, her throat cut, her eyes still open but dead, glassy. I recoiled. I stood up, probably too abruptly – felt the blood drain from my head. I lost balance – had to grab hold of the table. My hand left a bloody mark. I looked down: the sleeves of my shirt were smudged with her blood from when I turned her body. It wasn't a spatter of blood, see what I mean?

'Now I realise, I should've kept the bloody shirt. It'd show a different pattern – not a spatter, only smudges. But what did I know! I panicked. I pulled the shirt off my back and wiped everything I'd touched clean. My hands were covered in blood. I went to the bathroom to wash them. I couldn't risk leaving the cabin with bloodied hands. Wearing my vest alone looked suspicious enough. So, I washed my hands and gave the sink and taps a once-over. I wiped them I thought thoroughly. I didn't realise I'd left a fingerprint behind.

'I was in a rush. I lost track of time, couldn't tell if they could be already wondering where the hell I was. It all seemed so brief and yet somehow – so slow. Like in a dream – you don't know how long it's been going on for: it could be a few seconds, it could be a few hours.

'I ran back to our room, found a sweatshirt – the first thing I lay my hands on. If I was thinking rationally, I'd have put on another, similar shirt. But I wasn't thinking, was I?

'I then shot off to the deck and hurled the

bloody shirt overboard. I ran back to Sid's cabin. They were still playing the same hand. Stacey was doing well. Everyone was absorbed in the game. I was relieved.'

'Relieved that you got away with it?' Sam inquired coldly.

'I didn't! I swear I didn't kill Cordelia. You have to believe me!' Hywel screamed in his face.

Even Stacey was lost for words. She could offer her husband no consolation and no reassurance. Sidney was shaking his head dolefully. Sam puffed up his cheeks and exhaled his relief: the culprit had been unmasked. Of course, he didn't believe Hywel. Neither did Hatton.

'Hywel Edwards, I am placing you under arrest.' The Chief Security Officer put his hand on Hywel's shoulder. 'You'll come with me. You'll be placed under guard in isolation until we arrive in Helsinki where I will hand you over to the Finnish authorities.'

'Where have you been!' Maggie demanded when Sam finally returned to his cabin. 'I thought you were dead!'

'You didn't think that, Maggie – admit it,' Sam chuckled. 'If I were dead, you'd be the first to know. I'd be by your side in no time.'

'You'd be running to your mum.'

'Why? She wouldn't even know I was there. Only you'd be able to see me.'

'True,' Maggie conceded the point, looking pleased. 'But where did you go? You've been gone for two hours. I was worried.'

It was immensely gratifying to discover that Maggie worried about him. Sam sat by her and cupped his hands around hers. 'I've been busy tracking down Conti Lang's killer. The man is now in custody – still on this ship, but under lock and key. You can sleep safe and sound now, Maggie.'

'So who is it?'

'Hywel. He's confessed. Well, it's a sort of partial confession. He had no choice really but to confess–' and Sam relayed to Maggie the events of the evening, starting with Sidney's revelations and culminating with the arrest.

Maggie appeared slightly disgruntled. She obviously wished she had been the one to uncover the truth and bring the perpetrator to justice. Unfortunately, it had all happened in her absence. She wrinkled her nose, appearing pensive, almost doubtful.

'But he denies killing her?' She probed.

'He does, but with the weight of evidence against him I don't think even Stacey believes him.'

'Did he own up to trying to poison me too?'

'We didn't get to that, but I've no doubt it was him. You were getting too close to the truth for comfort. He must've noticed that you were watching him and Ollie, and he realised you were onto him. He decided to act before you put two and two together. Truth be told, without you Maggie we would've never thought of him.'

That last statement seemed to pacify Maggie. She pushed her chin up. 'True! I did have that strange feeling about him and Ollie, didn't I?'

'You did, indeed. And you told me, and the rest, as they say, is history.'

Her face crumpled. 'I suppose that means it's safe to return to my own room.'

Sam found himself the victim of his own success. He quickly back-peddled. 'Only if you want to. I'd much rather if you stayed.'

'I think I will. Just this one night.' Maggie beamed and her two little dimples made a welcome reappearance.

CHAPTER 28

Maggie's Journal

Not only did Stacey believe her husband – she stood with him shoulder to shoulder. I caught up with her on her way to deliver a takeaway meal to him. He was languishing locked up in a cell on the bottom deck. His cell wasn't that bad – not quite a dungeon with a bed of straw. It was a luxurious passenger cabin adapted for the purpose of his detention. But it was the idea of his incarceration that upset Stacey. She was in tears.

'Hywel isn't a killer, Maggie,' she sobbed. 'I'd know if he – a wife knows.' She pinched her nose to stop it from running. She sniffled and raised her head in a pointedly dignified fashion. 'If that night – if he'd killed anyone that night, I would've known. He wouldn't be able to hide it from me. He does everything properly – by the book, legally, everything above board. Why do you think he set up EFF? He's an activist, not a vigilante. He would never, not in a million years, resort to crime. To murder another human being of all things!' Her eyes welled up and tears broke the banks.

I put my arm around her and gently patted her back. I not only felt sorry for her, but I was plagued with guilt. Somehow, it seemed to me, it was my fault: Hywel being arrested and detained like a common criminal. What if he was telling the truth? What if Samuel and Vince Hatton were wrong? We had put that man through hell – we'd better be right! But assuming we were wrong, we'd be doing Hywel and his relationship with his son a great injustice. They had endured enough already.

The more I thought about it, the less convinced I was about his guilt. I didn't feel that sense of righteousness in my bones – that sense of justice being done. I felt rotten to the core. I told Stacey that I hoped this nightmare would be over soon and Hywel would be vindicated.

She blew her nose in a hankie I gave her. 'So, you don't believe he did it either? Or that he tried to kill you? Because, trust me Maggie, he didn't. He wouldn't. The thought wouldn't have crossed his mind.'

I didn't know what to think and I admitted that to her. I wasn't going to lie and assure her of her husband's innocence. I just did not know.

'But I do. You people have got the wrong man, and the real killer is out there, laughing at you. Oh well, I'd better take this to him before it gets cold.' She shrugged my arm off her back and wedged the tray with Hywel's dinner between us. Her lips were pursed tight.

'If I could talk to Hywel, we could straighten a few things up,' I suggested. I was eager to ask him a few questions, particularly about the scalpel. That scalpel had been bothering me since the start of this tragic saga.

Although Stacey didn't mind me coming along to Hywel's cell, I wasn't allowed in. The security guard stopped me at the door and informed me that on Mr Hatton's orders no one was permitted to visit the prisoner. When I insisted, the guard called Hatton on his walkie-talkie and conveyed my request to him.

'I said no one, especially not Miss Kaye!' Hatton's voice crackled on the poor wavelength. 'For God's sake, hasn't she caused enough trouble as it is!'

So that was me told.

I was disappointed. Samuel might be fancying himself Sherlock Holmes reincarnated – he had even quoted the famous detective at me earlier – but he could be wrong. I didn't begrudge him his moment of glory, I honestly didn't, but I wasn't convinced that he had got it right. I couldn't imagine poor Hywel plotting to murder me or having a vial of hallucinogenic potion at the ready in his pocket. Even if he had noticed me watching him and Ollie that night in the bar, he surely wouldn't have been in a position to act there and then. There was an element of premeditation in the attempt on my life. Hywel had no reason to want to kill me and to plan for it prior to the New Year's Eve ball. His actions would be spur of the moment. Even if he murdered Cordelia, I found it hard to believe that he was the one who spiked my drink that night.

Maybe I am naïve and give people more credit than they deserve, but I was struggling to accept that anyone would want to kill me. Me, Maggie Kaye, of all people! I am but a simple gal from the depths of the West Country. I am no threat to anyone. Who would go to the trouble of preying on my life? And why?

Deep down I harboured the hope that my poisoning wasn't a deliberate act but an accident: a slip of a drunken finger or a glass that had not been properly washed. I couldn't explain it away – not yet – but I was working on it.

And there was more. Reasonable doubts as to Hywel's guilt were nibbling at the back of my mind like a scurry of hungry squirrels. For starters, Cordelia was still rattling about, pursuing her unfinished business with earthly matters for all to see. Well, for *me* to see. She wouldn't be here if we had her killer.

When we sat down to dinner, Cordelia joined us. Her ghostly persona took a seat next to her son. As is the spirit world's unwritten convention, she showed no explicit interest in the goings-on around the table. She just sat there aloof and exotically beautiful in the prime of her distant youth. And this was what her presence had led me to conclude: we had the wrong man.

I didn't share my doubts with Samuel because I had no answers. After all, if it wasn't Hywel then who on earth was it? We had run out of suspects. Samuel had mentioned Vincent Hatton, but I couldn't bring myself to accept that a gentleman such as Mr Hatton would have asked me to dance in order to put poison in my drink. Not to mention that poison wasn't his style. He was a military man. He was more likely to shoot me or wring my neck, though of course such methods would be harder to conceal from public view.

My head was swirling with doubts, and in the end, I found myself dizzy and lightheaded. Perhaps I wasn't yet fully recovered. I leaned against the wall and recovered my breath. The chaos in my head began to settle. I blinked away the black dots that were spinning before my eyes and catching in my eyelashes. Slowly, staying close to the wall, I made my way to Samuel's cabin.

I would lie if I said I wasn't anxious. Assuming that someone was trying to kill me after all, and if that someone wasn't Hywel, I could still be at risk of losing my life. It was a chilling prospect. My veins iced over and I shivered, feeling really, really cold.

I opened the door to Samuel's room and slumped on the bed. Samuel hurried towards me, peering into my eyes with concern.

'Blimey, Maggie, your lips look blue. Are you all right?'

'I'm a bit cold, Samuel,' I said as calmly as I could. I didn't want him to worry for no reason. I was probably imagining things – maybe still hallucinating. Some of those nasty chemicals tend to linger in one's system for ages.

He threw a blanket over my shoulders and went to make tea. I wondered if he had any biscuits but before I asked he magicked up a pack of Digestives. He was a wonder man – my true guardian angel. He did so much more for me than just ride to my rescue on the odd occasion of my life being threatened. He was my permanent, unflinching, unmovable mainstay. I had only known Samuel a few years but already I could not envisage my life without him.

When he returned to sit by my side, a cup of fragrant Earl Grey in hand and a chocolate biscuit melting on the saucer, I inclined my head onto his shoulder and said, 'I'd love to stay with you in your room for the rest of this voyage, if that's not too much trouble.'

He hugged me and kissed the top of my head, 'Oh Maggie! It's no trouble at all. That was the plan from the start.'

'Maybe we could push our beds together?'

He gawped, baffled, but not dismayed, I noted.

'To keep each other warm,' I added, to clarify. 'You know – body heat comes highly recommended.'

'Absolutely! We'll do that. And tomorrow we'll be in Helsinki. There's nothing better for keeping warm than a Finnish sauna.'

We fell asleep in each other's arms, and at some point I became so hot that I had to throw the covers off my back. For a while I stayed awake pondering all sorts of outrageous risks and possibilities, but soon Samuel's soft and steady breathing lulled me into a peaceful, deep sleep. I was in good hands. And vice versa.

CHAPTER 29

Hywel Edwards was being escorted off the ship by Vincent Hatton and two Finnish detectives. To spare him and Stacey humiliation, he was not handcuffed. Nevertheless, being frogmarched under guard in front of his fellow passengers felt like running the gauntlet. He was red-faced and avoided eye contact with everyone, even his wife.

Stacey stood sandwiched between Barbara and Emilia. The two of them were doing their best to keep her spirits up. Barbara spoke soothingly into Stacey's ear. Coming from a sweet old lady, the words of wisdom and support were bound to help. Emilia hooked her arm with Stacey's and held on tight. Stacey was weeping. Her eyes were inflamed red from hours of tears and sleep deprivation.

Between her and Hywel, they had decided there was little point in her accompanying him off the ship in Helsinki. There was no telling how long he would be kept in Finland and where he'd be taken from there. For all they knew, he could be transferred to Riga the following day and Stacey would be left stranded. Therefore, she was going to continue on this cruise to get home to the UK. There she would organise legal representation for Hywel. She would move heaven and earth to have him released on bail and sent home. The task was daunting, especially for someone like Stacey who had no experience of navigating the choppy waters of the international justice system and competing foreign jurisdictions. It was a consolation that for the rest of this voyage she would be surrounded by friends. They were all there for her, including Oliver who, like her, refused to accept Hywel's guilt.

Sam and Maggie stood to one aside, separate from the others. Maggie looked unusually sheepish. Sam could understand why Stacey refused to socialise with them, but he had no qualms about having Hywel apprehended. He was prepared to sacrifice social niceties in the name of safeguarding Maggie. But Maggie was clearly disturbed by the snub.

On his way out, Hywel looked over his shoulder and shot them a pugnacious look. 'You've got it all wrong, you two! I'm an innocent man, damn you!'

Sam only shook his head, but Maggie responded in a most bizarre way. She broke away from Sam and darted towards Hywel.

'What about the scalpel?' She pulled his sleeve, forcing him and his minders to stop in their tracks. 'What happened to the scalpel?'

'What scalpel? What are you talking about!'

'Didn't you find the scalpel?'

'Someone, save me from this madwoman!' Hywel implored the detectives.

Vincent Hatton grabbed Maggie firmly by the elbow and pulled her away from the prisoner. He escorted her kicking and screaming back to Sam.

'Mr Dee, this young lady needs taking in hand. She can't be busy-bodying around, interrogating people and interfering with suspects.'

'I'm not interfering!' Maggie wriggled haplessly in the vice of Hatton's grip. 'It's important. The scalpel is important. I must know! Are you trying to hide something, Mr Hatton?' She paused to peer into his eyes, conflagrated and angry. 'Not you too!'

'Kindly take her to her room.' The Chief Security Officer growled, addressing Sam to the exclusion of Maggie.

Hywel shouted, 'This is madness! Hear me? Sheer lunacy!' and was forcibly ushered by the two detectives towards the police car waiting on the quay. Everyone remaining on deck stared at Maggie with a mixture of bemusement, concern and hostility.

Sam gazed apologetically at Hatton and then his gaze skimmed over the others. 'I'm sorry. Maggie isn't herself. It's the effects of the overdose ... um, the poison.'

'There's nothing wrong with me,' she protested, but weakly. All of a sudden her convictions and her energy had ebbed away, leaving her confused and lost. 'I think I need to lie down.'

'Come Maggie. You're not quite a hundred per cent yet.' Sam guided her down the stairs to his cabin. He made her tea while she muttered her disquiet and raved about the missing scalpel and it being the crux of the matter. Outwardly he agreed with everything she was saying, nodding and mumbling his unreserved consent. Inwardly, he worried that she would be in no state to leave the ship and go sightseeing in Helsinki tomorrow. He promised himself to make a doctor's appointment for her as soon as they set foot in Bishops Well.

By the time the tea was ready, Maggie was fast asleep. Sam took off her shoes and drew the blanket to her chin. He stood silently scrutinising her face. She looked peaceful – tired and pale but peaceful. This cruise had taken a lot out of her. It wasn't at all what Sam had hoped for. This holiday was a disaster.

'If we really have to wear something, Samuel,

it can't be a swimming costume,' Maggie was lecturing him. Having had her cat nap, she was full of beans and bouncing off the walls like the March Hare. She had gone to her cabin to refresh and came back wearing a flimsy t-shirt, and nothing underneath. That there was nothing under that shirt was abundantly clear – *abundantly* in more ways than one. Not that Sam was going to complain. Still, he had her modesty to guard in public.

'It's a mixed gender sauna.'

'So? Where does it say that clothing is mandatory?' Her eyes bulged in a challenging fashion.

'It's just, you know – common decency.'

'Oh, leave off, Samuel! What a pile of hogwash!' She folded her arms on her chest. 'Anyway, I'm only saying that Lycra cannot be worn in the sauna. That's all. I read somewhere that it reacts with the wood smoke in a bad way. While cotton,' she tugged at the hem of her t-shirt, lifting it slightly to reveal – to Sam's relief – that she was equipped with a pair of sensible knickers. Whether she would keep them on in the sauna was another matter, 'cotton, you see, lets your skin breathe and sweat out all those nasty toxins. And let's face it, I have a few nasty toxins to get rid of.'

That was true. A sauna was bound to have a therapeutic effect on Maggie's eroded health. Sam fumbled through his luggage in search of anything cotton and found a pair of pyjama bottoms that answered Maggie's specifications. She wrinkled her nose offishly but approved the article subject to a disclaimer, 'If you must. But if we see other men letting it all hang out, then I'd drop the PJs if I was you. You look … hm … octogenarian.'

The sauna was plush, but cosy. The lights were as red as the glowing coals. Several sweaty bodies camped in various comfortable poses on wooden benches. Some wore towels while some wore other articles of skimpy attire. A couple of women were topless but wrapped in towels. One man with a big stomach that was spilling into his lap may well have been naked, but there was no verifying that due to the folds of his tummy obscuring his nether regions. Sam wished he'd left his pyjama bottoms behind and worn his swimming trunks instead.

As they entered, Maggie tossed two ladles of water into the burner. The cabin filled with thick vapour. Maggie sighed with pleasure. Sam too relished the idleness and sheer bliss that penetrated his body from head to toe.

He and Maggie found spaces to sit opposite each other.

The cabin, though full, was silent. There was no chatter, no whispers, no giggles. Sam loved the relaxed ambience of this place and promised himself that he would look into installing a Finnish sauna cabin in his garden on his return to Bishops. He could do with a bit of pampering on a daily basis. Perhaps adding a sauna room to Badger's Hall could be an option. It would certainly enhance the B&B and attract more guests. He resolved to suggest that to Maggie later.

For a while he was sitting with his eyes closed, enjoying the peace and quiet. When he opened them, he realised that the water vapours had dispersed and improved the visibility within the cabin. This was evident in the image of Maggie poised before him. His eyes rested first on her flushed face and then travelled down to encounter the outline of her bosom. It transpired that the vapours had saturated her flimsy t-shirt and it clung to her curves, exposing them in all their glory. Sam exhaled slowly to steady his racing pulse. He changed his mind: he was now glad of his loose pyjama bottoms. Anything tighter would reveal way too much of his current discomfiture. He got up and chucked more water on the burner. The burning logs hissed and emitted a thick cloud of smoke. That helped with camouflaging his discomfort, but it did nothing to release it.

An enormous relief came when Maggie decided it was time to run outside into the snow to cool down. Sam was desperate for that. They burst out into the thick Nordic night. Distant stars teased the snow, which shone with its own uncanny light. They ran barefoot and their body temperature began to drop. Maggie hardly noticed. She pounced and skipped like said March Hare and started rubbing snow into her thighs and posterior.

'It's good for your circulation!' she shouted and threw a poorly formed snowball at Sam. It disintegrated before it reached him and he ended up with wet fluffy snowflakes on his face. At least the cold had a calming effect on his extremities and he was more or less back to himself.

Maggie discovered some sauna whisks made of birch twigs hanging on the wall. 'Come on, Samuel, I'll whip you first. Then you can do me!' And she lashed out at him.

Sam gave as good as he got. And even though Maggie's idea of gentle strokes left him stinging all over his legs and shoulders, he was finding himself at his happiest on this otherwise doomed cruise.

Back in his quarters, he was reliving the moment. Maggie had departed to her cabin to shower and change into something appropriate to wear for the evening. It was her idea. Sam would be grateful to have her wearing her flimsy t-shirt or a potato sack as long as she was nearby. He was already missing her. He had to hold himself back from texting or calling her mobile just to check that she hadn't forgotten to come back to him.

The engagement ring sat forlornly in his trouser pocket. If he'd had it on him in that stinging-cold snow, he would have gone down on his bare knee and proposed there and then. And he wouldn't have taken *no* for an answer. He scolded himself: he was a grown man, once a smooth barrister handy with a line of wisdom for every occasion, and yet he could not bring himself to utter a simple enough question. It wasn't fear or insecurity. He knew Maggie liked him a lot and she probably wouldn't say no. She was too soft-hearted to say no. So why was he being such a sad wimp?

He had to stop thinking about it and just do it. Now—

Maggie trundled into his room, looking agitated. She was waving her arms and shaking her fists, pulling faces and dancing on the spot.

'Oh Samuel, I can't stop thinking about it! I just can't get it out of my head.'

'Can't you?'

'We have to do something. This isn't right!'

'No, it isn't,' Sam agreed, briefly pondering the possibility of Maggie having developed psychic ability and reading his mind. 'We should do it – take a dive and do it!'

'Absolutely!' Maggie paced the length of his cabin, gesticulating with her forefinger to assist herself with her thought process. 'And I'll admit it without reservation – you were right in the first place. It's that scalpel, you see?'

The damned scalpel had made another entry. Sam's spirits started to sink.

'The murderer's plan was to frame Alvar for Cordelia's murder. That's why he used the same weapon.'

'The scalpel?' Sam resigned himself to abandon hope of ever going through with his plan to propose.

'Precisely! But Hywel couldn't have known about the scalpel. Like us, he didn't know about Nedim's death until after Cordelia was killed. Only Alvar knew and, of course, the crew. But they were ordered to keep quiet about it. By Hatton! That can mean only one thing.'

'I really doubt it, Maggie.'

She wasn't listening. 'We must get to the bottom of it! I have this terrible feeling that we've condemned the wrong man.'

CHAPTER 30

Maggie's Journal

We had a lot of back-peddling to do. It'd be down to me because Samuel obstinately refused to face the facts. It is my firm belief that men typically struggle with reality if it doesn't fit with their theories. Once they've made up their minds about something, they go blind, deaf and mulishly obstinate. They'd rather invest their energies in squaring the hole than exploring its roundness. I wasn't going to let Samuel stop me. The truth had to prevail in the end.

Unfortunately, even if it prevailed today, it would be too late for Hywel. We had stopped in Helsinki for only one night. The ship was on the move again, heading straight for the shores of the British Isles. Hywel was not on board. And he was not at the table when we convened for lunch.

Neither Samuel nor I contemplated relocating to a different table. We may be held responsible for Hywel's arrest by our fellow diners, but we wouldn't budge, on principle. Although my principle wasn't quite the same as Samuel's. He believed that he was right. I believed that he was wrong but that we had to face the music, and in particular – face Stacey. Reparations for the error of our ways would follow. We'd have to make it up to her. I had it all worked out.

We were the first at the table. Sidney and Barbara soon joined us, and offered a wooden greeting. Barbara gazed at us glumly. The disapproval in her eyes was tangible. I could feel what she was thinking: *I expected better of you, Maggie Kaye!* Sidney was less censorious. In fact, he slunk towards his chair like a stray fox who had just raided a chicken coop and was caught with feathers between his teeth. In short, he looked as guilty as I felt. And he should do – he too had a hand in Hywel's hasty arrest.

The speed of that arrest made me even more suspicious of Vincent Hatton. Not for one second had he given Hywel the benefit of the doubt. He wouldn't listen to my voice of reason and kept me away from the suspect. What was he afraid I would find out?

Ollie and Emilia arrived next, followed closely by Benedict. There was less reproach in their body language, but their earlier chumminess was gone. Ollie avoided eye contact with either me or Samuel. When he spoke, he would address Emilia or Benedict, giving us the cold shoulder. I shivered inwardly. I am not used having enemies, and if I inadvertently make them, I will go out of my way to undo the damage and rebuild the bridges.

Cordelia's spirit appeared unperturbed by developments, but that was normal. She was still around, in no obvious rush to depart this earth.

Finally, Stacey showed. Seeing Samuel and me at the table, she paused. She evidently couldn't bear the sight of our faces or the idea of fraternising with her husband's tormentors. She could come over and confront us, but what would be the point of that? What was done was done. She stood in the middle of the floor, hesitating.

I couldn't take it anymore. I hurried towards her. She clenched her jaw on seeing my approach and made to leave the restaurant.

'Stacey!' I stopped her. 'I realise it's too late for apologies, and that's not what I want to say. I believe Hywel's innocent, and I think I may just be able to prove it.'

That was one fat overstatement but it made Stacey stop in her tracks. She glowered at me, 'Why didn't you say so when he was arrested!'

'I tried,' I stammered, 'but Hatton wouldn't let me near Hywel. I tried to ask him about the scalpel, but he fobbed me off. I know it's not easy, but please give me a chance to sort this out.'

As soon as Stacey and I sat at the table, Pi materialised to take our orders. This was as good a time as any to secure the last piece of the puzzle: Hatton's motive.

Instead of giving Pi my order (and I didn't know what I was having anyway – my mind was too preoccupied to contemplate food), I shot from the hip, 'Do you remember when you told us that Mr Hatton had lost all his money on some dodgy investment?'

Pi blinked, discombobulated. Samuel kicked me under the table and fixed me with an unforgiving glare. I had no idea what his problem was. I ignored him and went on to explain to Pi, 'I'm only asking because it may have some bearing on the murder of Mrs Conti Lang. It's a question of motive, you see?'

He clearly didn't see. He was still blinking like a proverbial rabbit in the headlights.

'Well, do you remember or don't you?'

'Um … sort of. Yes, I do.' He gave a final blink.

'Can you tell us more? What kind of business was it? Who was behind it? Was it her? Was it Conti Lang?'

'I really, I don't … I …' Pi developed a sudden stammer. 'I can't remember the detail. I only knew he'd lost his pension savings. And I told you because you asked – what with him being so old and still working.' He shot sideways glances in all directions. He was checking who was listening. I realised he was scared. I realised why Samuel had kicked me.

'Never mind. Forget I asked. Sorry,' I apologised belatedly.

Pi scampered.

Everyone stared at me. Ollie asked, 'What was that all about?'

I had to tell them.

It was a long and convoluted account. They winced collectively when I began with the scalpel. But the scalpel was key to this case. Both Nedim and Cordelia were killed with that scalpel, in the exact same way. Alvar told me he had dropped the scalpel in the sick bay, and run away unarmed. Someone else had picked it up and used it to murder Cordelia. It could only be a crew member – only the crew knew about Nedim and how he was killed.

'He was killed with a scalpel?' Emilia was slow to catch up, poor lass.

'But what makes you think it was Vincent?' Benedict asked a rational question. Everyone else was grimacing at me in bewilderment.

'Well, for starters, he instructed all the staff to keep Nedim's death from the passengers.'

'That's true. He did.' Emilia was getting closer, but not close enough. 'But how does that make him a killer?'

'I think he was buying time.' I gave her a small hint.

'Time? What for?' She was falling behind again.

'To plan how to murder Cordelia and frame Alvar.' I explained it as plainly as I could.

'And then he tried to drug Maggie.' Samuel came to his senses and joined forces with me. I mouthed a grateful *thank you* to him.

'If it wasn't for Samuel, I would've never thought of Hatton. He comes across as such a darling old-time gentleman. He had me fooled.'

'He was best placed to spike your drink. And, unlike everyone else, he knew you were in touch with Detective Smilga. He was worried you already knew too much and might figure out the rest.' Samuel went on to tell them about our call to Riga when Smilga informed us that not only Alvar but also Ollie were out of the frame for murder. The real killer was on board the ship. Hatton realised we'd be looking for him.

'All the leads take us to Hatton,' Samuel concluded. It was a welcome change of heart. I would have to take back my allegation of his mulish obstinacy.

'But why would Vincent Hatton want to kill my mother in the first place?' Ollie threw his arms up with incredulity. 'His role is to look after the passengers. He'd be risking his job for what reason exactly?'

'That's the crux of the matter! Does he have a motive … One doesn't kill for the sake of killing.' I had to concede this small but sticky point.

'That's why Maggie questioned Pi. Though you did put the man on the spot! No wonder, he told you nothing.' Samuel admonished me for my lapse in discretion, and he was right. Poor Pi, I'd have to beg his forgiveness.

'Be it as it may – we're stuck without a motive.'

'I see,' Benedict interrupted me. 'I think I can help you with that.' And he relayed to us the very tragic story of the death of Vince Hatton's son.

Hatton Junior had not been a man averse to risk. Ten years ago, he had invested all he had in bitcoins from a dubious source. He had thrown his savings into it and even re-mortgaged his house. If that wasn't enough, he had also drawn his father into the scheme, promising him huge returns. At the time, crypto-currency was considered infallible. But it wasn't. Within months, he had lost everything. Vincent could not help his son to save his family home – his money was gone too. Unable to see his way out of it, broke and desperate, the son killed himself. He left behind a wife and two teenage daughters. Because of the suicide they weren't entitled to his life insurance. Vincent was forced out of retirement to support them. Whoever had duped the Hattons into buying that dodgy currency was guilty of the son's death.

'That's reason enough to kill twice over,' Sidney commented.

And that was when I remembered. I remembered Vera and Mary telling me about Cordelia when she first moved into Bishops Well. I recalled them referring to her as the Bitcoin Queen.

'Yes, you did tell me!' Samuel remembered too.

Our whole table froze with dread. We had found a compelling motive for Vincent Hatton to have killed Cordelia Conti Lang. We had the real killer. And he was on this ship.

'Hatton cannot find out that we know,' Samuel said. 'Not until we arrive in Southampton. He's a dangerous man. He may try to kill again if he knows we suspect him.'

'So, what do we do?' Barbara looked frightened. Her lips went white.

'We do nothing. We pretend everything's fine. We pretend Cordelia's murderer is under lock and key in Helsinki.'

'But he's innocent... Hywel is innocent. I never doubted it.' Stacey was weeping again, this time with quiet relief. She pulled me into her arms. 'Thank you, Maggie! You're an angel!'

I extricated myself from her embrace. We could not be seen hugging. That would alert Hatton. He expected Stacey to hate me. I spoke in a conspiratorial whisper, 'You always knew he was innocent – that's nothing new. Stay calm, Stacey. We have the real culprit and that's exciting. Of course, it is, to me, that is. But we must keep our emotions in check. Okay?'

She nodded keenly and wiped away her tears.

Meantime, Samuel was talking sense into Ollie. The young man's white fury was for all to see. His jaw twitched and he was cracking his knuckles. Samuel was telling him to contain himself – this wasn't the time to confront Hatton; his time would come. For now, he had to sit tight.

Ollie glanced at him, perplexed. He said, 'You don't get it, Sam. I'm not angry with Hatton. I am angry with my mother. She destroyed him – destroyed his family, his life. She deserved what she got. My mother was a monster. And Vince Hatton is just another victim in all of this.'

I gazed at Cordelia. She was still about, minding her own business. She seemed unmoved. Not a flinch. Not a flicker. She was sitting next to her son, gazing idly into space.

'What an utter bitch!' I said it out loud. I knew she could hear me.

CHAPTER 31

Maggie's Journal

As soon as we came ashore at Southampton, I asked an Immigration Officer to direct me to the nearest police station.

'If you have goods to declare, madam, you don't need the police. It can be done here. Just complete this declaration form.' The officer began in a bored tone and presented me with a slip of paper. He was no doubt used to overexcitable travellers snitching on their companions about smuggled cartons of Russian cigarettes and ninety percent proof vodka. He had droopy eyes with large puffy bags underneath. He looked like a bloodhound that had lost the will to live.

'No, no, no! You don't understand, Officer. We have a serious crime to report, and the culprit is still on board our cruise ship.'

'What sort of crime?'

'Murder.'

He smiled and explained competently, 'Ah, of course – the Hanseatic League cruise ... We know all about it. The port authorities have been notified. I trust those deaths didn't spoil your holiday, madam?' I wasn't sure whether I could hear genuine sympathy or sarcasm in his voice.

Samuel had been standing patiently behind the white line, his passport in hand, waiting to be processed. But as soon as he heard the man's flippant comment, he stepped forward.

'I'm travelling with his lady. And I'll have you know that an attempt was made on her life by the man we suspect. We have evidence against him and we'd like to share it with an appropriate law enforcement agency, if you wouldn't mind pointing us in their direction. Please.' Samuel stressed the last word which came out sounding more like a demand than a request.

Without further ado a security officer was called in and, for some unfathomable reason, instructed to escort us to Southampton Docks Police. I wondered why not Southampton CID, but refrained from questioning the Bloodhound's judgment. Probably the Docks Police headquarters was the closest station that was still operational.

The security officer assisting us had no idea why he was taking us to the Docks so he took the extra precaution of requisitioning a colleague to keep a close eye on us. With two uniformed men escorting us across the hall I felt like a right criminal. I was slowly developing a tension headache: the lights seemed too bright and the noise around me rang in my ears like tolling bells.

The security men passed us on to a uniformed policeman in the rank of sergeant. When asked what this was about, they claimed ignorance. Samuel embarked on an explanation.

It would be a very long story, I feared, and it was. The policeman offered us no refreshments: no tea, no biscuits, not even a chair to sit on. We were standing there like two supplicants, caps in hand, while he sat sprawled behind a littered desk, sipping freshly made coffee the aroma of which was rendering me faint. I left the talking to Samuel and concentrated on breathing.

Gradually, when the gravity of the situation began to sink in, the policeman invited us to a separate room where we could rest our weary bones in two plastic chairs. He told us he was not equipped to deal with the matter and that he would have to call the CID. It was precisely what I thought should have happened at the Border Control point. I had no energy to complain. My head felt like a walnut inside a nutcracker. I simply asked for a glass of water.

An hour, maybe ten hours later (I couldn't be any more precise. It felt like a lifetime of waiting), two plain-clothed detectives arrived. The younger one introduced himself as DC Gilliard and informed us that the older, grumpy-looking one was DI Sorkin. DI Sorkin frowned at that.

'I could do with a cup of coffee, sergeant,' DI Sorkin threw the remark at the policeman.

'We all could,' Samuel added.

Finally, coffee was served, but no biscuits. I felt fractionally revived.

DC Gilliard set up a laptop to record our conversation. We agreed to that and, once again, Samuel conveyed our suspicions and theories, and the evidence we had to back them. Having said it once already, he was much better at retelling. He was precise, to the point and controlled. I admired his calm. I would have made mincemeat of it if I was to put that whole nightmarish experience into words.

'So, if I were to get in touch with the Latvian police they'd confirm your involvement in this case?' DI Sorkin asked.

'Absolutely! And I'm not just involved – I'm also a victim of attempted murder. The detective in charge of the investigation goes by the name of Smilga,' I perked up. 'As a matter of fact, I do need to talk to him. He wanted to hear from me if I remembered anything new.'

'And did you – remember anything?' DI Sorkin was either dull-witted or given to mockery.

'Well – we just told you. A whole lot of stuff, actually!'

'I see. If you don't mind waiting, we'll contact our Latvian counterparts—'

'I've got his number!' I interrupted and handed him Detective Smilga's business card.

He looked at it down his nose. 'It's okay, Miss Kaye. We'll go through our own channels.'

Another wait commenced. Although we were given more coffee, I was beyond resuscitation. Samuel tried to keep me awake by going on about having a Finnish sauna installed at Badger's Hall. It was probably a good idea but I couldn't muster an ounce of enthusiasm.

At last, Smilga was on the line.

'I'll talk to him!' I grabbed the phone. After a brief but cordial greeting, I explained to him that Hywel wasn't his man and took him through the ins and outs of the scalpel saga and Hatton's motive that needed verifying, but was undoubtedly true. That was to say: Samuel and I didn't have any doubts.

'Yes, our British colleagues will check that for us,' Smilga confirmed. I was relieved: they believed us.

'Are you going to arrest him?'

'He'll be interviewed under caution.'

'And what about Hywel Edwards? His wife is beside herself. You've no idea the stress that woman's going through!'

'Don't worry, Miss Kaye. He hadn't been

charged so he was released yesterday. We couldn't keep him in custody for longer than thirty-six hours without charging him. He'll be on the next flight home.'

'You didn't charge him?'

'I had the same doubt as you: the reasonable doubt as to his access to the murder weapon.'

'The blinking scalpel!' Samuel laughed.

Our job done, we were finally going home. We still had our luggage to collect – that being my seaworthy trunk – so we returned to the main building. Our path crossed for the last time with Vincent Hatton. He was being accompanied by the same two security officers who had escorted us earlier. A police van pulled up outside the glass door. It had mesh enforced windows.

We stopped and stared at Hatton. Samuel nodded to him: sadly and with unspoken regret at his plight. There was no triumph or goading in his face. I too just looked at Hatton, too tired to say anything. If I had my wits about me I might have demanded an explanation. My disappointment with him trying to poison me nibbled away a big chunk of my faith in mankind, and particularly in old-time gentlemen.

He shook his head, and sighed. 'I should've guessed it was you, Miss Kaye – busy-bodying around. Let me assure you: just like the first time, you've got the wrong man. On all accounts. Someone's pulling your strings.'

'Did we?' I asked Samuel in the car.

'Did we what?'

'Get the wrong man? Again?'

'I don't know, Maggie. I don't think so. I didn't get any pleasure from this whole debacle. I'd rather Vincent Hatton was innocent, but it's not up to me, or you, to establish that. Let's leave it to the police.'

I agreed. This wasn't one of those cases where you'd really want the culprit brought to justice. The old man had suffered enough. Cordelia had been an utter bitch with more enemies than anyone could count. Hatton had done all of them a favour. Trying to drug me was probably a temporary lapse in judgment due to panic. Punishing him felt wrong. Frankly, I would have stayed out of it if I had only known that Hywel would be released without my intervention. Too late. I tipped my head back and closed my eyes. I was knackered. Thoughts of Vincent's dead son and his orphaned grandchildren stabbed my eyes and I welled up. I felt nausea building up in my throat. My head wanted to roll off my neck and hide under the seat, or better yet, in the boot. I wanted to follow it, but my trunk was in the boot and that left no room for either me or my head, certainly not both of us.

We didn't speak for the rest of the journey. We had a couple of hours driving in the torrential rain. Samuel had to concentrate. Vicious gusts of wind pushed gallons of water and other debris head-on at the windscreen. The wipers were going berserk on maximum speed, but achieved little. Before we left Southampton, we were told we would be heading into the eye of a storm. It had one of those innocent names, Kieran or Kailey, but you would come to regret it if you underestimated its evil intentions. If I were one of those meteorological people who christened hurricanes, I'd have called this one Beelzebub or Lucifer. That would reflect its true personality. I wondered how all the Kierans, or Kaileys, out there felt being namesakes with such a monstrosity. My well-proportioned trunk (which I might add was master-crafted in Britain) ensured that Samuel's Jag remained firmly on the highway, despite the tornado. Samuel now owed me a debt of gratitude, I concluded.

Pondering the weather, I fell asleep. I must have fallen asleep for, to my surprise, upon opening my eyes I saw the façade of Priest's Hole. Home, sweet home!

The security lights came on and Deirdre appeared on the doorstep. She wasn't dressed for the weather but seemed hell-bent on braving it. She leapt over a puddle and headed towards us, putting up a valiant fight against her umbrella. The umbrella fought back. Deirdre succeeded at opening it against all the odds but that was when the umbrella came to life and began flitting about, tugging and pulling at her hand. It would not stay still over the old lady's head to protect her elaborately set hair. By the time Deirdre made it to the car, her hair was set no longer. She had the look of the dragged-through-a-hedge-backwards variety.

'Mother, go back inside!' Samuel shouted over the howling wind. He snatched the umbrella out of her hand and folded it. He shoved Deirdre towards the house, politely but firmly. Looking over his shoulder, he told me to follow and to just leave my trunk in the half-open boot of his car.

I nodded. After all, my trunk was seaworthy so it was bound to be waterproof. I wasn't so sure about Samuel's Jag, especially if it was to be left open for the night. I got out of the car only to have the door wrenched from my hand and hurled back at me with great force. The top edge caught my cheekbone. It felt like a kung-fu kick. That storm was not Kieran, and definitely not Kailey – it was Devil himself. Or, judging by that high kick to my face, Bruce Lee reincarnated.

Inside the house was warm and quiet. We went straight to the kitchen – the safest place in any house, and properly stocked.

Deirdre had thousands of questions to ask,

all at once. Why were we late? How was the cruise? Why didn't we send any postcards? And finally: were congratulations in order?

'Congratulations?' I repeated. 'If the fact of me being still alive counts, then yes.'

'That's not what I mean, dear.' Deirdre took hold of my hands and inspected them. She squinted with disappointment and looked sharply at Samuel. 'Well?'

'I didn't get down to it,' he said mysteriously. Their faces dropped in synchronicity. Were those two talking in riddles or was I sliding into concussion?

'I'll talk to you later.' Deirdre lanced her son with a pointed glower.

'You've no idea what happened on that cursed cruise,' Samuel tried to deflect the blow. 'Maggie wasn't joking – someone tried to kill her. Two bodies … Well, firstly the ship received a distress call from a fishing boat—'

'It all started with the distress call,' I observed. 'If it wasn't for that and what followed, the murder wouldn't have happened. It was opportunistic, you see—'

'Right, you two, you can tell me about it later.' Deirdre interrupted. She toddled towards the oven and opened the door. A delicious aroma filled the kitchen. 'I've been keeping the blinking duck warm since lunchtime. It'll taste like wood shavings now, I'm afraid. It's your own fault – if you'd only called to tell me you were running late … Oh well, at least the Rum & Raisin Extravaganza fudge should make up for the lame duck.' She winked at me.

Deirdre had gone to the trouble of purchasing the life-saving delicacy. For me! She must have trudged through the flooded streets of Bishops, chancing the howling wind and the piercing cold to get it. Just the thought of it made my knees buckle under me. I may be an orphan, and trust me even at my age you never stop feeling abandoned and alone, but I couldn't remember the last time when I felt more loved. Emotions rose to my throat and gave in to an outpouring of … hm, I don't know what it was, but it shook me to the core.

Deirdre and Samuel started fussing over me. Samuel swept me off my feet (I was already falling so all he actually did was to catch me) and carried me to the sofa. In the better light of the living room, Deirdre noticed the cut on my cheek from when the car door had slammed into me. I didn't realise how bad it was.

'Lord Almighty!' She cried. 'I can see what you mean. Someone did try to kill you. My poor child! That looks nasty. Samuel, call an ambulance.'

I touched my face and found blood on my fingertips. I was as shocked as she was. And so was Samuel. He knelt by me, his face a picture of a thousand words. There was concern, fear, tenderness, anxiety and just about every emotion written on it.

'Don't call them. It's only the door. The car, the wind ...' I tried to explain, but I couldn't make myself coherent. I was in pieces. I curled into a small ball on the sofa and released the sobs I had been keeping locked inside me. I didn't even know they were there. I was crying, but not despairing. I felt safe, and loved, and looked after. And perhaps because of that I had no qualms letting it rip in front of the two people who wouldn't judge me.

Deirdre handed me a piece of fudge and I sucked on it like a distraught toddler would on its thumb.

CHAPTER 32

In Maggie's lounge an assortment of friends had gathered, most of them members of Bishops AA. They were waiting for Edgar's verdict. Vera's face was longer than it had ever been. By her feet, Rumpole sat equally worried. Despite the inviting warm rug under his paws, he could not settle down to rest. Cherie was pacing the room. She weaved between the window and the mantelpiece, with her hands bound behind her back, thinking dark thoughts. She had the air of Napoleon Bonaparte in exile on St Helena. Mary and Dan huddled together on the settee, holding hands. Mary was close to tears. Dan was fuming. That was his trademark answer to all adversity.

'She should've never gone on that cruise! Whosever's daft idea was that!' He declared, addressing a damning glare at Samuel.

'Hers, actually,' Samuel retorted but even though it was the truth he considered himself solely responsible. He was in no mood for a fight, not with Dan, not with anyone other than himself.

'Gentlemen,' Vicar Magnebu bellowed above them in his best preacher voice. 'We should not bicker amongst ourselves, or seek scapegoats, or blame one another, or point fingers!' These were all one and the same thing, but Quentin Magnebu was possessed of a flowery style of speech of which he was proud and which he found highly effective in getting his message across. 'Our Lord uttered these words, *He that is without sin among you, let him first cast a stone at her*. Is there anyone here without sin?'

Shifty looks were exchanged. Nobody had the faintest idea what the Vicar was getting at, but he certainly made everyone feel guilty.

'Sorry,' Dan mumbled.

Vanessa laced her plump fingers together and sighed, 'Dear Maggie – that it has befallen her of all people ...'

'To live in fear for her life for days on end, trapped on that damned ship! It would've sent the strongest of men absolutely mental,' James Weston-Jones illustrated Vanessa's point from a masculine perspective.

'Never mind the strongest of men. We're talking Maggie here,' Vera added. 'She's always been, um ... fragile that way.'

They all nodded, united in their concern. Maggie seemed to have suffered some sort of breakdown. She had been crying non-stop since her return to Bishops, gorging on an endless supply of Rum & Raisin Extravaganza and refusing to leave her bedroom.

Edgar came downstairs and joined the gathering in the lounge. Everyone's eyes were on him. He had just examined Maggie. Although he had checked her pulse, it hadn't been a physical examination *sensu stricto*, he had stipulated that from the outset. Edgar Flynn wasn't a general practitioner. He was a doctor of psychiatry.

'And?' Deirdre rounded on him.

Being the centre of attention didn't happen often to Edgar so he milked the moment. He poured himself a glass of water and drank it judiciously, pausing a couple of times to run his tongue over his lips.

'My mouth's dry,' was his first utterance.

They waited as he finished rehydrating, took off his thick-rimmed glasses and wiped them thoroughly with his handkerchief. Then he spoke.

'Yes, she has the hallmarks of mild PTSD.'

'The post-dramatic stress disease? You can't be serious!' Deirdre shrieked, disbelieving. That made Rumpole bristle with agitation. He heaved himself up and left the room to go to sleep on the doormat in the hallway.

'Post-*traumatic*, and it's a disorder, not a disease,' Edgar said. 'She'll need lots of tender loving care and reassurance. She may get better with time, but I'd recommend a series of therapy sessions to expedite the process. Whatever suppressed memories lurk in the depths of her mind have to be brought to light and addressed.'

'Suppressed memories? You reckon she's blocked some of her memories?'

'She may well have done so. I can tap into them. What do you say I pencil in a few sessions with her?'

Everyone agreed that it was a grand idea. Vera was happy to chip in to cover the therapy costs, and others reached for their wallets, but Edgar would have none of it. Maggie was his close friend too, he insisted, and he would help her free of charge. He had already started on his case notes, as it happened, and had a way forward planned broadly for his new *pro bono* patient.

Just as tea with cake was served by the ever-resourceful Deirdre, a stampede occurred on the stairs and down tumbled Maggie.

She was dressed – partially. She had thrown a stripy turtleneck jumper over her floral pyjamas. Her hair bore no description, but she looked perky – even bushy tailed. She glanced at the table laden with fresh cake. The box of Jaffa cakes did not escape her notice. She pounced on those and grabbed herself a pair.

'You weren't planning on having this party without me, were you?' She was munching on her Jaffa cake speedily, rotating it in her hands and nibbling at the edges like a busy little squirrel. That went well with her overall bushy-tailed appearance, Sam reflected with cautious optimism.

'Are you feeling all right, darling?' Vera inquired.

'Couldn't be better!'

'We thought you were a little … under the weather.'

'Don't get me started on the weather! It's worse than Judgment Day around here!' Maggie finished her first Jaffa, and attacked the second one. 'Anyway, I'm absolutely fine. I just needed a good-night's sleep. And the cakes won't go amiss, either. Who's having tea with me?'

Several weeks into Maggie's miraculous recovery, she was visiting Sam and Deirdre, and scouring the internet with Sam for reliable Finnish sauna providers. An agreement had been reached that a steaming hot sauna room would be installed in a purpose-built log cabin in the garden of Badger's Hall. Maggie noted with delight that the existing family of three birches would be an invaluable source of whipping whisks. Sam winced at the memory of his stinging legs, but welcomed the proposal. He had already acquired a pair of loose cotton boxers and had been practising sit-ups every morning to enhance his six-pack which at the moment was five packs short of the full rack.

Deirdre lamented over coronavirus and the

rapidly diminishing supply of toilet paper in Sexton's Canning supermarkets. She had been doing her weekly shop on Saturday and ventured into every superstore but was unable to cross the loo paper off her list. 'If this continues, we'll have to resort to recycling The Daily Mail.'

'You don't even read The Daily Mail,' Sam observed.

'I'll have to start then: give it a skim-read and then, you know, reuse it.'

'But you already subscribe to The Guardian,' Sam persisted. 'You may as well—'

'I wouldn't dream of using The Guardian in the loo,' Deirdre's face flushed crimson, 'What a preposterous idea!'

'I hear that hand sanitisers are also depleted,' Maggie said to end the newspaper debacle.

'That's all the same to me. I don't use them. What's wrong with soap and water, I ask?'

Maggie beamed at Sam. 'Do you realise, Samuel, how lucky we were to have gone on that cruise when we did?'

'I wouldn't put that cruise and luck in the same sentence.' Sam frowned at the memory.

'But if we had gone just a few weeks later, we may have ended up locked in our cabins, enduring quarantine like those poor people on The Grand Princess.'

'And dropping like flies!' Deirdre rolled her eyes.

Maggie's phone rang its bizarre, but

strangely fitting, apocalyptic tune. She answered it. Slowly as she listened, her face grew wider and wider in a huge smile. Finally, she blurted out, 'That's great news! Of course we'll be there. And, oh my, congratulations.'

She rung off and gazed at Sam with rounded eyes. 'Guess who it was!'

Sam mumbled his wild guesses: Her Royal Highness the Queen? Dalai Lama?

Maggie squinted her disapproval and said, 'It was Ollie!'

'As in Oliver Conti Lang?'

'Precisely. He and Emilia have just moved into Forget-Me-Not. They got married last week – in blinking Vegas!'

'Blimey, there's no business like showbusiness, I say,' said Deirdre.

'And they invited us for dinner tomorrow, at six-thirty.' Maggie peered apologetically at Deirdre. 'Just Samuel and me, sorry.'

'Why would they be inviting me? They don't know me from Adam.' Deirdre shrugged and turned on the TV for the latest news on the toilet paper rationing.

Oliver moving back to Bishops Well followed naturally from the fact that he used to live here with his mother and had now inherited the Forget-Me-Not estate. However, Sam wasn't happy about this development. He would much prefer it if Conti Lang Junior had sold the house and taken himself and his new in-laws elsewhere. In spite, or perhaps because, of what Sam knew about the dubious reputation of Benedict Raw-blinking-botham, he was feeling insecure around that man. The thieving swine used to be Maggie's lover, shared her bed at night, and maybe planned his future together with her. Even now, who was to say that he wasn't concocting schemes to win her back? That didn't sit well with Sam's own plans for and Maggie and himself.

To Sam's horror, when they arrived at Forget-Me-Not at six-thirty on Monday, Count Dracula was already there. And it seemed he was there to stay.

It didn't help matters that Maggie looked particularly stunning that evening. She must have raided her seaworthy trunk for she was wearing yet another brand-new gown (which she hadn't had the chance to showcase on the cruise). It was a glittering black mini-dress which exhibited Maggie's shapely legs in all their loveliness. As much as Sam relished the look, he didn't want Rawbotham to enjoy it too. In his quietly raging jealousy, Sam stood behind Maggie, chewing his bottom lip and eyeing his rival with distaste.

Effusive greetings and hugs followed their arrival at Forget-Me-Not. Emilia and Ollie seemed over the moon to see Maggie and Sam, and were apparently looking forward to being their – several times removed – neighbours. Even Hywel decided to let bygones be bygones and embraced them.

'I'm ever so sorry about your … arrest,' Sam muttered sheepishly when he shook hands with Hywel.

'Don't worry, mate!' Hywel slapped Sam's back. 'I don't think about it. You did what you thought was right. It was a close call for Maggie. I would've done the same if I thought Stacey's life was in danger. I know how much you care about Maggie – we all do!'

Maggie produced a quizzical look – she was the only one who had no idea how Sam felt about her. Rawbotham caught Sam's eye and smirked in his typical slimy fashion. Sam wished he could do something to wipe that smirk from the man's face without having to have to go jail for it. He would have to think of a way. For now, he shook Rawbotham's cold hand. It was like holding a dead fish.

'Good to see you, Benedict.' He nearly choked on that sentence. 'Visiting for a few days?'

Dracula's toothy smirk widened to a full-blown grin. 'I've moved in with them permanently. At Emilia and Ollie's insistence. It's a big house after all.' He kissed his daughter's forehead with mock tenderness – at least Sam judged it to be mock. 'It's high time to put cruises behind me. I'm too old for that. I'm contemplating starting a small enterprise –

magician-slash-entertainer, that sort of thing. Kiddies' birthday parties, and so on. I think there's money in it.'

There's money in everything you touch with your sticky fingers, Sam mused bitterly. He could feel misery creeping into his veins. Maggie was again at risk of being snatched from under his nose.

They were shown to the dining room, the same dining room where only a few years ago Richard Ruta had collapsed after being poisoned. He had been Sam's good friend. The memories of that day flooded back. Sam's unease grew by the minute.

Meantime Maggie was thriving. She discovered a middle-aged woman with an electric-grey mass of shoulder-length hair, and threw herself into her arms.

'Sabine! My God, it's been ages!'

'Maggie, darling!'

The two women embraced most cordially and kissed on both cheeks.

'What are you doing here? A family friend? I had no idea you knew the Contis,' Maggie blathered. 'Samuel, this is Vera's cousin, Sabine. She lives in Parson's Combe.'

Sam offered a friendly *how-do-you-do* and Sabine responded with a wink and an oblique comment, 'So I meet you at last – Maggie's mystery man ...'

'My neighbour, actually,' Maggie hastened to

clarify.

'And her neighbour?' Sabine smirked. 'Great to meet you. Who would've thought we'd bump into each other here! It's such a small world.'

Sam responded with a bewildered *pleased-to-meet-you*. He mentally placed Sabine in the same league as Maggie. She had an exulted and effusive manner about her, but at the same time seemed as sharp as a razor and spoke what was on her mind without regard for conventions. Her dress taste was a cross between a Mayan priestess and the bag lady.

Oliver stepped in to answer Maggie's question. 'Emilia and I invited Sabine. We decided to make a small donation to her retreat. As soon as the probate is complete.'

'Small?' Sabine chirped. 'A mere three million pounds sterling, darling!'

'Oh my!' Maggie cried.

'A retreat? What sort of retreat?' Rawbotham looked surprised. It was a gratifying consolation that he wasn't in on the plan.

'It's a spiritual retreat for people who need to take stock of their lives – a halfway house for victims of domestic abuse, recovering alcoholics and drug addicts,' Ollie explained.

'The sort of place my mother could've done with,' Emilia said in a small voice. She raised her eyes to her father, addressing him directly, 'My mother was an addict and died of an overdose.'

'You know?' Rawbotham stared, nonplussed.

And so did Maggie, Sam observed. Both were shocked, and it didn't appear that they were shocked to discover that Emilia's mother had been a drug addict, but that Emilia knew about it.

'I know now,' Emilia nodded. 'I found out a year ago. Ollie was recovering from his addiction – we took all the help we could get. We met this guy – he works for The Samaritans. We chatted about this and that, and it turned out that he knew mum. He told me about her because – apparently – she never stopped thinking of me. She'd been desperate to find me, but Dad had hid me away so efficiently …' Emilia folded her hands over Benedict's to stop his from shaking. 'I don't blame you for keeping it from me, Dad. I understand you wanted to spare me the shame – and the pain of knowing my mother was a junkie. It's no reflection on you. I'm fine with it.'

Yet another lie you told your daughter. First, the locket, now this, Sam mused savagely.

'So yes,' Ollie summed it up neatly, 'we decided that if we couldn't help Emilia's mother we would help other addicts, and let's face it, my mother's ill-gained dosh needs to be redistributed. Not that she'd approve.' He gave a loud guffaw, but a false note rang in it. It must have hurt knowing his mother had destroyed so many lives to make her fortune, and that his inheritance was tainted. 'I feel like a bloody Robin Hood,' he added.

Everyone was impressed. Maggie buzzed,

'You'll definitely make up for your mother's sins, Ollie. How exciting! Wait till I tell Vera. Please don't tell her, Sabine. Let me do that.' Maggie relished being the bearer of good news, or any news for that matter.

Ollie was happy to accede to Maggie's request. Emilia offered aperitifs, and Ollie went about helping her with that. Maggie leant into Sam and whispered, 'What is she still doing here?'

'Who?' he whispered back.

'Cordelia!' There was an exclamation mark in Maggie's hush response. 'I thought we put her to bed – in a manner of speech – when we exposed Hatton for her murder.'

'Perhaps she has other unfinished business on this earth,' Sam speculated helpfully.

'Or maybe we were wrong. Again.'

Soon after they sat down to dinner, Sam asked Oliver about any new developments in the murder investigation. If anyone knew, it would be Ollie who, as the next of kin, was being kept up-to-date by the police.

'Oh yes! You won't believe it,' Emilia said. 'Vincent Hatton's off the hook.'

'Out on bail?' Sam thought that to be the only reasonable interpretation of her statement.

'No, not on bail. The charges have been dropped against him. Tell them, Ollie.'

'It's true. The night of my mother's murder

– all night – they have Mr Hatton on CCTV, either with the ship's captain or some other crew member. The captain and Mr Hatton were coordinating the search for that escaped man who held you hostage, Maggie—'

'Alvar.'

'Yes, him. So, the search was going on all day and all night. They were keen to find him before they'd have to break the news of the other man's death to the guests. Mr Hatton's movements could be traced throughout the night. At no time did he come anywhere near my mother's cabin.'

'That's great!' Maggie chirped away. 'I'm so pleased for Vince. I always knew he couldn't have done it. He was such a gentleman, wasn't he? I guess we got it wrong again, Samuel, just like he told us. In fact, I've only just suggested the very same thing to Samuel.'

'Oh? What was that?' Rowbotham inquired.

'That we had the wrong man. We must write to Vince to apologise. Oh, what a relief it must be for his family!'

'All is well that ends well,' Sabine commented.

Sam wasn't relieved in the least. He froze, injected with sudden dread.

'But that means the murderer is still out there.'

CHAPTER 33

Just as Edgar Flynn was leaving Maggie's house after their first therapy session, DI Gillian Marsh arrived. They ran into each other on the doorstep.

'Has Miss Kaye commissioned you for criminal profiling of herself or of someone else?' She shot from the hip in her habitually brusque manner. No greetings, no manners whatsoever.

Edgar's first impulse was to raise his eyebrows and shake his head with dismay. But he held his tongue. He was a freelance profiler for Sexton's CID. His income depended largely on the irascible Marsh. He was also good friends with Michael Almond, her long suffering boyfriend whose motives for dating the woman remained a mystery even to an experienced psychiatrist like Edgar. He replied in a civil way, 'I can't tell you that, Gillian – professional privilege.'

'So, the woman needs a psychiatrist after all. I always suspected that may be the case.'

Edgar ignored the remark. 'And what brings you here?' he inquired politely not expecting any constructive answers.

And he didn't get any.

'I can't tell you that, Edgar, but it isn't a social visit.'

'I didn't think it was.'

They parted ways: Gillian charged into Maggie's house; Edgar proceeded to visit Sam next door by prior arrangement. Sam was dead keen to know if Maggie had remembered anything new, which naturally Edgar wouldn't be revealing to him without Maggie's consent. A nice cup of tea and a social chat with a friend would however be welcome before Edgar drove home to spend the rest of the day – and his life – with his mother. Edgar was what one would refer to as a *confirmed bachelor.* But then who needed a wife where a mother could do. Edgar refused to consider any Freudian implication of his elected lifestyle choices.

DI Marsh barged into Maggie's living room just as Maggie switched on the telly to indulge in daytime TV. Edgar had scrambled her brains and she needed to unwind and recover her wits. The arrival of DI Marsh would not be conducive to that process. The mere sight of her sent a cold shiver down Maggie's spine and threw her mind into even more turmoil.

'DI Marsh!' Maggie recoiled. 'What have I

done now? If it's anything to do with that unfortunate kerb parking, I've already paid the fine. I'm not contesting it.'

'Your parking or driving offences are of no interest to me, unless of course they result in fatalities.' Marsh pinched her lips and added, 'Which I wouldn't put past you.'

Maggie was puzzled, but hospitable. 'May I offer you a cup of tea? I even have coffee. And I could find some biscuits, I'm sure. Would you like some?'

After a short internal battle, Gillian Marsh surrendered and accepted the offer of coffee and the *rest of it*, as she put it. When Maggie returned from the kitchen, bearing the sustenance, Marsh got straight to the point.

'This is concerning the attempt on your life,' she started and with her mouth full muttered under her breath, 'Why didn't it surprise me ...'

'Oh, that ...' It wasn't a memory Maggie wished to re-live – and re-*living* it bore a particularly sinister meaning in this context – but she was curious as to what new developments may have transpired since she disembarked from the ship.

'So, the Russian authorities have now shared with us the toxicity report on the substance found in your bloodstream. Pink.'

'Pink? As in the singer – Pink?' Maggie blinked.

'Yes, Pink – an opioid counterfeit of

Oxycontin.'

'Oxy- con- tin,' Maggie continued to blink. She had long left her comfort zone. Whatever it was, it sounded evil.

'Yes. A particularly nasty version, with traces of fentanyl thrown in for good measure. It's a small miracle you survived.'

'Well, there you go. Who would've thought – someone going to all that trouble – especially for me. Well, not exactly *for me* but to ... to kill me, rather.' Maggie was thoroughly unsettled and close to tears. Again! She wanted Marsh gone so that she could crawl back to bed and turn off the lights. She was prepared to forsake daytime TV. 'Thank you for stopping by to let me know, Miss Marsh.'

'That's not all. I didn't come here just to inform you. I could've sent a lower-ranking officer to do that.' Marsh still sounded curt but she was looking at Maggie with a hint of sympathy. 'I came to let you know that I've taken over the investigation into your attempted murder. I'm not planning to let whoever it was that tried to kill you get away with it.'

'Thank you, you're very kind,' Maggie mumbled.

'It's not out of kindness,' DI Marsh grimaced. 'Anyway, I had the ship searched from top to bottom, sniffer dogs and all. We found a stash of Pink disguised as quinine tablets in the medical bay. The same composition, same batch as the drug used to – you know – on you.'

'It was left on the ship?'

'The perpetrator didn't want to risk taking the stash off the ship in case they were searched on arrival in Southampton. They played it safe. No fingerprints so evidently they expected us to find it. They won't be coming back for it.'

'Could the drug have been brought on board by the smugglers – the people we rescued?' It seemed like a logical guess.

'No. I had Alvar re-interviewed. They had thrown their cargo overboard. All of it, and to his knowledge, they did not carry Pink.'

'So it was somebody from the ship – a passenger or more likely a crew member?'

'Yes, one of the crew. Alvar has a faint recollection of seeing a man, not any of the medics, but another person. He says he thought it was Nedim. The man looked like Nedim: slim built, average height, dark hair. Alvar thought Nedim followed him down the corridor after the fight. But it can't have been Nedim. Nedim was dead within seconds of Alvar opening his carotid artery. He couldn't have followed anyone. So there was someone else there. Alvar ran away and didn't take a good look at him, sadly. We're stuck on this one. Alvar's description is vague. Maybe he didn't even see anyone – just imagined Nedim in pursuit of him.'

'But if there was someone—'

'It could've been our man. It was a man. That

much Alvar was sure of.'

'It could be the person who found Nedim's body, couldn't it?'

'Nedim's body was found the next morning. By a medic who doesn't resemble Nedim in the slightest. A large Scotsman with a copper-red beard. Our man was cleanshaven, wiry and swarthy. Anyway,' DI Marsh finished the rest of her coffee in a quick swig. 'I'll keep you posted on my progress. If you remember anything, get in touch. Otherwise, you don't have to do anything. In fact, I strongly advise you to do nothing.'

She left.

Maggie sat numb for a few minutes. Her body was ossified. Her brains were even more scrambled now than they were before. Deep down she had been harbouring the notion that perhaps no one intended to spike her drink in St Petersburg, that perhaps she was an accidental casualty caught in the crossfire of some Russian gang war, that her G&T had got mixed up with somebody else's. But now, she couldn't deny the facts any longer. She needed comfort. She needed brain food. She needed to stock up on Jaffas and Rum & Raisin Extravaganza. Coincidentally, it was Thursday – Bishops Well's market day since the time the dinosaurs ruled the earth. Kev and Jane Wilcox would have their pink-and-cream stall erected in the town square, selling the best fudge on the planet. Provided of course, Maggie reflected with growing trepidation, that the market wasn't cancelled due to the coronavirus outbreak. That would be the end of Maggie Kaye – a strangling lockdown without fudge or Jaffa cakes in the pantry. Sudden death! If only her intended killer had thought of that, he would have succeeded.

She dressed hurriedly in suitable winter clothing and ran into town.

Sam was entertaining Edgar in his study which overlooked the shared driveway. Idle chat aside, Sam was deploying his well-practised witness cross-examination tactics to extract from Edgar everything he had so far elicited from Maggie.

An experienced psychiatrist and nobody's fool, Edgar was a hard nut to crack. He knew the constraints of doctor-patient confidentiality, and wasn't letting much out. He skilfully – and annoyingly – kept the conversation on a superficial level.

'There're always benefits, Sam. Introspection is something we should all engage in regularly. I'd compare it to your daily hygiene rituals, like brushing your teeth or combing your hair. Only this is your mental hygiene. I do it every day in the morning, after my stretching exercising – I adopt the lotus position and meditate. It does me a world of good. Emotional stability. A fresh perspective on life …'

Sam was close to nodding off. It was probably intentional on Edgar's part to lull him into submission. The droning of Edgar's voice was soothing. It was possible that Edgar was hypnotising him, but Sam had no strength to fight back. He began to surrender.

'Sandwiches are on the table,' Deirdre's voice pierced the nirvana. She stuck her head in the door, followed closely by the aroma of baking. 'And the scones are in the oven. Come on, then, you can't sit here sipping tea all day!'

Edgar appeared startled. Sam was positively discombobulated. His mother had the knack for a dramatic entrance.

'You two look like rabbits in the headlights!' Deirdre observed, bemused. 'And by the way, Edgar, what did you find out from Maggie? Did she remember anything new? Go on, tell us!'

Edgar straightened his posture like a schoolboy on encountering the headmistress. He said, 'No, nothing yet, but I think we're getting there. She's beginning to relax. Another two or three sessions, and we will break through to her deep subconsciousness.'

'Keep working on it.'

At that very moment, Sam heard Maggie's front door slam. He peeked through the window. Armed with her *Teachers are Good!* jute bag, Maggie was obviously heading for the market. It was a great sign to see her return to her usual routines.

An hour later, standing on the doorstep, Edgar was thanking Deirdre and Sam for their hospitality and for the doggy bag of fruit scones for his mother. 'She'll be delighted – she loves a cream tea. As much as the doctors tell her to lay off the cream – it sends her cholesterol through the roof – she just can't resist it.'

'We all have to die of something – we may as well enjoy it while we're at it.' Deirdre wasn't one to take doctors seriously. She had survived the war and rationing without once having to see a quack. She had given birth at home between breakfast and lunchtime, and when she was finally forced to visit a GP it was only to be threatened with being at high risk of having a stroke or heart attack. So be it, she thought, I'll take my chances – I've had a good innings anyway. And that was the last time her foot crossed the threshold of a doctor's surgery.

Maggie burst into the driveway and, head down like a charging rhino, disappeared inside her house. Unsurprisingly, she didn't even have to pause to find her key under the terracotta pot – she had left the door unlocked. Sam despaired. She had learned nothing.

Sam saw Edgar off and they agreed to meet at the rugby clubhouse the next day when Bishops Well were playing the Harlequins. James and Michael would be there too. They could stay on for bangers and mash and a pint after the match. They had a lot of catching up to do. In fact, Sam had a few queries of forensic nature to raise with Michael, not to mention how curious he was to find out about the reason for DI Marsh's flying visit to see Maggie.

Before Edgar put his key in the ignition, Maggie shot past them. Again, she didn't even look up to say hello. She appeared seriously distracted.

CHAPTER 34

Maggie's Journal

I was in luck. The Thursday market was up and running. The crowds were on the thin side however, but that could be on account of the gusty wind and spells of rain rather than the invisible microbe. Adversity of all shapes and sizes notwithstanding, Jane and Kev Wilcox were there and so was their legendary fudge. I didn't even have to queue. They were both there to serve me.

'The usual, Maggie?' Kev asked.

'Yes, but I may as well stock up. Let's make it a pound of Rum and Raisin.'

'Why don't we?' Kev grinned and in his usual style flung twice as much on the scales, and tied the box nicely for me with a pink ribbon.

'How are you coping, Maggie?' Jane peered at me anxiously. Her slim face was crestfallen.

'Just fine, thank you, my darling.'

'You don't have to pretend in front of us, dear. We've heard.'

'What bastard, excuse my French, would want to bump off such a lovely lady as yourself!' Kev was incensed.

'Oh that!' I waved my hand dismissively. 'It's nothing! The police are looking into it.'

'So it can't be nothing then.'

'Well …' I conceded the point.

'Why don't you try our salted caramel toffee. New recipe!' Kev shoved under my nose a seductive looking piece of toffee on a silver cake slicer.

'Don't mind if I do.' I took the piece. It tasted divine, so I decided to buy half a pound. I always make the effort to try new things in life, though buying toffee can't really be classified as an effort.

'That'll be on the house. Take care, Maggie.'

As the longstanding Bishopian tradition has it, after my market errands, I pop into The Old Stables for refreshments. Vera and Rumpole were already there having a toasted teacake with butter – well, Vera was having it, Rumpole was catching crumbs. Soon Mary joined us. She had some news – she had been headhunted to teach makeup artistry at the Sexton's branch of Wiltshire College. She wanted a few tips from me about handling teenagers. I told her a few horror stories based on my real-life upheavals with Thomas Moore amongst others. *Forewarned is forearmed* is my motto. Mary's enthusiasm seemed to be fading by the minute. I advised her to just be herself – nobody would dream of upsetting such a sweet, gentle lady as her. Then, I thought twice about what I had just said and remembered the exact same words Kev had uttered in relation to me. It's a cruel world we live in, I concluded glumly. Vera agreed.

We promptly changed the subject and began to wonder where Vanessa was. She always joins us for tea and cake at The Old Stables on Thursdays. We didn't have to wonder for long. Vanessa burst into the café, looking haunted. She didn't even stop at the counter to order anything before she swooped upon our table. She collapsed into a chair, breathless.

'You won't believe this! It's Oliver Conti Lang! Alec and I saw an ambulance heading their way – literally forty-five minutes ago,' Vanessa paused for breath. She inhaled deeply, clutching her chest.

'To Forget-Me-Not?' I asked. If anyone could witness any strange activity at the estate it would be Vanessa and Alec Scarfe. Their converted barn house was along the same dirt road as Forget-Me-Not Hall, halfway between Bishops Well and Nortonview Farm.

'Yes. It went straight in, blue lights and all!'

'It could be for someone other than Oliver.

His father and a few other guests are staying there.'

'Oh no! It was definitely for Oliver. A drug overdose. Alec was called soon after. If it's a drug overdose, the hospital has a duty to inform the police. It was an overdose.'

'Is he dead?'

'Critical. He's fighting for his life.'

'The youth and drugs these days,' Vera sighed. 'Drugs are the scourge of this earth.'

'What made him do that?'

'Too much money, I say. A young man sitting on a fortune and not very much to do with himself, that's what it was. Bored, looking for easy thrills, etcetera, etcetera.'

'But he wouldn't take drugs!'

'Don't be naïve, Maggie. He's well into drugs. I remember when I saw him for the first time – when they moved in to Bishops: he was as high as a kite most of the time. Never touched the ground!'

'He beat his addiction over a year ago!' It didn't make sense.

'It's not that easy to beat a drug addiction, Maggie,' Vera was quick to point out. 'One mistake, one moment of weakness and you're back in its clutches.'

'Only last week he made a donation to your sister's retreat – three million pounds!'

'Sabine's got a donation? Three mills, I never!'

'Yes, I was going to tell you – I forgot! Anyway, he and Emilia gave the money away to help struggling addicts. He's been clean for over a year, and now, all of a sudden, he's taken an overdose?'

'Incomprehensible!' Mary exclaimed.

'There is no logic to addiction,' Vera declared. 'Poor boy. Let's hope he pulls through and learns something from his moment of weakness.'

Walking home, I was feeling nauseous. I couldn't believe it. Ollie suddenly succumbing to his old habit wasn't just illogical – it was incongruous with everything he had been through and the new direction his life had recently taken. *He* had recently taken. He had defeated his demons and found love. He'd reconnected with his father. He was happy with Emilia. They had great plans for the future. They were in a good place and had their whole life ahead of them – bright and wonderful. Overdosing was the most surreal – most bizarre thing to do. Admittedly, I didn't know much about the psychology of drug addiction, but—

But I could not believe he would have done it!

I don't remember how I got home. I dropped my shopping on the floor and slumped on the sofa. I couldn't think straight. I took out the box of fudge and untied the ribbon – picked my first piece of Rum & Raisin Extravaganza. Orderly thoughts began to form in my head as I bit off my first mouthful. Ollie had overdosed. It implied a deliberate act on his part. But the same had been said about me in St Petersburg – that I had overdosed. I wouldn't know how! Someone had spiked my drink. I reached for another fudge. And that was when everything became clear. It hit me like a dazzling light. I experienced a brief and sharp flashback: lights, darkness, nausea … I not only knew what happened – I remembered!

Benedict opened the door. I had been banging on it relentlessly; my knuckles turned red. He didn't look pleased to see me.

'It's not a good time, Maggie. Ollie's in hospital.'

'I know. News travels fast in Bishops.'

'They all went with him. I'm a bit behind, sorting out a few things, but I'll be on my way in a minute. Like I said, it's not a good time.'

Sorting out a few things, I shivered at the euphemism. What he meant, surely, was *covering his tracks, getting rid of evidence* – that kind of sorting.

'I don't think you'll be going to the hospital, Benny. The last person they want there by Ollie's side is you. I know you did it. I know you killed Cordelia. I know you tried to kill me, and now Ollie. You are a cold-blooded murderer, Benedict Rawbotham!'

Alarmed – an emotion even a professional

magician-cum-confidence trickster could not conceal – he ground his teeth and peered apprehensively over my shoulder.

'The police are on their way,' I said. They may have been, I crossed my fingers. I was hoping they would be sending officers to search the premises for drugs. That would be the routine procedure, right? I hoped so. Because they wouldn't be here on my instigation. I had not called them. Unwisely, as soon as it had all become clear in my head, I had rushed here to confront my former fiancé. I don't know what I was thinking. The man had already tried to kill me once. All I can say in my defence is that my emotions – my anger, my indignation, my hurt, my shame – had made me take leave of my senses.

'I know you did it, but don't know why. Why the killing spree? I totally understand that you are a thieving, dishonest and callous bastard, but murder?'

'Come inside, Maggie. You're upset. But you're wrong, I assure you. You know I couldn't have done anything of the sort. Let's talk calmly.'

'Can't you see where you went wrong?'

He shook his head, trying to appear baffled, innocent and thoroughly misunderstood.

'Just one *accidental* overdose too many! Can you see now? It made me think and it made me remember. The first time you gave it to me was that night when Cordelia was killed – when *you* killed her.'

'I didn't even know the woman—'

'Yes, you did!' *Down boy!* I wanted to scream at him, *I'm talking now!* 'I didn't put it all together at the time, but the symptoms, Benny – they were the same that night and then again when you slipped Pink into my drink in St Petersburg.'

'Pink?'

'Yes, Pink. I know it was Pink – they police told me what it was.'

'They had it analysed, of course ...' He muttered under his breath. The twitch of his jaw betrayed his panic.

'Confusion, intermittent loss of consciousness, blurred vision, weird hallucinations, losing track of time, nausea, and in the end, gaps in my memory so huge you could drive a horse and cart through them. You gave me just enough to put me out of action the first time. You didn't want me dead then. You wanted me unconscious and spaced out. I was your alibi. I thought I was plastered – just drunk, too drunk to stay awake and that's how I explained the blackout to myself.'

'You were pretty sloshed, Maggie. We both were. We both passed out.'

'No, not you. You were sober and you were busy killing Cordelia.'

'I was with you all night!'

'No, you weren't. I woke up – I needed to

puke. My stomach woke me up in the middle of the night. You weren't there. I remember now. I staggered, looking for the toilet. I couldn't see you. I asked where the toilet was, but you gave me no answer. Because you weren't there! I bumped around your cabin until I found it. I threw up and passed out again. And I forgot the whole episode – forgot that you were not there.'

'I was there, passed out – all night,' he repeated obstinately.

'You weren't. When I came to, when Emilia rushed in to tell us they'd found Cordelia dead, I saw your hair was wet. I didn't think much of it then, but now I know why – you had to shower to wash away the blood. Apparently, when you open the carotid artery the blood gets pumped out like from a fountain. You had her blood all over you so you showered.'

'It's nonsense, Maggie. Just listen to yourself!'

'That confused, floating feeling ...' It was all coming back to me. 'That's how I felt that night, on New Year's Eve in St Petersburg, when you slipped Pink into my G&T. I experienced the same confusion, distortions to my vision, mad, mad hallucinations – except that night you wanted me dead, so you gave me enough to kill me. Only I'm like an old weed – I keep getting up and coming back, Benny. You thought you'd put me behind twenty years ago, stole from me and moved on. But I came back to haunt you, Benny.

And I'm here to stay. This is my turf.'

'Utter fantasy, Maggie. You aren't making any sense. Please, listen to me—'

I wouldn't. Not anymore. Not ever again would I listen to him. I went on, 'And if you had stopped there and then, I may have never put two and two together, but you couldn't stop, could you? You went for Oliver. What did he do wrong, I wonder. What did he do to hack you off? Could it be that he decided to give his money away to some charity for junkies? His money was now your daughter's – and in your sick mind it was also yours. Am I on the right track? I can read you like a book. You like money, don't you Benny? You like money way, way too much to share it with anyone. Even if it isn't yours in the first place. So Oliver is now in hospital, fighting for his life, just like I was six weeks ago. But you know what? He'll pull through. Because he is young and strong, and Emilia is by his side. When she finds out what you did, she'll disown you. You will be as good as dead to her.'

A black shadow crossed his face and for a split second I had a glimpse of his true face: evil, hateful and cruel. The real Benedict Rawbotham, the conman. He gazed at me hard and bared his teeth in a grimace that was intended as a benevolent smile but came across as a snarl. 'Oh Maggie, Maggie... it's all in your head. Pure speculation. You've always had a rich imagination. Alas you can't prove any of it. And that's where this conversation ends.'

'Alvar saw you, Benedict! He saw you heading down the corridor towards the sick bay. He described you to the cops – slim build, dark hair, wiry.'

'That could be anyone. My hair is grey, actually. The black – that's just stage dye.'

'He'll recognise you when they show him your picture.'

'Ha!' He laughed, but it was a nervous laughter. He was losing confidence. 'So they haven't yet?'

I pressed on. I was like a bulldozer – I just wanted to level the bastard with the ground. 'They will – I'll suggest they do. And he'll identify you.'

'Right you are!'

'But if he doesn't – You see, Benny, it doesn't matter, because you as much as admitted it to me. That evening when you told me Nedim was killed with a scalpel. How did you know?'

'The crew knew and so did I.'

'They all knew Nedim was killed, but nobody knew how – with what weapon precisely. Nobody except the killer knew of the scalpel.'

He shifted uncomfortably, walked towards the window and peered through the curtains. Did he hear the sirens? Had the police arrived at long last?

Transparently not. His attention returned to me, 'And how did you work that out?'

'Alvar dropped the scalpel in the sick bay after he cut Nedim. By the time he took me hostage, he was wielding an axe. Because he'd lost the scalpel. He thought it was lying on the floor in the sick bay. And if it had still been there in the morning when Nedim's body was found, it would have been secured in evidence. But it wasn't there! Hatton and his men didn't find it. They didn't know anything about the scalpel, not until I started asking about it. And I knew about it because you told me. You – Benedict! You told me before Alvar did! That evening we were sat in the bar, before we went to your room, you told me about Nedim's death and about the scalpel. How would you have known about it if it wasn't you who had found and removed it from the scene? And then you used it to murder Cordelia Conti and to frame Alvar. One more dead body on his tab, who was counting, right?'

Benedict steepled his fingertips and pressed them to his lips. Then, with a deliberate, measured slowness he began to clap. 'What do you know? Miss Marple lives on! Well done, Maggie! I never had you as a particularly bright spark. How wrong I was! Yes, I made a stupid, stupid mistake telling you about the bloody scalpel. When I realised it—'

'You decided not to take any chances. You had to kill me before I worked it out.'

'Correct again! I was so disappointed you didn't die though. You didn't drink the whole glass. You passed out too quickly. Oh well, a lesson learned. Next time I'll be thorough. I may have to think of a different method.'

His last sentence, uttered with unperturbed calm, filled me with dread. At that point I was under no illusion that he wouldn't let me out of the house alive. I had to get him to talk until the police arrived. And I had to pray for that to happen, which was in all honestly like praying for a miracle.

'I can understand why you wanted to get rid of me, but Cordelia? What had she ever done to you?'

He sat in an armchair, propped his elbows on the arms, laced his fingers on his chest and crossed his legs elegantly. He was relaxed. He must have realised that the cops weren't coming. They would have been here by now. He may have made a big mistake telling me about the scalpel, but I had made a stupendous one by coming here on my own and without any backup.

'Ah, that bitch! She demanded to have a word with Emilia. She was fuming over her and Ollie. I said she'd have to talk to me first – I was the girl's father. She laughed. I don't take kindly to people taking the piss out of me. She called my daughter all sorts: a whore, a gold digger … No one insults my child and gets away with it. She offered me money to keep Emilia away from Oliver. I refused – would you believe it? I, Benedict Rawbotham, rejected a bribe. A hundred thousand bob!' He smiled, amused. 'Of course, I rejected it. Emilia stood to get ten times – a hundred times – more than that. I told Cordelia to go to hell. She threatened me. Said she'd dig up every possible dirt on me and Emilia, and destroy us. No dirt to be found on Emilia, but me ... That was a different proposition altogether. I had to take the old bag seriously. When I saw that dead man in the sick bay and that scalpel next to him, well ... I had my solution to the Cordelia Conti Lang problem. That boy already had one person on his conscience. What difference would another body make?'

'So you framed him.'

'He walked into the trap by himself. Ran into it, to be exact. I saw him fleeing from the sick bay, covered in blood. Perfect!'

'What were you doing there in the night?'

'In the sick bay? Well, let's say I was feeling sick,' he laughed.

'Or is that where you kept your supplies of Pink. In plain view, so to speak?'

'What better place?' He scrutinised me with renewed interest. 'You're not as stupid as you make yourself out to be, love.'

'So you've been dealing on the ship.'

'A small sideline – pocket money, really.'

'After Emilia's mother died of an overdose!' I could see no limit to that man's depravity.

'Who do you think had started her on drugs in the first place?'

He was a monster. I despised him.

He rose from his chair and headed for the bar. There he poured a couple of drinks, added some ice and stirred. He carried them across the room, handed one of them to me. 'Let's have a G&T for old times' sake.'

I shook my head and backed into the sofa. 'I'm not accepting a drink from you. It's probably laced with rat poison, or worse!'

He shrugged and put his own glass on the table. 'Very wise, Maggie. In that case, we'll have to try something different. Something less elegant.'

He approached the window again, but this time he didn't look out. Instead, he pulled a cord from the curtains and started towards me, weaving the cord menacingly over his closed fist.

I pressed my back into the sofa, but there was no escape. He leaned over me, wrapped the cord around my neck and pulled. I should be fighting him, but my hands instinctively went towards the cord, scrambling without success to loosen it. My eyes bulged and my throat spasmed as, suddenly, his whole body jerked back and slumped onto me like a felled log.

CHAPTER 35

Sam lifted his hand to wave goodbye. He did it automatically but he wasn't looking at Edgar's car as it exited onto the road. He was watching Maggie's doubled up figure diving off the driveway with extreme urgency. She didn't even glance in his direction.

Sam stood hapless for a while, staring, until Maggie disappeared round the bend. He dragged his feet home, feeling unwanted and bothered.

'Where on earth was Maggie rushing off to? She's only just come back from the market.' His mother was waiting in the doorway, her arms folded on her stomach. She too had her reservations about Maggie's behaviour which was more bizarre than normal.

'I've no idea. She hasn't said a word to me all day.'

'Don't you think you should follow her? God knows what trouble she's going to get herself into in the state she's in. Didn't Edgar say she was on the verge of doing something stupid?'

'He said she was on the verge of remembering.'

'Splitting hairs!' Deirdre fixed her son with a stern glare. 'Well, are you going to go and check on her or do I have to put my coat on?'

Hurrying along the High Street, Sam wondered where to from here. The stalls in the Market Square were being dismantled and the commotion of traders and last-minute buyers was in its final throes. Sam searched for Maggie. His educated guess was that she had forgotten to get something vital to her staple diet – more fudge? – and returned for it before the market closed. That would explain the urgency of her step and her failure to acknowledge him. Fudge meant a lot to Maggie.

Sam approached Kev Wilcox, Maggie's sole fudge supplier.

'Have you seen Maggie, Kev?'

'Yeah, over an hour ago. She's been round getting fudge. And some toffee too. Our new recipe. Would you like to—'

'Thanks Kev, but not right this minute. I need to find Maggie. Haven't you seen her in, say, the last ten minutes?'

Kev shook his head, slightly disappointed by Sam's snub of his offer of toffee. Jane however came over to save the day. 'I did see her. Yes, fifteen-twenty minutes ago – she was heading in that direction, took that alley,' she pointed towards the pedestrian pathway that cut through The Old Stables building, leading ultimately to join the country lane to—

Forget-Me-Not!

Sam broke into a steady jog. He was in no doubt as to where Maggie was going. Why she was going there, was another matter. A pang of jealousy stabbed Sam in the chest. Was she having a secret rendezvous with Count Dracula? Had the swine charmed his way back into her favours? Sam had a bad feeling about that man since the day he'd first laid eyes on him. That was during Rawbotham's so-called magic show when he'd presented Maggie with the red paper roses.

Of course, Sam had no right to interfere. Maggie was free to see whoever she chose, but, Sam was reasoning with himself, Rawbotham couldn't be trusted and it was Sam's duty to watch out for Maggie. Otherwise, he would have to admit to being no more than a jealous old fool. He'd much rather resume the role of a knight and saviour. That was what he was telling himself to justify his intrusion on Maggie's, God forbid, romantic date.

He reached the entrance to Forget-Me-Not. Ashamed of his infantile spying, he decided to jump over the wall instead of proceeding through the gate which was likely to be monitored by an overhead camera. He went straight for the tradesman's door at the back.

He knew that route well. It led to the kitchen and was frequently left unlocked. Praise be to Bishops Well's customarily lax home security practices!

As anticipated, he found the door open.

He went in. If asked what the hell he was doing here, he would have to come up with something plausible, though right this very minute nothing came to mind that made sense. He hoped to remain unnoticed and unchallenged. He traversed the empty kitchen and climbed the stairs leading to the hallway. He peeped through the door before entering. No one was there either, but he could hear voices in the sitting room. Maggie's voice was quite distinct. She was speaking fast and furiously. Rawbotham responded in the more measured fashion. *At least all they're doing is talking,* a thought crossed Sam's tormented mind. He crept closer in order to establish what exactly they were talking about. A small voice nagged at the back of his skull that he was plainly and simply eavesdropping.

His heart stopped. It did stop literally for a fraction of a second when it jumped to his throat and got stuck there. Sam watched speechless. Maggie was lying on the sofa, and Dracula was on top of her. Where they having—

Sam's heart skipped a beat, dislodged itself from his throat and plummeted to the depths of his stomach. He felt bile come up to his mouth.

He should have spared himself the pain and walked away, but something held him in place. He took another look.

And only on that closer, more sober inspection did he notice the cord tightening around Maggie's neck.

He swept into action: shot into the room, fetched a poker from beside the fireplace, pounced towards the couple on the sofa, and – with the greatest of pleasure – smashed the poker on Rawbotham's head. Rawbotham stiffened and flopped.

It felt wonderful! Gratifying. Perfectly correct. It felt like the ultimate triumph of good over evil.

Sam stood spellbound, admiring his handiwork. Rawbotham was slumped and seemingly lifeless. Hopefully he was dead.

Maggie coughed and began to wriggle from under her attacker. She pushed his form off the sofa and sat up. Her fingers were clutching her throat. She gaped at Sam.

'Samuel?' she coughed out his name.

'Are you all right, Maggie? Was he trying to – to rape you?'

'If only – *cough, cough, cough...* He was trying to kill me, Samuel! And not for the first time!'

'It was him?'

'Oh yes! This time I'm absolutely positive – *cough, cough, cough.* Can I please have something to drink. My throat is in a spasm. I don't think I'll ever sing a high note again.'

Sam reached for a glass with some colourless liquid and ice standing on a table.

'No, not that!' Maggie cried in horror and broke out in a volley of coughs. When she recovered her breath sufficiently to speak, she said, 'I bet that's laced with Pink.'

'Pink?'

'It's a long story. I'll explain later. Firstly, Samuel darling...' The *darling* bit uttered in conjunction with his name felt like a gentle tummy tickle. Sam rejoiced. 'First thing's first: could you fetch me a glass of water from the kitchen? Then we need to call the police.' With her foot she nudged Rawbotham's limp body. 'He may still be alive so we'd better hurry before he comes round.'

An ambulance took Maggie and Sam to the hospital. Maggie was the patient but Sam was determined not to leave her side, no matter what. On arrival, they were asked if they had any symptoms of coronavirus or were likely to have come into contact with anyone who had. Having assured the medics that wasn't the case, they were seen by a doctor. Well, Maggie was seen – with Sam in attendance. She was told to say nothing (easier said than done in her case) in order to preserve her vocal cords from further strain. Her neck was bruised and angry-red, the imprint of the curtain cord for all to see. Sam was mortified to think how close she had come to dying in the last couple of months. Something had to be done about that, and soon – before it was too late.

'She'll live,' the doctor told Sam when his examination was over.

'Let's hope so,' Sam smiled, and again reflected about Maggie's odds not being that great.

She on the other hand looked pleased with herself and her swift return to full health.

'We must visit Oliver!' She demanded in total disregard of the doctor's orders just as they were heading for the exit.

'I don't think—'

'We must tell him – all of them – about Benedict. I want to do that before the police speak to him. I'm not having DI Marsh take the full credit for solving this case!'

So, like it or not, Sam followed Maggie to inquire about Oliver Conti Lang's whereabout and then to find him conscious in his hospital bed surrounded by his loved ones. He appeared delighted to see them and thanked them for the visit.

'That's not why we're here, darling,' Maggie started relaying to him and everyone present the story of the case she *single-handedly* solved at great risk to her own life and limb. She had half the ward captivated for a good hour.

They caught a taxi back to Bishops Well. Maggie smiled mysteriously and said, 'Cordelia was grateful to me – really grateful! For the first time in her life, I imagine. Well, if not the first then definitely the last time, but she did thank me.'

'Was she there?' Sam wasn't surprised in the least to hear about a dead person interacting with his neighbour. This was Maggie Kaye speaking after all and no conversation with her would pass without at least one dead person making an appearance.

'Oh yeah! Sat by Ollie's bed. She took it all in – all I had to say and then, believe me because it's true, she nodded to me as if she was saying *thanks, Maggie, much obliged.* Then she took herself off, I'm guessing, straight to hell.'

Sam chuckled. Maggie was back on form. Most certainly, the temporary withdrawal of oxygen from her brain when she was being strangled had not affected her wit.

Maggie insisted on going fifty-fifty with Sam on the considerable sum the taxi driver demanded when he dropped them off in front of Priest's Hole. Sam wouldn't have any of it. And he wouldn't let Maggie return to her house – not until *he had his say.*

Expecting a serious telling-off for her solo mission against a vicious killer, Maggie plodded behind him and perched timidly on the edge of a chair by the dining table (where incidentally

Deirdre had prepared quite a feast acting on some sixth sense that told her to expect them home at this very hour). Sam however wouldn't let Maggie touch it – not until *he had his say*. He was going to do it. Now. Before something else happened to derail him yet again.

He went to his bedroom to fetch the well-travelled engagement ring. He returned to the dining room and, unwaveringly this time, plonked himself on one knee in front of this thoroughly annoying but also thoroughly loveable woman.

'You'll have to marry me, Maggie. I love everything about you: top to bottom. Um, you know what I mean! I want to take care of you. And frankly, I simply won't take no for an answer. So there!'

THE END

ABOUT THE AUTHOR

Anna Legat

Anna Legat is best known for her cosy crime fiction, The Shires Mysteries, and her legal crime thrillers, Goode's Law and the DI Gillian Marsh series. Murder isn't the only thing on her mind. She dabbles in a wide variety of genres, ranging from historical fiction, through magic realism to dystopia.

A globe-trotter and Jack-of-all-trades, Anna has been an attorney, legal adviser, a silver-service waitress, a school teacher and a librarian. She has lived in far-flung places where she delighted in people-watching and collecting precious life experiences for her stories.

She lives near Bath.

annalegatblog.wordpress.com

@LegatWriter on Twitter

@AnnaLegatAuthor on Facebook

@LegatAuthor on Instagram

BOOKS IN THIS SERIES

The Shires Mysteries

Death Comes To Bishops Well

At Death's Door

Cause Of Death

Death On The High Seas

Death By Misadventure

BOOKS BY THIS AUTHOR

The Inheritance

Bloodlines

Complicity

Buried In The Past

Life Without Me

Broken

The End Of The Road

Swimming With Sharks

Nothing To Lose

Thicker Than Blood

Sandman

A Conspiracy Of Silence

Out Of Sight

Paula Goes To Heaven

Printed in Great Britain
by Amazon